The Revolution

S. L. SCOTT

To my awesome readers.
You ROCK my world!

The Revolution

Prologue

THE WOMAN I'VE fantasized about is finally in my bed. The one who's starred in my dreams and I've imagined when fucking others. She's here, lying next to me and I can't sleep.

My chest hurts while watching her. She's the most beautiful woman I've ever seen and equally the most fascinating. She teases and jokes, flirts... and she trusts me. She trusts me with her life. That's what brought her here tonight. I would do anything for her and she knows it.

I sit up and scrub my hands over the way-too-long scruff that covers my face. She stirs beside me, making me want to stay. I really should, but I just can't stay here any longer...

A promise is a promise and all that. But some promises are worth breaking. *This is one of them.*

1

Lara Kessler

STUPID MUSICIANS!

Stupid, sexy guitarists in fitted shirts that highlight muscles and accentuate abs that should not be hidden behind cotton nor confined under it. But when muscles become eight-packs that's what happens. Score one for him. He's got my complete attention and it's so annoying.

"Lara?"

I look back over my shoulder. Rochelle smiles while adding an accusing lifted eyebrow. Damn her and her all-knowing self.

"What?" I reply as innocently as I can.

"Really?" Crossing her arms over her chest and the stagnant stare tells me I'm not fooling her. "You ready or do you need a few more minutes to stare at the band?"

Caught.

Did Rochelle really think bringing me backstage to The Resistance sound check would be a quick in and out? I want to see the guys. Johnny Outlaw, the lead singer, may be the one most clamor to see, but not me. Everything about him oozes sex appeal, but despite that, my attention tends to go elsewhere. Dex, the drummer, is hot, but he and Rochelle... I'm not sure what's going on there. The other guitarist, Derrick, is cute, but definitely not my type. Kaz on the other hand... I let my gaze linger on his ass in those tight jeans, the holes at the knees formed naturally, literally torn from wear. *So freaking hot.* "A few minutes," I joke. Kind of.

She laughs, pulling the band around my topknot out before I can stop her. My long brown hair comes tumbling down over my shoulders and she says, "Fine, I'll meet you at the car." Teasing as she walks away popping the band she just stole from me, she adds while pointing at my hair, "That's much better too."

"Hey there." And there it is, the voice I was longing to hear.

Before I have a chance to mess with my hair, I run my hand down the front of my purple silk shirt hoping it's not a wrinkled mess. Not like guys care about that. Not that I should care about that. But I do when it comes to *him*. When I turn back around, Kaz is standing in front of me. His smile is sweet, one I haven't seen him reveal in months, maybe since our beach encounter. I don't kid myself though. I'm more practical than that. I'm probably one of many he's actually shown it to, but I like to think it's just for me. "Hi."

"You coming to the show tomorrow?"

"I wouldn't miss it."

Tommy, the band's manager, calls him from the dressing room and waves him over.

When Kaz's caramel-colored eyes are back on me, the corners dip down along with his smile. He looks frustrated. "Guess I should I go. We've got some stuff to do before the show. I'll see you tomorrow?"

I'm honestly not sure what the game plan is, but I won't miss this opportunity either. Nodding, I reply, "For sure." I give a little wave and turn with a big smile on my face. I push through the double doors and am instantly blinded by the sunlight. When my eyes adjust, I see Rochelle's SUV and walk to it. I've just closed the door when she says, "You're gonna get yourself into trouble if you're not careful. You need to be very clear with Mark, and do it today."

Exasperated I'm still dealing with this mess, I lean my head against the seat. "I have several times. He refuses to listen."

Her annoyance is clear, even though I can't see her eyes behind the large designer sunglasses hiding them. Her head tilts and her smile flattens into a straight line. Rochelle is stunning even when she has no patience for things like her friends' terrible relationships. "Make him listen. It's not fair for you to live like this—"

"This? I don't want to hurt him, Ro."

"You know how I feel about everything that's happened. You also know what's happened to me. Don't waste time on things, or people, who don't make you happy." She shifts the Escalade into drive, and turns her focus forward.

I've felt many emotions over the last few months, but the one that stands out is fear. I've felt it deep inside, yet it's one I've not spoken of before, so I whisper, "I'm scared."

Smiling sympathetically, she reaches over and squeezes my hand before returning it to the steering wheel. "It won't be easy, but you've wanted this for a while. It's time to move on with your life, Lara."

"I know. I'll do it soon."

She drives through the parking lot toward the guarded gate while circling back topic-wise to where we began. "In the meantime," she starts as a security guard presses a button and the gate lifts for us to leave the arena, "Tomorrow, we party. It's been forever for me. I need a night out."

"Me too." Kaz crosses my mind and I wonder if how I'm feeling about tonight, about seeing him, is wrong. Flipping down the visor, I open the mirror to see how much I really embarrassed myself with Kaz. My hair is a wild mess of waves I can live with, and the charcoal gray eyeliner that rims my blue eyes is still in place, thank goodness. I push the mirror closed and lean back just as we pass a billboard advertising season tickets for the local major league baseball team. "It will be fun." When I glance her way, I add, "Don't let me drink too much."

"I won't. Or I might. I'm thinking you need a night out just as badly as I do." She's my friend through and through. She may freely give her opinion, but she won't hold it against me if we differ. Following a laugh, she says, "I like Kaz. I'm just worried what your boyfriend might think about this friendship forming with him. Mark's known for two things: homeruns *and* his temper. He wasn't happy the last time you brought him around the band."

Mark flipped out on the band manager for talking to me a four months back. I haven't brought him around since. "I'm allowed to have friends. Separate friends from him. Besides, Mark and I haven't been coupling since the playoffs began."

"Coupling?"

I shouldn't share my sexual secrets but it's one of the reasons I'm leaving Mark, and I trust her with the information. "There's no intimacy."

"You don't have sex?" The shock is heard through the higher octave of her voice. "Lara Kessler, please tell me that's not the case."

"Did you just full-name me?"

"I did. Now tell me you haven't gone without sex."

I shake my head. "I've had sex, though it's been longer than I'd like to admit, and there's no intimacy. It's about him getting off and getting his body in tune to play. Sex is something he does for himself. Not me. It's all about the sport—baseball and sex."

"But I thought players went at it like rabbits in the off-season?"

"Everything in Mark's life revolves around pre-season, the baseball season, and the playoffs. All else is considered a distraction to his routine, including me."

"I'm sorry. I had no idea."

"It's sort of embarrassing to admit, so I don't talk about it."

"When was the last time you... you know?"

"Speaking of rabbits," I laugh, "can we stop at the store? I'm out of batteries."

Rochelle doesn't laugh, but her grin shows her amusement. "Definitely. I'll even buy the bulk pack for you." Traffic in LA sucks so she takes advantage of the time. "Mark has a competitive streak when it comes to pro baseball, but his jealous streak rivals it when it comes to you. Again, not to hound, but make a clean break before you flirt with disaster."

She's right. He's very protective of me because he believes we're meant to be, but the feeling isn't mutual. "Is flirting with disaster a reference to Kaz?"

It's too hot today, so I pull an elastic from my purse, and twist my hair back into a knot on top of my head. Her lack of answer causes me to say, "I was afraid of that."

"Your friendship with Kaz is not wrong."

She's right. *Of course.* So for myself, I say, "We're only friends. He's a great guy, but we're *only* friends. I'm not looking to jump from one relationship into another."

"What if Mr. Right shows up?"

"I don't need Mr. Right. I'm just looking for that damn elusive O. No matter how many batteries I go through, I'm not able to find him. *It.*" I correct. "I mean it, not him."

She laughs along with me, but it lulls as we both realize what I mean. Then I just feel sad. "My mind is a mess these days."

"We need our minds romanced as much as our bodies. The O will come. But not until your mind is free. You need to get yourself in a good place mentally." Touching my hand again, she says, "Things work out how they're supposed to, Lara."

"Is that how you feel about Cory?" I shouldn't have said that and I know it, but I'm curious and usually too afraid to ask. My defenses lower as regret sets in. "I'm sorry."

"It's okay." Her fingers tighten around the leather wheel, but her face remains neutral. "Things work out how they're supposed to," she repeats, her shoulders and tone much more stoic than her façade of calm.

MARK'S DRIVEWAY IS long. I've often thought it was a source of pride for him, as if he believes we are judged by the entrance to our homes instead of our hearts. He chose the former to highlight in life. I chose the latter. Another reason in a long list that we were never meant to be more than one hot night on Mulholland.

Stars are hidden behind clouds, or smog, making my night even more ominous than it already felt. The gate closes behind me and I'm left pulling up to a house that is grand and over the top with hideous Greek columns and an ostentatious Roman fountain with pissing cherubs. This house has a Hollywood legacy of a famous showman from before films existed through famous actresses who held huge society parties in the 1950s. More recently it was a porn producer's home until he went to jail for tax evasion. The mansion was put on the market and Mark scooped it up below value. He transformed the place and made it grand again. It's a symbol of his success and makes him feel important in a town full of players. I get it. He's known for his homeruns and ego. After meeting some of his teammates, it's clear he's not unique in this way.

But this house sets him apart. It's a status symbol that many other players can't afford. Mark's marketability affords him luxuries most will never experience.

Sometime in the last month I realized I was another status symbol like this house. I was a pretty package he could display in front of cameras as the doting girlfriend. I'd foolishly fallen for the charade and had played my part. The role of trophy without the wife title never sat well with me.

I may not be wealthy, but I make a good living and am recognized in my industry. Mark's never appreciated my achievements. He's paraded me up and down red carpets, World Series, and parties. It was fun, at first. In time, the real Mark Renner was exposed and his dark side wasn't pretty. We weren't real. I know that now. Sadly, I had changed to become what he wanted, what he demanded not so subtly. I barely recognize myself anymore.

And for what? *Fame?* I don't need fame. *Money?* I don't need money at this level. *Happiness?* I don't even remember when I gave that up. *Integrity? That's* what I most long for, what I desire to recapture. I may have lost my soul to the darkness of Hollywood, but I believe I can get back to a place where I feel proud of myself again, where I sleep at night without the help from a glass of wine to relax. Where tears and exhaustive arguments are no longer part of my daily routine. Where dreams replace the nightmares I've had longer than I remember.

We're not meant to be.

I didn't see the differences soon enough to stop this train from wrecking. He parties too much and I don't like the changes I've seen in him. From tabloid photos of him with other women while on the road to drunken fights on nights out with his buddies—he's a disaster and he's dragging me down with him.

Now that I've been investing into *my* life, and me, my friendships have strengthened again and hope is on the horizon. He may have been able to talk himself out of any situation before, but my instincts tell me not to believe him anymore. And I'm good with this.

Tonight I will walk away from his world, out from his shadow, and start living my life again.

After parking, I walk toward the house. Rap music penetrates the glass and iron front door. It's locked so I use my key and let myself in. The music is louder when I enter, the bass bouncing off the marble entryway. "Mark?" I call, shutting the door. "Mark?"

I leave my purse on the foyer table and make my way into the large living room with ornate and gaudy framed paintings. I don't have the heart to tell him he was had in Vegas when he bought what he thought were original masterpieces. They're knock-offs. Any fool can tell with one glance, except Mark.

When I round the corner to the kitchen, Mark is rapping at the top of his lungs. His back is to me as the blender runs giving me this last look at how handsome he used to be to me—broad shoulders and dark hair, golden skin from hours of practice outside. He's not the same man I met. The brightness that used to fill his eyes—joy from the game, excitement from being with me—has dulled. Now, online images show eyes that spark from alcohol and easy women. Even the way he stands is different to me now. He's weaker in my eyes, and I'm convinced I need to end this relationship. "Hi," I say loud enough for him to hear, but not startle him. He's not someone you want to surprise or sneak up on. Lately, he has been edgy. His size alone is intimidating, but his speedy reactions would land me in the hospital if he were startled.

He looks over his shoulder. "Hey, babe." Pointing at the stuff in the blender, he offers, "Protein shake?"

I soften under the endearment and the offer, and shake my head. "No, I'm good. Is that dinner?"

His bright white smile is engaging as he stops what he's doing and comes to hug me. "We can order a pizza if you're hungry."

"I ate earlier."

"Without me?" He looks hurt just from the thought.

"You weren't around earlier when I called."

"Coach started two-a-days today. I needed the extra cage time so I stayed later." He lifts my chin and the gesture is so caring that I almost forget why I'm here. "You okay? You look troubled."

This.

This is the Mark who charmed me into bed that first night. This is the Mark who had waffles and crispy bacon ready for me when I woke the next morning. This is the man I fell for never thinking twice that it was a side I'd rarely see. Seeing this man before me now, I feel sentimental as I forget the bad and warm from the good we have had.

SOMETIMES I SABOTAGE myself. I've been working on it for a while, and when I gave in after he guilted me into staying, I realize I'll be working on it a lot longer. To his dismay, we didn't have sex. He wanted to break our streak, but I didn't. Sex isn't only physical for me. It's in my head and my body. Hence no orgasms in longer than I care to think about.

I'm having trouble sleeping. Again. Being awake in the middle of the night is no joyride, so I pick up my phone from the nightstand, careful not to wake Mark, and scroll through Instagram. As a decorator who's established a name and reputation in this town, I have many celebrity clients who have become friends. Their posts are exactly what people expect from them—parties, schmoozing, exotic vacations, and everything else most consider glamorous. Although I'm not rich, I have lived among the uber-wealthy long enough that I'm used to seeing the most amazing photos of incredible adventures. I used to get envious, but I see beyond the bright selfie lights. Their lives are, for the most part, superficial and highly coordinated. They don't order takeout without their manager's approval and their publicist's press release. It's suffocating, even to me as an outsider looking in on their lives.

As I scroll, I come across a photo posted by Mark. It's a pic of him working out with no shirt on. His body is amazing. He works hard for it and it shows. I just wish he didn't have to show it all the time. He has over three-thousand likes on the photo and at least one hundred comments, most from women—some vulgar, some flattering. All annoying.

Scrolling past Mark's, I don't bother liking it. I don't want to encourage more shirtless shots. His ego is big enough already, and he wouldn't notice my like anyway. Next is a photo of Rochelle's boys and I smile. Then I spy a photo of Kaz. It's a photo Rochelle posted. By the look of their clothes and the background, it was taken backstage earlier today. Their arms are around each other and their smiles are genuine. The lighting sparks in their eyes, revealing their happiness. I understand why Rochelle posted it. It's real. They're real. So different from the world I'm engulfed in right now.

"Turn off your phone and go to sleep," Mark snaps. His voice is gruff, short-tempered. He's warned me before about it, so I deserve it since I woke him.

I set the phone on the nightstand and slide down under the covers. "Sorry," I whisper, sad to see the sweet Mark gone so quickly.

He turns his back to me and within minutes he's snoring loudly. Half a year into our relationship and I don't feel the love I should for him. The spark was gone too soon for my liking. I was supposed to come over and break up, but I hate hurting people. *Even if it means hurting me in the process.*

I'll have to do it tomorrow.

"I'VE GOT A crazy day today, so I'm gonna head out," I say with the shower curtain between us.

"Okay," he says from the other side before burying his face under the spray. "I'll see you tonight."

I pause. "I'm not sure about tonight. I have the concert with Rochelle."

Just as I turn to leave my wrist is grabbed. "Hey, what's up?" His hand is wet, the tendons in his forearms bulging from his grip.

I turn my arm and try to wiggle free. Fear doesn't enter my psyche from the way he's holding on to me until his eyes narrow and his grip tightens. My mind wars with itself as I struggle internally to decide if it's fear I'm feeling or something else. I can't pinpoint the other emotions running rampant so I settle on fear and say, "Nothing. I have a long day ahead with a job in Malibu."

"I want to have dinner with you. Come by the gym." His fingers loosen around my wrist.

"I can't. I have the concert afterward. I'm already going to be late for it."

"Come over after."

"Maybe. I'll text you."

Bunched eyebrows. A disdainful snort. *He's irritated.* "Don't make this a habit."

My hair rises from his authoritarian tone. "Don't make what a habit?"

"This. Last night. This morning. Tonight. I barely see you these days and you haven't blown me in months."

My head jolts back from the slap of his words. "Blown you? I'm sorry. I must've been under the impression that I was more than a mouth for your pleasure."

"God, Lara. Don't be such a bitch all the time. You know I'll fuck you if you want me to, but you don't seem to want that. Maybe we should be talking about that."

Checking my watch, I say, "I've tried." Looking back at him, he stands naked before me, half in the shower, half out. "You had no interest in talking to me and last night I wasn't in the mood."

"Is this what last night was about? You're so uptight lately, I'm

14

afraid you'll bite my head off if I touch you."

"I highly doubt you're afraid of much, much less me."

"Fine, let's do it. I wanted to last night."

Offended, I say, "I don't want to *do it*. I want you to realize I'm more than this hole or this one." My hand goes from my mouth and then points below my belly. "You used to—"

"Fuck *used to*. I don't want to hear it." He ducks back into the shower stall and allows the water to drown me out. He shouts over the water, "Go be a cunt with your friends."

What the hell?

There are times in our lives that someone pushes you too far. There's an imaginary line that's been drawn in the sand of your mind that you're not even aware of until you're pushed over it. I just discovered my line.

With my fists balled at my sides, I yell, "We're done." I turn quickly, fear and excitement coursing through me, and escape the house. I finally did it. Not the way I planned, but the only way he would hear it. I mentally blur the line, hoping never to return to the other side again.

I'm done with him.

We're done.

The deed is done, and as I watch the gate close behind me, I release a long-held breath. My hands begin to shake in disbelief. I finally did it. It's done. A smile filters its way onto my face as I drive away.

I'm finally free.

3

"GUESS WHAT I just found out?"

I don't even have time to say hello when I answer, so I take the opportunity now. "Good morning, Ro. And how are you?"

"Fabulous. Good Morning," she says, laughing. "And how are you?"

"Excellent. Thank you for asking." I laugh too, life feeling lighter by the minute. "So, what did you find out?"

"A mutual friend of ours just bought a house. You know what that means."

"I do know what that means. They might need a decorator."

"Ding. Ding. Ding."

"Who's the mutual friend?"

"Kaz Fabian."

An involuntary smile sneaks onto my face. "Oh really? Are we supposed to know about the house yet or is it still a secret?"

"I read about it online. I knew he was looking and had bids in on two properties. I guess the deal was finalized between the lawyers last night at Spago. A blogger overheard and leaked it overnight."

"That sucks on the leak. I know he was sharing a house in West Hollywood with Derrick and wanted his own space, so it's good news on buying."

"Want me to ask about the house and see what he plans to do with it?"

Rochelle is someone I've always been able to rely on, a friend of a friend who became my friend. We just clicked and two years later, here she is thinking of job opportunities for me. "That would be awesome. Thanks."

"No worries. Where are you going this morning?"

"I just left Mark's. I'm driving home. I have a job in Malibu today."

Her voice lowers, the subject calling for it. "Did you do it?"

"We'll talk about it tonight. I need to get my head out of that space or I'll be crying and I just don't want to cry over that asshole."

Her silence is telling, so I let it stay, speaking for us.

She finally asks, "New client in Malibu? And anyone I've heard of?"

"You might have. Calliope Mathers."

"Wow. Hot actress of the moment. That's a good job to have. Maybe you'll get some press out of it. We all know how much she loves the attention."

"She's not that bad once you get past the fur-lined robes and teased bleach-blond hair. She's actually sweet sometimes."

CALLIOPE STAMPS HER high heel on the marble flooring, the tantrum proving her point. "See? There's an echo. I don't like that."

"But you'll get that with any flooring other than carpet and you said you thought carpet was, and I quote, 'Gross.'"

"I never said that," she protests with a toss of her highly hairsprayed hair. It doesn't move though her hand continues the motion.

"You did when I brought the samples. You said you didn't want a 'beach-themed' house. You wanted expensive and over the top. That's what the whole design was based on."

She walks past me into the kitchen where a uniformed maid hands her an espresso. "Latte?" she asks me, holding her cup to her lips.

"That's an espresso, and no, I'm good. Thanks."

"I thought the tiny cups of coffee were lattes?"

"Lattes have milk—" I stop myself from continuing on this ridiculous path. "The marble is stunning and it's custom. It was imported from Europe. If you want to dampen the sound, we have rugs on order that will do that. Don't stress. Let's stick with our original plan and then decide once everything is in place."

She comes closer and hugs me unexpectedly. "Fine. You're right. You're always right, Lara. What would I do without you?"

I'm starting to question her sanity, but in this city, I'm considered the odd one out. I return her hug, thinking she just might need one. She leans back and looks me in the eyes with a small smile on her face. "You know, because you're my friend, I'll totally get you an appointment with Stanz, my fab hairdresser. He could knock the dull right out of your brown hair. It does wonders for the self-esteem and all the guys in LA would be after you. Well, all the guys who aren't coming after me that is."

My grin is tight, but my annoyance is kept buried. "Thanks, but I'm swearing off men for a while."

"What about your soccer player?"

I don't bother correcting her. "I'd rather not talk about him right now."

"Soccer just isn't that popular though. You could really land someone bigger. You have such a pretty face." In other words, my ass is big, but thank goodness my face is pretty. *Ugh.*

I can't deal with her today. Taking a step back from her, I grab my purse, and say, "He's a *major* league baseball player, and I'm all set on the hair, but thanks anyway." Totally irritated, I head for the door. "The rugs should be in next week. I'll see you then."

"Tootles."

Clueless.

I cringe when I see the time. *Damn it.* I'll be sitting in rush-hour traffic for the next two hours. I settle into my Range Rover and turn on Vivaldi to keep me company on the trek back to Hollywood Hills. I've moved so much of my stuff into Mark's that I forgot the small detail of removing things before I broke it off with him. Now I'm stuck with my clothes in his closet. My saving grace is that I know he's at practice so I'll be able to slip in and out with a few armloads of clothes before he returns later tonight.

Like an LA miracle, I get to his house sooner than expected. I walk in and dump the keys and my bag on the table in the dining room before being startled by Mark in the living room. "Hey," I say, grabbing my chest. "I didn't think I'd see you."

"But we had plans," he says. His fingers are steepled and he's glaring at me. His look is intense, his tone tight. The rigidness of his body makes me nervous.

His brusque behavior gives me pause, and I worry if honesty is not the best policy for my safety. I venture there first though, testing the waters. Keeping my voice calm, I ask, "I have the concert tonight. Remember?"

"Oh right," he says, playing it off as he sits back and lowers his hands to his thighs. "But you can skip it. Some of the team are getting together with their girlfriends down at O'Malley's to watch the Red Sox preseason opener."

His ease causes irritation as he discounts not only my plans, but dismisses what I told him this morning. "What are their wives doing?"

"I'm not going to argue with you, Lara." Mark's not amused by the snarky joke. He can't argue it, though, since a few of his teammates actually do have girlfriends on the side, if not most. I used to wonder if he did too. Now I just want to move on from him. "Get dressed."

"Don't tell me what to do. We are no longer a couple. I'll collect a few things tonight and be out of your way shortly." He's on his feet before I have a chance to turn away. My wrist is grabbed, the tips of his fingers like spears to my skin as he digs in. "Mark!"

Pulling me close, he holds me tight against his side. "I will not be embarrassed. You will come with me tonight." With one strong shove, my knees hit the hard floor and the palms of my hands slap down roughly. The smart is instant as pain shoots through me, breaking through the shock of what just happened. My eyes well, but my anger rules. I swing my head around and my hair flies to the side when he reaches for me. "Get away from me."

"I'm sorry," he says, but there's no feeling behind the words. His tone is the same as before he pushed me. He stands and says, "We're not broken up. No one breaks up with me."

Despite the pain, I get to my feet, stand tall, and face him. "I just did." Pushing past him, I head for the door. Forget the clothes and everything else. I need to get out of here before something worse happens.

He steps back and to the side to block my way. I look up, straight into his eyes. "Move out of my way, Mark."

A cocky smile that had come easily to him is replaced with a scowl. "Look, I'm sorry if I hurt you." He comes closer. "I care about you. I don't want us to be over."

"Too late," I say, keeping my expression straight and my tone firm. "This isn't working out. You can go out with your friends and meet all the women you want. They'll be thrilled to hear you're single."

"No."

"What do you mean, no?" I back away from him toward the door. Quickly, I turn and unlock it, holding it wide open, something in my gut telling me to just in case I need to scream.

But whatever made his demeanor confrontational before is

gone, the nice guy that wooed me months earlier has returned. "Lara," he says, his voice soft. "Don't do this. Give me another chance. I don't want to lose you. Please. One more chance."

I gulp, debating if I should make a run for it or stay and try to leave on good terms. "I think it's best we go our separate ways. I'm never going to be what you need. Trust me, you'll meet the girl of your dreams, but I'm not her."

Disappointment settles into his features. "We can work this out. Please be open-minded. We are everything together and nothing apart."

Starting to feel bad, I acquiesce. "I'm not going to change my mind."

He stops in front of me and rubs my wrists where he grabbed me earlier. I'm not scared, but I recoil involuntarily. When he sees me flinch, he frowns. "I'm sorry. I'll make it up to you. I promise. We'll talk tomorrow."

We're done. So done. There's no way I'm changing my mind, but to keep him calm, I nod before walking out.

As soon as I shut the door to my car, I lock it, and breathe for what feels like the first time in minutes. Inhaling slowly, my lungs burn. *No one breaks up with me.* Trying to regulate my pounding heart, I exhale even slower to release the tension in my body. *I will not be embarrassed. You will come with me tonight.* I start the car with shaking hands. *No, Mark, I won't.* Even though the signs have been there since before the playoffs, I shouldn't have ignored them; I've never seen him that aggressive. I'm not sure why he's become more aggressive, but I can't stick around to find out either. At six five, he's a big guy. I cover my wrist with my hand and rub. It hurts. *He* hurt me. I need to leave, so I ignore the pain and back down the driveway.

AFTER GETTING PAST three different bouncers, verifying my name, and flashing my badge, I'm finally backstage. My stomach is still upset from earlier, my head still spinning, but I try to shake it off and enjoy the night.

Lifting up on my toes, I search for Rochelle amongst the chaos. A familiar face pops up in the crowd when she jumps, then waves her arm. Holli comes over and hugs me, the smile on her face welcome. "Good to see you, Lara," she says warmly. "Glad you could make it."

Holliday Hughes—gorgeous, smart, and down to earth. She's the most put together woman I know. She's definitely someone to look up to. And as if she didn't have everything already, she also owns the heart of the one and only Johnny Outlaw—the front man and lead singer of *The Resistance*. I've always liked her, but everyone does. She makes it easy and is the kind of person people gravitate toward. "Good to see you," I reply, embracing her while protecting my wrist. "I'm excited to see the show. I love the new CD."

"God, so do I. I know I'm partial," she says, smiling, "but I think it's their best album yet. Are you looking for Rochelle?"

"Yes, I'm late. Have you seen her?"

"I think she's with the guys. I'm not sure if we should disturb the preshow routine, but we can get a drink at the bar and wait for her, if you like."

"Sounds good."

"How's business?" she asks, weaving through the crowd.

"Busy. I've been working on a job in Malibu that has me pulling my hair out some days, but it's finally coming together beautifully. How about you?"

We reach the table set up outside their dressing room. It has bottles of liquor and mixers, cups, and ice. We start making our drinks as we continue to chat. "I flew to New York and Chicago recently. I'm supposed to head to Miami next week." She stops pouring the vodka and looks up at me, and whispers, "Dalton is not happy about it."

"Dalton?"

"Johnny. I call him Dalton." She carries on making her vodka tonic. "My marketing director is pushing another campaign. More photo shoots and models. I'm not sure, but I'm testing the waters by exploring more of the ideas and locations."

"Sounds exciting."

She shrugs. "Sometimes. I'm not convinced I need to be in the ads to sell Limelight products."

"You're beautiful, so I see why they'd want you."

I'm sure it's something she hears often, but she smiles genuinely. "Thanks. Guess we'll see." She laughs, looking down, and then sips her drink.

Tommy opens the dressing room door and looks out. When he sees Holli, he nods toward the door. "C'mon in."

Holli touches my hand, and says, "Let's go in for a minute. I want to talk to Dalton real quick."

I follow her inside and watch as she heads straight into his arms.

The way he looks at her is the same look I dream about, hoping one day a man looks at me like that. It makes my heart ache with envy. *Did Mark ever look at me like that?* I fell for his attention because he was so different from anyone I had previously dated. What I realize now is he didn't want *me*, he wanted to own me. I still have no idea why he chose me. I learned a hard lesson though: desire to me was power to him.

Johnny kisses her as she wraps her arms around his neck, then she whispers into his ear. I turn away, feeling like I'm intruding on their intimacy.

I'm grabbed from behind and turned quickly, flinching in the process. Rochelle is all smiles to my startled expression. "You're here," she says, fortunately not noticing. "You're late, but I'm glad you came."

"Me too. It wasn't easy, but we can talk about it later. I just want to enjoy the show."

She nods, understanding my need to keep the heavy at bay. She starts to tug me toward the door, when Dex stands with his sticks in hand, he says, "Good to see you, Lara."

"You too. I'm excited to see the show."

"Thanks." He maneuvers next to Rochelle, and whispers, "Stay close to Lara and Holli."

"I will," she says. Warmth softens her expression as she looks into his eyes. "Break a leg."

Rochelle opens the door and turns back. "Let's wait for Holli."

I lean against the wall by the door, taking in my surroundings and this unprecedented opportunity I've been given. This band is a legend in their own time. Through hits and tragedy they have fallen and risen to the top again. Biographies have been written about them, and a movie has been made. They are the reigning kings of rock 'n' roll and I'm standing in the same room as them as if I belong.

Kaz comes out from a back room. When he sees me, he doesn't smile but I see something in his expression that draws out mine.

"Hey," he says, adding in a singular tilt of his head.

"Hey," I reply quietly.

He walks over and everything goes quiet in my world. Or that's just my world grinding to a silent stop. My heart is racing watching his body move like he knows how to use it. He's a beautiful man, the word handsome insufficient to describe his dark features: hair like midnight at the beach, eyes like caramel candies melting from the heat of the sun, and skin tinted by the southern California weather. Then the door next to me opens and he says, "See you after," as he passes.

I want to die. Die of embarrassment. I mentally facepalm that he just caught me daydreaming about him while staring at him.

"Yeah, okay," is all I manage to squeak out before Derrick passes, then Dex and Johnny. Tommy follows them and I'm left with Holli and Rochelle, both of whom are shaking their heads at me, and then start laughing.

I'm so busted.

Holli heads for the door, and states, "He is really cute."

I roll my eyes, my face heating from humiliation. Rochelle adds, "Super cute." She wraps her arm around mine and turns me so we walk out together. "Don't worry. I don't think he caught the sexual fantasy playing out all over your face when he walked by."

"Ugh. Was it that obvious?"

She answers with a laugh.

"Just kill me now."

Tapping my drink, she says, "Drink up, Buttercup. You need it."

"And about five more to erase this embarrassment." *And the situation with Mark earlier tonight.* I rub my wrists and look down, making sure the leather bands hide the redness. It should be gone by tomorrow. Hopefully. Now, I just need to settle my nerves.

"Ah, good ole alcohol. The great eraser. I've used it before, but it only relieves temporarily. Trust me on that." Her arm drops and she hurries to catch up with Holli. Looking back over her shoulder, she says, "C'mon. I don't want to miss Dex's opening. It's my favorite part."

I have to get over what just happened and decide to laugh it off. What does it matter? Millions of women have fantasies about him. I'm sure Kaz Fabian is used to it. One more won't make a difference to him. I join the girls and we go down the stairs and around a gathered group of men in suits. After bypassing them, we cross through a red velvet curtain and out a door. A large bodyguard takes to Holli's side and leads us to a section in the front. The lights go down and the crowd goes quiet.

Rochelle grabs my hand and squeezes. I can tell she's nervous. When I look over, she's biting her bottom lip and staring at the stage. The first hit on the drum kit gets my attention and I search the darkness on stage until a spotlight hits Dex, who is pounding his intro solo to his own beat. Rochelle screams and so do I; the beat is contagious. The excitement is invigorating.

As soon as Johnny starts singing, a spotlight hits him and the crowd goes wild. The lights flicker to the chorus and the stage lights up revealing Kaz and Derrick flanking Johnny.

Kaz is on the opposite side from us, too far for my liking, but I enjoy the song and move to the beat anyway. Drinks are delivered to us three songs in and the girls and I toast to the night. I'm swaying my hips and closing my eyes, letting the rhythm dictate my moves. Rochelle hip bumps me to get my attention. "Look up."

When I do, Kaz and Derrick have switched sides. He has his eyes focused on the guitar as he plays but then glances in our direction. When his eyes meet mine, he smirks with a little head nod before leaning back and getting back into the music. The muscles in his arms are buff and the veins strain from the intensity as he strums. He's passionate about playing which is incredibly sexy and intoxicating, making me want to discover what else he's passionate about.

During the next song, Derrick and Kaz swap sides again and my view is partially blocked by Johnny. Not that it's not a great view, but he's taken. Another forty-five minutes pass and I continue to watch Kaz, captivated by the way he moves his fingers over the strings and holds the guitar pressed against his body. He's sweaty and sexy and—

"Let's get another round before the encore," Holli says, taking our hands.

Probably best. I'm getting too hot anyway.

Rochelle and I follow her backstage to the bar set up on the table outside their dressing room. She pours a large glass of water just as the guys, surrounded by bodyguards, start walking toward us. She hands Johnny the water and he takes her by the hand with him into the room. Rochelle makes a drink for herself and I refill my glass, giving the band their space. Just as I look up, Kaz winks at me and follows the other guys into the room.

Rochelle leans against the wall and says, "Sometimes I like to stay out here."

She gets reflective, her thoughts changing her expression. While she looks down at the floor, I start to wonder so many things about when she's back in this environment and if she's okay or not. I worry about her, but do I need to? "Do you still think of Cory?"

Her reaction is a smile and bright eyes. "All the time. He was such a great songwriter and guitarist. It's hard not to think of him when they play one of his songs." She pushes off the wall. "But the band has lived on long after he did." After taking a sip of her drink, she adds, "Dex has really helped me." Her smile grows and she blushes. "There's just something about that bad-boy drummer..."

Kaz and Derrick replaced Cory, who was one of the founding band members. I just thought it would always be Cory and Rochelle and their sons. But things change, things outside of our control. I've thought a lot about them over the last month. Knowing I couldn't waste my life being unhappy, I knew I had to breakup with Mark. We're not in so deep that we can't crawl back out with only minor damage. I believe in love, which means I'm open to finding the real thing. My heart and head know it's not going to be found with Mark.

I take a long gulp, the stress of a "talk" with Mark still weighing me down. Turning to Rochelle for support, I whisper, "I did it."

"Did what?" she asks.

"I broke up with Mark."

Her eyebrows go up and her eyes go wide in shock. "You did it? Like finality, *finito* did it?"

"This morning and then again tonight. That's why I was late. I went to get some clothes and he was there." I look away. "I thought he'd be at practice, but he was there as if nothing had changed, demanding I go out with him."

"Oh honey, are you okay?" She moves over to the side of the table where I'm standing and sets her drink down to hug me.

"It was a long time coming, but doing it was hard." A memory from earlier still haunting me—*my wrist is grabbed, the tips of his fingers like spears to my skin as he digs in.*

"I'm sure it wasn't easy, but you're so much better off. I didn't want to say anything, but I saw an Instagram photo of him and some woman the other night. If I was with him, that would have been it for me."

"He tried to explain that photo, but she was on his lap and her hand was touching his inner thigh, so yeah, I didn't believe him. We had a huge fight over it. That's why I don't know why he's fighting so hard to stay together."

"What do you mean? He wants to keep dating?"

"Yeah. He wants to talk again. Tomorrow. He didn't seem right tonight. It was odd."

She looks surprised. "No, that's not a good idea. You broke up. It's done."

"It's not that easy, Ro. He has some of my things and I want us to end this amicably."

"How will it end amicably if he doesn't want to breakup?"

The door opens near us and Tommy walks out. The bodyguards come over and the band walks back toward the stage. Holli follows them out, but stops to make a cocktail. "You girls ready?"

29

"Yep," I reply.

She waggles her eyebrows once and says, "This should be good. Dalton's all fired up."

Rochelle laughs. "You always have a way with him." She dashes off suddenly and slaps Dex's ass as she passes. Holli and I trail behind laughing.

HOLLI AND JOHNNY rarely come to the after parties from what I hear and Dex and Rochelle do some of the time. Tonight Rochelle said she wants to party, so she grabs me, and Dex is right there with her. He's got it so bad for her. He has for a while, but it's new for them. It will be interesting to watch how they maneuver through their relationship. I'm in a Suburban with them, Derrick, Tommy, and Kaz. Kaz is sitting in the front and I'm sitting next to Rochelle who is whispering to Dex. His hand is rubbing her shoulder as he listens intently. Tommy and Derrick are in the third row discussing some ancient artifacts exhibit in Washington, D.C. that they want to see when they fly out there for the tour.

It's weird being in a situation like this, knowing I'm fresh from a breakup. I'm left feeling caught between being a fifth or sixth wheel and awkwardly wondering what I should be doing or if I should just be sitting here quietly. From my position I have a full view of Kaz. He's showered and changed. His hair is still damp and I don't know if he washed it or it's from sweat but I'm intrigued enough to want to find out. Guilt overrides the fun. Mark has a way of inserting himself in all aspects of my life, even when he doesn't have the right any longer.

When Kaz turns, he catches me watching him, so I turn to look out the window instead. The lights outside are suddenly the most fascinating things in the world. I shouldn't be thinking about him the way I do... the way I have for a while now, if I'm honest with myself. Nobody wants to be a rebound. *Is that what Kaz will be?* I haven't had sex in so long that he just might be a bound at this point.

It's amazing to think I even have the option. I glance back at him. Our eyes meet and he stretches his arm and rubs the back of my jeans-covered calf. "I'm glad you came."

My whole body warms from his touch. "Me too."

He turns back and I sit there melting in all the swoons for the rest of the ride. I had no idea he'd even noticed me before the other day or even in the last year. Sure, we've been around each other more than a few times, but the only time we talked was during group settings, parties and such, or backstage with other stuff going on. Except this one party Rochelle took me out at Carillo Beach, the night before I met Mark...

Everyone was dancing on the beach, drinking, roasting marshmallows. A few were even skinny-dipping. If the rest of LA only knew how many celebrities were out here right now, this state beach would be overrun with groupies. Tonight, the band, the actors, and the models, they were just people out for a bonfire with their friends.

Rochelle went back to the house to get another round of drinks for us. I remained outside because the music was too loud in the house to enjoy any kind of real conversation, and I liked the sound of the ocean. The group thinned when Derrick went looking for weed and the Brazilian model hanging on his arm accompanied him. Kaz stayed.

He always seemed preoccupied with others when I was around or with the band. I've seen women flirt with him. I've seen him flirt in return, but when I really think about those times, they were more on the courteous side than returning their interest.

That night it got chilly as soon as the sun set, and I shivered. He moved closer and set his beer down in the sand. Taking his leather jacket off, he wrapped it around my shoulders. Surprised by his gesture, I said, "You'll get cold."

Kaz shoved his hands in his pockets. "I'll be okay."

"Thank you." I set my Solo cup down and slipped my arms into the sleeves. The worn leather smelled like warmth if warm had a scent—comfort and musky, cognac, and sunsets. I then looked at Kaz differently. I watched as he stared into the fire, the flames' reflection flickering in his irises.

He glanced my way and a small smile made its way across his mouth. I'm sure he's used to people staring at him because of his fame and because he's gorgeous. I looked away after holding the connection a few seconds. I didn't know what to say, the loss of words coming with a loss of breath from his nearness.

"This is the first time we've had a chance to talk," he starts. After pausing, he turns back to the fire. "So you're a deco—"

"Dude! Kaz, c'mere!" is shouted from a group nearby. Derrick. "Kaaaazzzzz! Get the fuck over here."

Kaz stares into my eyes. "I'm sorry."

"It's okay."

He nods, appearing as disappointed as I feel. I start to take the jacket off, but he moves in front of me, fists the front and tightens it closed again. "It looks good on you. You should hold on to it. You can return it next week after the show."

"I'll be there." I still don't know how I was able to speak with him so close, his warmth filling my lungs.

Rochelle returns laughing and handing me a drink. "God, the line was insane." She begins telling me a story about some guy hitting on her and Dex almost getting in a fight, but I don't hear it. I just watch Kaz walk away. He turns back once with a sexy smirk and then joins the guys in the band.

I never made that concert. Mark had a game and he wanted me to be there to watch him play. Rochelle returned the jacket for me.

This is our second chance. Remembering that time at the beach and how he's looking at me now, it's not the same as he looked at the women frequenting the parties or the after-parties. There's more in his smile for me. The tilt of the right side of his lips is more suggestive. There's more emotion behind his brown eyes. There's more in the way he touches me, as if *he* might be the one to get burned.

Inside the bar, the lights are so dim that it's hard to see beyond the table we're sitting around. We have a corner to ourselves and the table seats at least twelve. Other celebrities have stopped by to talk to the guys and tell them how great the concert was. Women have tried to talk their way into the VIP area and failed, so they linger near the bouncer, hoping they get spotted and invited in. I don't blame them. All the guys are good-looking and they're rock stars, so what's not to be attracted to? I feel fortunate to have inside connections to get to hang with them, and really lucky I get to hang out with my friends. Speaking of, I elbow Rochelle. "Hey, talk to me."

"Sorry." She laughs.

I look at my glass that's empty. "I need another drink. Wanna come with me?"

"I'll come with you." We both look across the table following the offer to find Kaz smiling. He holds his glass up and adds, "I need another and the waitress hasn't restocked the bottles yet."

Rochelle practically pushes me out of my seat. "Yeah, go. And order me a white wine while you're at it."

Kaz stands and offers me his hand, helping me up. He holds my hand high in the air as we move over everyone's heads until we're standing together at the end of the table. "What are you drinking?" he asks.

"A greyhound with a dash of orange juice and a twist of lime."

"Sounds complicated." We reach the edge of the bar and he leans on it, looking right at me. "Are you complicated, Lara?"

I answer honestly. "I'm not sure anymore."

That makes him chuckle. "Okay."

I lean on the bar next to him and ask, "What about you?"

"I try not to be, but shit happens."

Nodding, I agree. "Yep, it sure does." We place our orders. "I heard you bought a home."

"I think everyone has heard that. For some reason the press finds every move I make very interesting."

"Well," I start, but suddenly feel awkward, and I never feel awkward talking about my business. I'm successful because I have a great eye for making generic spaces unique and comforting, modern and homey. *So why am I now hesitant, almost shy?*

"You decorate houses, right?"

Feeling relieved by his lead in question, I reply, "Yes. And other spaces, some offices, but mainly homes."

"I could use your help. Do you have time in your schedule to look at it?"

"I'd love to."

"I have no idea what I'm doing and I don't want to just throw inflatable mattresses everywhere."

Laughing, I tease, "Yeah, don't do that. Anyway, they're bad for your back. Just let me know what your schedule looks like and we'll set up a date... I mean, time."

I'm not sure if he caught my flub, but if he did, he lets it slide. "The owners are getting the rest of their stuff out today. I have a show in Indiana on Sunday and then we're back. How does Tuesday night look for you?"

"I usually don't work nights, but I know you're busy, so I'll make an exception."

The drinks are set before us and he tells the bartender to add it to the tab. Turning back to me, he clinks his glass against mine. "Sometimes the exceptions are what the journey is all about."

I swear my heart flutters from his words, or maybe it's just his proximity to me thinking he might make an exception for me too. "Are we still talking about decorating appointments?" I ask coyly, my cheeks flaming hot.

Full of confidence, he leans down until he's eye level with me. "Not at all."

And just like that, I have a date... I mean a *meeting* with Kaz Fabian.

5

"COME SIT BY me," Kaz says. "We won't have to yell to talk."

My cheeks heat again and I'm starting to think this might be how it always is when I'm around him. I should use less blush, if this is the case. I'm also not sure why I'm so goofy over this guy. I mean, sure, he's hot with his longish hair and soulful eyes that seem to be from another time. His body is rock hard, and he's a musician, which speaks my body's language, seeping under my skin. But it's the way he looks at me. His eyes speak to me without him saying one single word.

I'm breathless as I slip into the seat next to him. My heart pulsing in time with the music, my thoughts releasing the guilt I was carrying earlier. I'm free. Free to do whatever I want, and right now, that's Kaz. Leaning in so close his lips touch the shell of my ear, he whispers, "I hear you have a boyfriend."

Not really a question, so I let it lie there between us long enough to take a sip. I know he's recently single, but I don't know the details of the breakup. Kaz's phone lights up on the table in front of him, but he ignores it. "You can answer it if you need to," I say.

He doesn't look at the screen to see who's calling before replying, "It's not important."

"You didn't even look."

When his eyes hit mine, they penetrate deeper than the surface of the conversation we're having. "Nothing's more important than living in the moment. And this moment is worth being present."

His words momentarily stun me, then I ask, "You sure you're only twenty-six?"

With a laugh under his breath, he looks around again. "I'm pretty sure and I like that you know my age." Leaning closer, he adds, "As for me *only* being twenty-six, I've lived a lifetime or two in those years."

"I don't know much about you," I say, pushing my fingers through my hair and hoping I don't come off like a groupie. But the way he listens to me puts me at ease. "I've learned a few details over the last year from being around you, but I'd like to know more."

His smile falters as he sits back. "I'd rather hear about you."

"Nice role reversal. Are you shy?"

A wry grin pops into place. "Do I seem shy to you?"

I shake my head. "Why are you so mysterious?"

"Am I?" His brow furrows. "I find it hard to be mysterious in LA or when you're in a band as big as *The Resistance*. My face is in the tabloids. Paparazzi seem to be everywhere. And my private life has been used for entertainment purposes by the media. So mysterious isn't really a word that comes to mind when thinking about my life." Resting his arms on the table, he adds, "But I have a few skeletons I'd like to keep in the closet. Now you on the other hand..."

Looking down, I turn the glass in my hand. "There's nothing special going on here."

"You don't see what I see." My gaze darts up, and I see his eyes set on mine. "Tell me about your relationship with the baseball player."

"Why do you want to know about that?"

"I like to know about my competition. It's easier to assess the opportunities."

Competition? Opportunity? Is he really interested in me? I laugh, liking his attention. "I've been warned about boys like you."

He leans in really close, so close that the scruff blanketing his jaw tickles the skin behind my ear when he whispers, "I'm no boy, babe." His words are drawn out and husky, his dulcet tone making me tingle all over.

When I turn, our lips are so close to touching that I start to move, but his hand captures the back of my head, and he asks, "Want to get out of here?"

I suck in an uneven breath, but manage to nod without fainting from swooning. Quick to his feet, he takes my hand, taking me to my feet with him. Rochelle looks between us. "Leaving?"

"We're gonna go."

She smiles and sits back. I trust Kaz, but I know Rochelle, and if she approves, it's okay to go with him.

As we work our way toward the exit, Kaz looks back at me as if making sure I'm still there. He flashes a smile that is somewhere between pure sex and the sincerest of grins. I have no idea how he does that, but it must get him laid a lot. I'm not sure which one I prefer, but I really like the way his hand wraps around mine—gentle and secure, possessive and with purpose. With the smile and that hand holding together, I'd follow him anywhere he wants to go. How is that even possible? I'm not frivolous with my emotions, but here I am, eager to follow.

I tried carefree with Mark. That didn't turn out well for either of us. Nothing about the way Kaz touches, speaks, or looks at me feels careless. It's all ground, just like Kaz, with meaning, a depth that goes beyond good looks and talent. I'd venture to say by how our skin feels pressed together that it's heart deep.

I hold on to him even tighter, knowing I have started to slip, maybe even begun to fall for him.

Out front, we get a cab, leaving the Suburban for the rest of the band to have when they're ready to leave. We slide in and he looks at me. "Your place?"

I tell the driver my address and lean back. Kaz puts his arm around me and we ride in silence. I have so many thoughts rushing through my head, so many feelings running through my chest. I'm free, I remind myself. Free to do as I please, *like Mark has done when he* wasn't *free.*

Kaz traces figure eights up my thigh, building the anticipation of what's to come. Hopefully that will be me. My breathing deepens. It feels good to be touched—*desired*—the sensations sparking every nerve to life. This cab ride has got to be the longest fifteen minutes of my life.

After hitting what seems like every red light between the club and my place, we finally arrive. I practically trip out of the car to get him inside.

Kaz gives the driver a wad of bills and tells him to keep the change and we hurry to the door. He grabs me by the hand and spins me around until I'm pressed against him. His lips meet mine, his other hand rubbing my cheek gently. We're out of breath when our lips part, our eyes bright from excitement. He says, "You never answered my question."

"About?"

"The boyfriend."

"We're not togethe—"

My words are cut off by caressing lips and a tempting tongue. My back falls against the wood of the door, and the shattering of glass fills my ears.

We jump apart and look down. "Shit," he says. "Sorry about that. I'll clean it up."

I'm still confused to what it is until I see a note amongst the red roses. "What is it?"

"A vase of flowers. My bad. I didn't see them."

"Me either." I reach for the note and Kaz guides me over the broken glass. All I need to see is the one name for me to want to avoid this altogether—Mark. I drop the note back down and unlock the door. "Let's get inside."

As soon as we step inside, my purse is dropped and I'm grabbed, then pinned to the wall before the door even shuts. His mouth is on mine. He tastes of whiskey and the faintest of mint, and I can't get enough. My nails run gently through his hair as his hands lift me up. I wrap my legs around his middle and kiss him hard while holding on to him tightly. I come up for air and open my eyes. Looking at him, I feel reckless, wild and crazy, *free*. There's that word again and it feels so good. "The bedroom," I mumble. "Down the hall."

Kaz turns quickly, holding me to him, but I straighten my legs and he sets me down. I turn and this time I lead him, taking his hand, and walk to the bedroom. He grabs me right before I enter the room and spins me around. With my back to the doorframe and my breath coming out harshly, I look up at him wondering why he stopped us. "Hey," he says, searching my eyes. "You sure? Once we go in there—"

I don't need to think twice, I'm sure. "Yes. Are you?"

"More than sure."

He picks me up and I scream as he tosses me over his shoulder. He's about to toss me onto the bed, but he stops and holds me there. I'm squirming and squealing, but then I stop and hang upside down laughing. "Are you going to put me down?"

His hand runs over my ass. "I'm liking the view from this angle."

I slap his ass as hard as I can. "Wait until you see it naked—"

I'm tossed to the mattress in one quick motion and he falls with me, landing over me, and looking down. "I don't think I can wait much longer."

The lamp on the nightstand is on, and something about what I'm sharing with Kaz makes me want to leave it on, to see everything, to watch him as he fucks me. With my eyes locked on his, I whisper, "Then don't."

He falls to the side. In a frenzy of flying clothes, we undress ourselves. Within seconds we're naked and back in our original position. Our breathing is fast, our hearts beating harder, and our desire mutual by the way his expression is reflecting how I feel. "Scoot up," he says. His voice is huskier than before, lust occupying some of the deeper notes.

I move until my head is on the pillow and knees bent with my feet on the mattress. He comes closer, tapping his fingers on the underside of my thigh. "Do you have condoms?"

"Yes. Nightstand."

He reaches over and pulls a few foil packets out and rips one off. I watch as he rolls it down his cock—smooth and long, thick, and if I wasn't so turned on, I might be worried by the size. He continues to fit the stereotype of rock stars quite well. My bottom lip is pressed between my teeth as I gaze down. He peeks up and smirks. "You ready for me?"

The question seems more loaded than the simplicity of the physical connection and I start to wonder if an emotional connection is possible between two people who share an intense attraction. Mark wounded more than my pride. He made me doubt if a deeper bond between two people is even possible.

Kaz moves to his knees and touches my chin. "Hey, you here with me?"

I push all else aside and focus on the feeling tightening in my belly when I look at him. "I'm here with you." And I am. I feel wanted. Desired. *His.* And I realize I need this. I need this attention, even if it's only for one night.

His hands spread my legs apart enough for him to settle between them. His tongue runs over his bottom lip as he looks at my breasts. He kisses each and then reaches up for my mouth and kisses the corners. His breath is hot, his body heated like mine. We're infernos. Our bodies become combustible together as the sparks fly between us. We tried for gentle, but quickly work our way into shameless and wanton. I move beneath him, my body reaching its own desired accord. I want to feel him, all of him. I want his cock pressed between my legs, deep inside. I want to come and then I want him to fuck me until I come again. *God, what is this man doing to me?*

Kaz Fabian makes shameless feel refined. His body presses between my legs as calloused fingertips slide down the curve of my breast, dipping in at my waistline and out over my hips. Pulling back, he looks down between us. "You're so fucking sexy."

Two fingers slide into my most intimate of places, making me want him even more. Heaving beneath him, I plead, "Kaz, don't tease."

"I'm not teasing. I'm appreciating."

As if all the other stuff wasn't enough, for that alone I'd kiss him again, and I do. His fingers rub and splay until I'm weak to him. I'm so close. His touch... the intensity in his expression... It's all for me. *For my pleasure.* My body starts throbbing inside, my mouth falling open, and a moan escapes as long-sought-after waves rolls through me. "Oh God."

I want to thank him, thank him for putting me first and making me feel so much that I've become grateful for an orgasm like it's a present from the gods. Instead, I try to show him how appreciative I am. I push lightly on his chest until he rolls to his back, and I say, "I want on top."

"You can have me however you want me, babe."

I straddle and position him, his cock so hard just for me. My tongue rolls over my bottom lip before leaning down and sliding it over his. He cups my breasts, kneading them while admiring them. This is it. There's no going back and I don't want to. I'm feeling something real for the first time in forever and I need more. Sliding down his length, I go slow, enjoying the fullness as he fills and stretches me, making me realize how empty I've been until now. His eyes close and he mutters, "You feel amazing." *And so does he. So amazing.*

Rocking back and forth a few times, I start slow, not wanting my body to tear like my soul has been torn. We start moving together, his hands sliding down my back and grabbing hold of my hips. My head drops back as our passion picks up. A moan and then another escapes as each breath is thrust out. I move my hips while holding his thighs. "You feel so good," I say between jagged breaths. He starts to move faster and I drop my hands forward on his chest, using his body as leverage as I join his rhythm, rocking hard on top of him. My eyes meet his and this time with my hair hanging all around me, the tips touching his chest, I smile. "You really do feel amazing, Kaz."

He bites his bottom lip and sits up quickly, his hands going around to my back. "C'mere," he says, and my lips meet his. Our tongues entwine as our bodies gyrate together.

Rolling us over, he licks my neck before sucking. I don't think there will be a mark, but I start wishing there was so I'd have something tangible tomorrow to hold on to. I moan loudly as he thrusts harder and harder. "Fuck!" he exclaims loud enough for me to know he's close.

I start moving, exhilaration blooming throughout my body. Holding on to his strong arms, I open my eyes and see the beauty in the pleasurable pain he's experiencing. I'm right there.

Right. There. With. Him.

He drops down on top of me and bites my shoulder, this time leaving a mark as he comes. It hurts too good to stop him and it'll be something I'll savor in the daylight, a memory that remains from tonight.

IT'S JUST PAST four in the morning. Kaz fell asleep less than an hour ago, but he's already sleeping soundly, his breaths regulated and deep, his face handsome and at peace with the world. My heart feels full as much as my body feels worn out in the *best* of ways.

I'm not experienced in one-night stands. The only other one I've done ended up in a long-term relationship I ended yesterday. So I need to contain the emotions that blanket my heart in something that feels like more than a friendly fast fuck.

I don't even know what he thinks of me, especially now after I slept with him so quickly. Am I now categorized as an easy fuck or a groupie? Mark thought I was easy when I had been sincere in my interest in the beginning.

Strings weren't discussed but it was clear neither of us wanted any attachment. But talking about it and preventing it are two different things when the heart is involved. I'm sure I'm another number on his bedpost, but tonight I'll snuggle into his side and enjoy the time we do have together.

Tomorrow I won't pressure him or make it awkward. I'll let him figure out what he wants and I'll move on either way. *Even though it was so good. Even though he said I felt amazing.*

I've been on my own since I was eighteen. I created a life that most would call lavish. I call it earned. I break hearts before they break mine. So I'll lie here against the warmth of his body and enjoy this night whether it leads to more or leads to another lesson learned.

THE SUNLIGHT MAKES its way across the room until it hits my face, then stops and decides to stay there until I can't deny it's morning. The inside of my eyelids are red from the brightness and I silently grumble. When I reluctantly open them, I look down and see two well-defined arms cocooning me. The heat from Kaz's body warms my backside, and his large endowment is pressed against my ass. This is more than spooning. He's holding me like he never wants to let me go. I relish the comfort.

"Let's stay in bed all day." His voice is deep, rough from sleep, his hold tightening even more. He drags the bridge of his nose along my neck, then kisses me. "You smell good."

"I probably smell like sweat from the concert, beer, and sex."

With a soft chuckle against my neck, he says, "Like I said, you smell good."

I laugh softly, closing my eyes again and enjoying his arms around me. I wake up two hours later. I open my eyes and see him beside me. The blinds are closed this time, I assume by Kaz, and he's asleep next to me. I watch how he sleeps, how he breathes, each breath powerful in the rise of his chest. I wonder if he always sleeps this well or if last night wore him out because of the show. Performing like they do must be exhausting.

He stirs, rolling toward me, and slowly opens his eyes. "Good morning."

"Good afternoon," I whisper.

"I'm working on evening with you."

I giggle and reach over to stroke his cheek, dragging my nails lightly down his neck. I like the feel of his scruff. Mark is always super clean-shaven. I shouldn't compare, but I always was a little weak to a bad boy. I smile, thinking about how special he's made me feel. Kaz may not be that bad of a boy. He matches the image, but has a heart of gold. If I'm not careful like Rochelle keeps warning, I just might fall a little in love with the man. It would be so easy to do. "Any plans today?" I ask to distract myself before my heartfelt thoughts get away from me.

Taking my hand in his, he kisses my fingers one by one, and replies, "I have lots of plans. All of them include you, this bed, maybe a little nourishment, this bed, and you."

"Do you treat all your one-nighters this well?" I look down, his attention making me blush.

His fingers gently pinch my chin and he lifts it until my gaze meets his. "Is that what you think?"

"I don't know what to think."

His hand dips under the covers and finds my hip. "Look, Lara, I know you had a boyfriend. I've asked around. We've been flirting and whatever, but I knew you were in a relationship. Last night you said you weren't taken, and I'd apologize for taking advantage of a recent breakup, but I'm not sorry. With that said, I've still been expecting your boyfriend to barge in here all night long and well into this morning. It's the afternoon and he isn't around, you're not calling him, and I'm still naked in bed with you. I'm not sure what's going on and I'm not that eager to leave, but if you want me to, I will, but know it's because you asked me, not because I want to."

"Why are you so nice? Don't you have a rep to uphold?"

He shakes his head. "No, no rep. Just me. You get what you see."

"I like what I see."

"I like you more and have for a while."

Annnnd I die a slow swooning death. His honesty affects me. How does he confess his true feelings so easily? "I don't know what to say to that."

He turns onto his stomach and buries his face into the pillow. When he peeks over at me, he says, "You don't have to say anything." *God, the man is cute.*

"I told you last night that I don't have a boyfriend. We broke up."

"I heard otherwise, so I wasn't sure."

"If you weren't sure, why'd you sleep with me?"

"Like I said, I've liked you for a while." He sits up and leans forward. With his eyes on me, he runs his fingers over the open palm of my hand.

His touch sends shivers through my body. The attraction is more than skin deep and I'm starting to want to see that cute little dent in his chin more often. I sit up and lean against the headboard, taking my hand away from his.

"What's wrong?" he asks. "Did I upset you? I don't like to lie, but maybe I said too much."

"You didn't. What you said was... I liked it, Kaz."

"Then what's wrong?"

"You're dangerous to my heart."

"I don't want to hurt your heart and I won't hurt you."

"I know. That's what makes you so dangerous."

His tongue dips out and slowly slides over his lower lip before he bites that same lip and looks away. He repeats what I said earlier, "Now *I* don't know what to say."

"Don't say anything at all," I say trying to recapture the ease of a few minutes earlier. "Just kiss me."

A smile runs across his face as he turns and takes me in his arms. "My pleasure." He makes love to me again and then I bring him to his knees with some of my own tender loving care before we fall back asleep.

The best conversations happen on lazy days.

There's a spark in his eye, a fire from within that drives his soul. I could listen to him talk all day and night. Every once in a while I hear a slight twist on a word, an accent that doesn't seem to fit. But he's entirely too captivating to stop to ask. "You probably understand the high you get when something you created from your thoughts, your time, you own abilities comes together."

Bringing my knees up, I snuggle into the covers a little more while facing him in bed. "I didn't know you were a songwriter."

"I'm a musician who likes to create."

"I call it blood love. You do something you love so much that you bleed your passion to life."

"Very visual," he jokes. "But true. I bleed for music. I do every time I perform." *That's exactly what I saw when he played last night.*

"It shows. You're amazing to watch."

"So are you," he says, dragging his hand over my shoulder. I love the way it feels, like he can't keep his hands off me. It's as if he has to find ways to touch me.

"You never told me what you did before you joined the band."

"You never asked."

"I asked you to tell me about you."

He rubs his eyes as if the topic is either boring or annoying. I can't tell.

"My life before *The Resistance* was a life not worth living nor mentioning." Rolling onto his back he takes some of the covers with him so I cuddle against him and rest my head on his chest. "I was living in an excuse. Saying and doing anything to avoid the expectations placed on me."

"I think most of us spend our teen years rebelling. What were you rebelling against?"

"My parents."

"Did they want you to become a doctor or a lawyer or something?" I laugh.

"No, worse—a professional musician." He smiles this grin that borders on cocky, but fully embraces sexy.

"You suck at rebelling, you know that?"

"Ha!"

"So you failed." It's fun to tease one of the most famous musicians in the world.

He sighs heavily as if there's more to the story. "If you only knew." He looks at me again and says, "Lie with me. I leave tomorrow and want to remember this."

I nod, letting the topic of his past go... for now, but hoping I get another chance to ask him about it later. I snuggle with him, wanting to remember this too.

I SHUT THE door and lock it behind me, smiling as I walk into the kitchen for another cup of coffee. Kaz and I had our first cup this morning and now after having a too-long-to-be-appropriate goodbye to him, I'm left lingering in my kitchen not sure what to do. He's only been here once, but his presence has taken over the whole space. And I like it. I like him.

Damn him and his enticing ways.

My phone rings. *Kaz.* "Hello," I answer aloud while swooning inside.

"I was thinking we should do it again." His voice is free-spirited and I'm reminded of his sexy smile.

"I'm up for *it* again."

His chuckles fill my ear. "Yes, that too, but I meant I want to see you again."

"I thought we were, on Tuesday?"

"Oh, yes. I'd almost forgotten the business at hand, too sidetracked by the business of you."

"I hope I'm not too distracting." He's too much fun to flirt with. "I could send my assistant over instead?"

"No. You're just the kind of distraction I've been looking for."

"Are distractions really a good thing?" I ask, smiling.

"In your case, most definitely."

"You can be very charming, you know that, Mr. Fabian?"

"I do, Ms. Kessler."

"And so humble," I tease. "It's a good combination."

His laugh initiates my own. "I should go before we end up taking this conversation a whole other route and the driver overhears what I plan to do to you next time.."

"Yes, I wouldn't want that." Oh my God, so much. I want to know what he wants to do to me so much. I'm looking forward to seeing you on Tuesday. Drive safe and talk soon. Bye, Kaz."

"Goodbye, Lara."

He's cute all right... yep, dangerously so.

LATER THAT EVENING, I sink into a tub full of hot water and bubbles. I sip my wine and lie back. Closing my eyes, my head fills with naughty thoughts of the rock star too delicious to not think about.

The serenity in my bathroom is ruined when my phone rings. When I see the screen and Mark's name, I try to hide my cringe. I hadn't really thought of him in the last twenty-four hours, which seems like a lifetime considering he used to try to control every minute of my day. He's trained me well and I push the answer button before I have time to think twice. *Shit*. "Hello?"

"Lara, where are you?" he asks.

"At home."

"You're coming over, right?"

"Why would I come over?"

"You didn't call me yesterday. I left messages. You promised we'd talk."

"Oh. Um. I'm sorry. I had my phone off so I could sleep. I guess I forgot to turn it back on." More like I was too caught up in bed to even think about my phone.

"Practice sucked. I want you to come over."

I let out a heavy breath. "I'm sorry."

"You're sorry? That's it?" he asks, his voice wavering between aggravation and hurt. "You're not coming?"

"I just want to take a bath, go to bed early, and read tonight. I have a busy Monday."

"You were never here for me when I needed you."

"I was there for you every night, even when you weren't. This weekend was the first time in a long time I was home for me."

"You must be starting your period. You're acting bitchy."

"I am not. You're just being an asshole." I hang up the phone, fuming from his remarks.

I finish my wine, then dry off, and trek into the kitchen for more. There isn't a bottle big enough to tamper my hot-temper tonight. Working my way back to the bathroom, my anger hasn't ceased, but increased. Mark better be damn glad he hasn't called back.

I have absolutely no doubt that I made the right decision in ending us. This is the ugly side of relationships, the ones that don't work out. I slip back into the hot, sudsy water, lean back, and close my eyes again. My exceptional time with Kaz is at the forefront of my thoughts, taking over completely.

When the water cools, I get out, and dry off again. After pulling on some cotton underwear and a tank top, I crawl under the bed covers. I can smell Kaz's cologne and take a deep breath, inhaling his scent from the pillow, and then smile. Giddy from the thrill of this new relationship and excited to see where it leads, I lie there with a smirky grin on my face and anticipate *our* next time.

My phone rings again. *Mark.* Nope. Sending to voicemail. I refuse to let him ruin my good mood. It's sad to see what had so much potential early on deteriorate so quickly, but it's obvious we were never meant to be.

We used to be fun... Mark Renner was coming off a winning season, voted MVP for his team, and had just been re-signed with a big pay raise. We met at a party in The Hills. The attraction was instant and mutual, but I'm thinking it might have been more physical than mental. Emotionally, we're very different, want different things in life, and expect different things from a partner.

Partner—that's the problem. He never wanted a partner. He wanted a shiny trophy for his arm, a prize to add to his collection. I'm more than my looks. I'm not unaware that I get attention for the superficial stuff, but I've worked hard to build my business. I've earned every accolade I've won.

I take a gulp of wine and lean back against the headboard, fuming. How dare he call me bitchy just because I didn't cater to his whim? *Spoiled!* He's spoiled and believes his own hype. I roll my eyes.

My phone rings, startling me. Moving to see the screen, the sheets bunch at my feet, sheets that Kaz and I were tangled in all night. Seeing Mark's name on the screen ruins my memory. No way am I answering it. I'm already too riled up to deal with his shit again. Then the banging on my front door begins.

Grabbing my robe, I wrap it around me as I make my way to the front door. I peek through the peephole. *What the hell? When has he ever come after me like this?* Never. Possibly because I always turned up when he beckoned. My mistake. Another lesson learned. I take a deep breath, steadying myself and my thoughts, then exhale and open the door. "What are you doing here?" I ask, no patience for this man.

He pushes past me. "Is someone here? Is that why you've been ignoring me?" He walks around the living room and then into the kitchen searching for suspects while I remain at the front door with it held wide open.

"You have no right to be here. I want you to leave."

His eyes narrow, a vein exposing itself in his forehead. It's one I only see when I've seen him in playbacks of his losing games. It means he's pissed. This time though he's pissed at me. That bulging vein is aimed in my direction. "What the fuck, Lara? Who's here?"

I close the door not wanting the neighbors to hear the fight I can feel brewing. "You need to leave. Now." He takes off down the hall and kicks my bedroom door all the way open. Running after him I yell, "Stop searching my house and leave. I mean it, Mark."

He turns in an instant and pins me by my shoulders. My breath escapes me as my back slams against the hallway wall. "Are you cheating on me?" There's a rage running rampant in his eyes that turns my blood cold. I was scared before, but now I'm terrified. My hands fly up to push him away. My wrists are grabbed and ground against the stucco wall, the rough surface scratching my skin as his thumbs rub harshly over the veins on the underside. "You're so... breakable. Perfect and small."

"Mark," I start, my voice trembling. I clear it, needing to gain my composure, concerned for my safety if I don't calm him down. I've seen him mad, but now it's channeled completely at me. "You're hurting me. I know you don't want to hurt me." I wiggle my wrists until his grip loosens.

His breathing is jagged, but in his eyes I see the moment the man I cared about returns. A slow intake of air calms him enough to reason what he's just done. "Lara..." He backs away, his own back hitting the other wall, as if invisibly pushed off me. "I'm sorry. I don't know what came over me. I'm sorry."

I look down and rub my wrists one at a time. They're scratched and raw. When I look back up, my voice no longer shakes. It's firm and direct, "You should go."

"I'm sorry." He shakes his head like he hopes his better judgment comes back. "I didn't mean it."

Shaken, I fight the tears wanting to appear and walk back to the living room and straight for the front door. With the door held open, I see the roses. "I want you to leave and take your damn flowers."

When he walks to me, I back away with my eyes lowered. My hand is gripping the doorknob so tightly that it's starting to hurt.

"Please let me—"

"Please, Mark. I don't know what just happened. I don't want to make things worse by arguing."

"I had this crazy thought that you were blowing me off because you were cheating."

I look into his eyes, scared to say the words I know will upset him, but I need to make myself clear. "We're not together anymore."

He nods, his head down, his shoulders slumped forward. All six five of him crumbling in shame right before my eyes.

He deserves to live in that shame for the night. The nerves in my wrists lick with fire as they pulse with pain. Just as I look down at my right wrist, he says, "I love you."

The shock of hearing him say this after months of holding back, throws me, sending my heart and head into a tailspin. "Please go, Mark." That's all I can muster while holding back the tears desperate to fall in protest. I can't believe he would say those three words because of duress from the situation instead from love and happiness.

Finally, he walks out the door, but stops on the mat, and says, "Call me when you wake up. Okay?" When I don't respond, he insists, "Okay? Promise me."

"Okay," I quickly agree, but only to end this. I shut the door, locking the three locks, and activate the alarm system. I go to the kitchen and run my wrists under cool water. I'm gentle as I run my fingers over them. There are a few scratches and there might be a little bruising added to the other ones, so I dry them and pull two icepacks from the freezer.

I wish I could call Rochelle or talk about what just happened, seek another opinion, or find reasoning in his behavior. But no one can know about this. One leak and this would be bad for him. *Don't embarrass me, Lara. It's bad for my career.* His career...

Did I do something wrong? Am I missing something?

Although my mind is blurring with emotions, I'm willing to chalk it up to a moment of insanity on his part. My tears finally fall.

I angered him.

He acted from fear of losing me when he was already feeling rejected. He's an athlete, used to being physical, so he got a little rough. I know he didn't mean to hurt me.

"You're so... breakable. Perfect and small."

I know in my heart he didn't mean to. I'm just... small. Easily hurt.

He didn't mean to hurt me.

A GRANDE COFFEE is set down on my desk, and Lane, my lead designer slash assistant, says, "You were late. How is that possible when you live here?"

"Good morning to you too, Lane. I needed a coffee that I didn't have to make." I needed to get tested for STDs because of Mark's philandering, and thankfully, my doctor's office squeezed me in. That's the truth I'll lie about this morning. "Thank you."

"You're welcome. Hey. What's with the throwback to Madonna "Like a Virgin" and bangle days?" He leans against the desk while I finish attaching a swatch to the board, my bracelets jingling. "Are we not talking about it?"

"About what?" I look up at him, hoping my wide-eyed innocent expression will throw him off the scent.

He walks around behind me and hovers over my shoulder, judging the board with a silent chin rub. "New client?"

It worked. "Yep."

Moving back to the chair in front of my desk, he sits, and crosses his legs as he would say, "at the ankles like a proper lady."

"Fine, I'll drop harping on the '80s wardrobe throwback so you can fill me on the client."

"Kaz Fabian."

"*Ooohhh*, Kaz Fabian. I like the name. *So sexy*. Now where have I heard it before?"

Taking the coffee in hand, I sit back in my chair and sip the hot brew, then smile. "Kaz Fabian is a guitarist in the band *The Resistance*."

"*Ahhh*, the boys in the band. How are they doing these days?"

"They're busy, but getting a break soon. Kaz just closed on a house and he wants us to start immediately."

Lane takes the electronic tablet from my desk and starts taking notes. "I'll need the address, his phone number, any house regulations, limitations, expectations. Remodel or only design decorating? Timeline? Deadline? Rush or standard? When can I see the house? What's the code to get in if gated? Does he have any pets I need to be aware of, and, last but certainly not least, is he cute, single, and gay?"

I burst out laughing, and am so glad I wasn't drinking at the time or it would surely be spewed all over the visual board I just created. "You're very on top of things this morning."

"You should have seen what I was on top of last night."

My eyes dart to his and I raise an eyebrow. "Wow, and frisky too."

"Frisky, caffeinated, and happy."

"It's working for you. Direct that energy into design and we'll have a kickass week. As for the other information, I've seen online photos from the realty site, but I won't see the property until tomorrow night when he's back in LA. Also, he's very cute and very straight." I can't hide the smile I get just thinking of Kaz, so I start gathering the papers spread out on my desk as a deterrent.

He does an over-the-top eye-roll, then starts typing again. "Well, that doesn't do me any good. So not fair."

"Half of LA is on your team, so I think that leaves us pretty dang equal."

"I love when you use dang. You're adorable like that."

"Dang. Dang. Dang," I say and stick my tongue out at him.

When he looks up from the tablet, I busy myself with the crap on my desk again. "That desk hasn't been cleaned in months."

"I know. That's why I'm cleaning it."

"You only clean when you're hiding something or you're avoiding a topic because you're not ready to share. Which is it?" He leans forward conspiratorially. There's a giddiness to his tone when he says, "So how'd you land the Fabian account? Did you have to sleep with him?"

I about choke on my own spit, and start hacking. Lane jumps up and hits me on the back until I manage to say, "Okay. Okay. Stop."

Walking around the desk back to the chair, he mumbles, "Just trying to help."

My hands feel cool against my heated cheeks as I try to regain my breath again. I clear my throat and look away from his suspicious eyes. "Thanks for the vote of confidence by the way."

"Oh, come on. Two hot singles in the City of Lost Angels—"

"I never said he was single."

"You didn't have to. I think the choking, cleaning of the desk, red face, and avoidance techniques kind of say it all, don't you think?" This time he raises an eyebrow at me.

I slip my fingertips around the bangles, silencing them. "You know when it comes to business I keep it professional."

He turns the tablet toward me, showing me a large photo of Kaz. "Dammmnnnn. Look at that yumminess. Mm-hmm. Why do all the good-looking ones have to be straight?"

"You know. My girlfriends and I say that about gay guys. Once again, greener grass not so green on the other side." I look at the photo and let myself smile in front of him, knowing he'll always protect any secrets. But I don't think I'm quite ready to reveal *these* secrets quite yet.

"Actually, I take that back. We do have cuter guys." Laughing, he stands up and heads for his desk in the other room. "But let's face it, Mark Renner, hot player extraordinaire, is the luckiest of them all to have snagged you, my dear."

My wrists begin pulsing from the mere mention of his name. My heart starts thumping in my chest as I look down at the bangles.

I feel something on my shoulder and scream. The back of my chair hits the windowsill as I grab my wrists protectively.

"Lara?" My eyes bolt up to see Lane. "What happened? Are you okay?"

Snapping out of the memory from last night that held me captive seconds earlier, I try to smile for him, to ease the worry written on his face. "I'm sorry. I forgot something in my bedroom." I stand and rush to the stairs. "I'll be back in a minute."

He lets me leave in silence, which is so unlike him. I'm relieved as I turn at the top of the staircase and head up to the main floor of my place, and run for my bedroom. As I pass the spot where I was pinned in fear, my hands start shaking, so I fist them to steady myself and hurry away. I head straight to the medicine cabinet in my bathroom. The Xanax aren't hard to find, but I don't use them much. Once I needed a few after a car accident I was involved in. I couldn't sleep or eat, reliving the accident over and over in my head. This feels a lot like that same post-traumatic reaction.

I down a pill and follow it with water I have cupped in my hand over the sink. I don't want to think about last night, and attempt to blow off my overreaction by the lack of sleep getting the better of me. I lean toward the mirror, palms flat on the marble, wrists aching from the pressure, but I push through it. "I will be fine. I will be fine." I say it one more time, hoping to believe it if said again. "I will be fine."

Swallowing hard, I raise my chin and lift my hands, my wrists aching from the memory more than his grasp. There's minor bruising that can be easily hidden by makeup or bracelets. As for my emotional state, it's a little more damaged, but easier to hide. My heart steadies and I close my eyes, then exhale. A light knock on the door draws my attention. I look up and straighten my hair quickly, and exhale.

Lane pokes his head inside, just as I turn around. "Hey there. Just checking on you. You okay?"

"Fine. Fine," I reply, "Sorry. I'm tired. I didn't get much sleep over the weekend. We're too busy for me to be tired though. I'm fine now."

He nods as if he believes me. "I'm heading over to Calliope's. Her end tables, the two large entryway mirrors, and dining room set have arrived. I want to inspect each piece before the delivery guys leave."

"Thanks." I nod to ease his concern for me. "Touch base with me. I'm scheduled to go over later for the bedroom furniture. Can you confirm the appointment for that delivery while you're out there?"

The concern never leaves his face as his eyes glance to my wrists and back up. "No problem. Talk later." He leaves, but comes right back, and says, "If you ever want or need to talk without the usual witty remarks, you know you can talk to me, right?"

I smile, for him, to put him at ease. "I do. Thanks." *And I do.*

"Okay. Catch ya later, Chica-bee."

"What are you doing?"

Kaz's voice fills me with joy. "Thinking about your house and tracking down a rug for a very demanding actress. What are you doing?"

"I like that you're thinking about my house, but I can't help but want you to be thinking about other things of mine."

"Is this you flirting, Kaz?" I sit back in my chair and start a slow spin, loving that he called me.

"I suck at it, don't I? Maybe that's why I don't have a girlfriend."

"You don't suck... well, sometimes you do, but I liked it." I bite the end of the pen in my hand, grinning.

"I do suck better at some things than others."

"As a firsthand witness to your sucking, your sucking does not suck at all, just so you know. And I like your flirting. Go on..."

"I'll go on and on when I'm back tomorrow. I want to see you."

My heart eats up his deep voice and playful words. "Is this a professional call or personal?"

"Can't it be both?"

"I don't normally mix business and pleasure."

He chuckles. "I thought we already had this talk about exceptions."

"Ahhh yes, you are definitely one worth making an exception for."

"You're not too sucky at this flirting thing either, Ms. Kessler."

"Thanks. I've had many years of experience."

"And here I thought I was special." He sounds pouty on the other end of the line. "How much experience are we talking about anyway? Girl-next-door innocent or Call Girl?"

"Those are my choices? Wow, you don't leave much gray area. How about Catholic school girl?"

"I'm impressed. You were wild then."

"I'm wild now," I joke, spinning around again in the chair.

"You're beautiful too." I bite my lip, not sure how to follow such sweetness. He lowers his voice. "Too soon?"

I'm shaking my head though he can't see me. "No, you've got perfect timing."

He lightens the conversation back up and says, "I am a musician. Timing is everything."

"Yep, timing is everything. As for the house, I'd love to see it."

"Oh yeah, the house. Dinner at the new place around seven?"

"That works for me. I'll need to take measurements and pictures for reference."

"Are we still talking about my house?"

I burst out laughing. Repeating what he once told me, I say, "Not at all."

"Good because we have all night."

"Perfect. I'll see you then."

His tone gets husky, an element of appeal that conjures naughty thoughts of the last time we were together. "Goodbye, Lara."

As I type the appointment into my planner and sync my phone with the program, my stomach fills with fluttering butterflies of the most wonderful kind.

I still have so much to process with my love life. The butterflies for Kaz have definitely jaded my thoughts toward Mark. I stare out the large window overlooking my backyard and realize Mark jaded my thoughts when he hurt me, not Kaz. Surely Mark can't think we'll get back together after what happened or with how bad things were before we talked. Everything happens for a reason and thinking back on what Kaz said, timing is everything, and maybe *our* timing is perfect.

MY TEST RESULTS came back clean and I can finally relax. Or so I thought...

Flowers start arriving around two o'clock and don't stop until nine when the final bunch is hand delivered by Mark himself.

"I'm sorry," he says, shoving the bouquet at me.

With flowers against my chest, I wrap one arm around them and keep one hand on the door. I stand there in shock that he has the nerve to show up like this. "What are you doing here?" I hold the flowers out, not wanting them. "And take these. I don't want them."

"You said we could talk."

"I did say that, but I don't see the point."

He walks past me without my permission and I step back, intimidated by his stature. Holding the flowers out to him again, he sees the change in my expression. He must see the fear I wear so obviously as my hands shake. His eyes set on mine, and he says, "You know I didn't mean to hurt you. You know that, Lara. I wouldn't hurt you. Not ever. I love you. You believe me, right? Right?"

"Mark—"

"Don't say my name like that. I can hear the change in your tone." He quickly grabs hold of my arms and the bouquet falls to the ground. His grip is firm as I cower down. "I love you," he pleads, shadowing me. "My love for you is real, Lara. You have to believe me. I've never felt like this for anyone."

Fear snowballs in the pit of my stomach. "I believe you," I whisper, not sure if I even hear my voice. His hold on me loosens just enough for me to slip out and back away toward the couch. I'm hoping to make it to the other side, to have something large and solid between us. "We can talk. All right?"

"Sit," he commands.

I sit down knowing I can't get to my phone in the office downstairs without him catching me and doing who knows what to me.

"Thank you," he says, sounding calmer as he sits in the chair across from me. This is the Mark I know, but I'm guarded by the sudden turn. "I don't know what happened last night, but I promise it won't happen again."

"Or after the other incident? How can you promise that when you don't know what happened?"

"Lara, please. Just trust me. You know I would never hurt you on purpose—"

"You hurt me last night and it seemed like it was on purpose. I have bruises to prove it." I push up the sleeves of my robe and show him the scratches on the top and bruises where his thumbs dug into me. "You hurt me just now."

He sucks in a breath. It stutters in his throat as he stares at the bruising. His head shakes. "I didn't do that."

Confused by his reaction, I reason, "You did, Mark."

Standing up, he looks down at me. "I'll make this up to you. Flowers won't heal this mess."

I hold the arm of the couch, bracing myself. "You don't have to heal this mess. We're not together anymore."

"No." He stands there looking strong, his chest appearing bigger than a moment earlier. "What happened last night won't happen again. I promise you. I had a rough day and you weren't there. I was upset. Practice sucked. I was benched half the day. I just want us together." Kneeling down in front of me, I see the desperation in his eyes. Seeing this strong man breaking before me is hard to watch despite the incident from the night before. "Please, Lara. I need you." His head drops to my knees and I hear him sniffle.

"Mark—"

"Please don't say my name like that. Say it like you used to, like when you loved me."

"I can't. I'm here, but only as a friend." *Friend* is being generous, but I'll say what I need to right now. *I just need him to leave.*

He wails in distress and I'm not sure if I should try to comfort him or not. "Please don't do this. I'll be good."

Refusing to kick someone when they're down, my defenses crumble. "Maybe you can be better. Maybe you won't hurt me again, but my heart is not in this, Mark. Please. You have to let me go and move on."

"I can't. We're so good together. I screwed up and I'm sorry. I promise I'll be better."

My heart's not racing from fear, and my hands aren't shaking anymore. Seeing a man of his size—of his demeanor—break is heartbreaking in itself. I do what I know I shouldn't, but can't help. I stroke his hair as his head lies in my lap.

THE NEXT DAY I walk into the restaurant and hang my purse by the strap on the back of the chair. Exasperated, I say to Rochelle, "I have so much to talk about."

She laughs. "I have so much to talk about too, but you go first."

I slide into my chair and scoot up to the table. "Did you order wine?"

"I did. Of course. This isn't my first rodeo." I laugh just as two glasses of wine arrive along with the bottle in an ice bucket. "You go first," she says.

"I spent the night with Kaz and then I spent another."

"That was fast," she says, relaxing back with the menu in hand as if she expected it all along. Maybe she did. "How do you feel about that?"

I reach for my glass of wine, needing someone else's perspective on the situation. Rochelle will never utter a word to anyone about it, so I know I can trust her. "I like him, Ro. Is it too soon? Am I just confused because of the breakup with Mark?"

She leans forward. "Not too soon if you don't regret it."

"I don't, but I feel like I should."

"Why? You're both recently single, young, hot. You're both creative types. Sounds like a match made in Hollywood Heaven."

The waitress arrives, takes our orders, and tops up our glasses. When she leaves, Rochelle says, "You've dated someone famous and understand the baggage that comes with that fame. Be upfront with him and demand the same from him. Secrets destroy happiness."

"That's why they're secrets."

Our salads are delivered, but my stomach is in knots. She adds, "You've worked hard to build your reputation and career. It's very admirable."

"Thank you." Thinking of Kaz, I ask, "Are we moving too quickly?"

"You both just broke up with your others, but that doesn't mean it should dictate your future relationships. Do what feels right."

I nod in agreement because she's right. "Maybe we should slow down." I'm starved and start eating like it's going to be stolen from me.

"So what if you didn't. We're adults and if it felt good and no one was hurt, just keep doing what you're doing. Anyway, I like you two together. And Mark is on the same page now?"

"I think he understands we're done."

"You think?" she asks, her fork clanging against the porcelain plate.

"We are. We're done."

Her eyes are set, her complete attention on me. "What is going on, Lara?"

"Nothing," I lie, not wanting to expose the dirty details with Mark. "I told you. I slept with Kaz, and it was great."

"You actually didn't tell me the sex was great, so good to know, and ick. He's like a brother to me."

I laugh, and roll my eyes. "One minute you're pushing me on him and the next you're grossed out."

"Yeah, I want you together, but I don't want the details." Now she's laughing.

"Good, because I don't want to share them."

The laughter stops and a wave of heaviness rolls in. When I look up she asks, "Are you sure you're okay?"

"I'm sure." I'm lying. I'm shaken and a little wounded on the outside and a lot on the inside, but my shame feels more powerful at the moment. I never thought I'd find myself in this situation. It's embarrassing to admit, so I put on a smile for her, and say, "I'm fine."

"It's good to see you happy again. You deserve it. You deserve someone who treats you with respect. As for the details, maybe a few. I need to live vicariously for a few minutes before I return to mommyhood."

In minutes, spending time with my friend has turned around my whole day. I feel so much better than I did after saying I would be Mark's friend last night. My relationship with him is thick with deceit. It's nice to have the reprieve.

I PARK JUST inside the gate. There are no other cars at Kaz's new house, so I'm not sure if I should wait in my car or see if the door is open for me. I decide to get out and walk up. The house is great, a beautiful Mediterranean. From the outside, it's one I'd be interested in if I was in the market to buy a new house. Deep green vines cover the walls on either side of the entrance that are anchored by large planters and that house large black wooden doors that look old from time instead of design.

After being on Calliope's project for months, it's a nice break to work on a man's house. The lines and design tend to be less over the top, even with the history of the home coming into play.

I check the front door and it opens, so I go inside. I cross through the foyer and enter the main room; large dark wood beams highlight a vaulted ceiling that gives the space an airy, but impressive feel. There's a back wall of what appears to be glass pocket doors showing off the beauty of the landscaping. I love the warmth and see why he bought it.

The only piece of furniture in the room is not furniture at all. A beautiful black baby grand piano is tucked in the corner. No guitar like I expected, but he's not moved in yet. The bench is protected between the wall and the instrument. Drawn to it, I admire the shiny lacquer and the scale. It's perfect in this room.

"The house has been well maintained," Kaz's voice greets my backside.

I turn with a smile, my back against the piano. "It has been. It's beautiful."

"So are you." He comes closer. "It's good to see you."

I can't help feeling coy, and I know I'm blushing just from his smile. "It's good to see you, too."

Leaning in, he kisses me on the cheek, then whispers, "I can't stop thinking about you."

Just as he's about to move away, I hold him and kiss under his jaw. "You've been on my mind since you left."

We stand in the middle of the room. His body is relaxed under my hands and his scent is masculine and calming. His hands are on my hips and our bodies close the distance. I can feel his heart beating steady and mine steadies in sync.

The back of my head is stroked and the gesture is so loving that I close my eyes, wanting to stay in this moment for as long as I can.

A sharp inhale is heard and his breath covers my neck followed by a sweet peck. He whispers, "Would you like to eat or have a tour first?"

"Give me the tour and start with this," I reply lowly, weak to this man.

A smile plays on his lips, tempting me to kiss him. He says, "The piano is one of the few items I own. It's a Steinway. Other than the house, it's my biggest splurge."

"Do you play?"

"I play."

"Will you play for me now?"

"I doubt it's in tune after being moved in yesterday."

"Maybe another time?"

"Definitely another time." He starts toward the stairs. "Ready to see the rest?"

"Lead the way." It's still daylight and our voices echo in the empty house, but there's an intimacy he maintains when he takes my hand. I grab my measuring tape from my purse and leave the bag on the floor.

Signaling to the stairs, he says, "We can start in the bedroom... or mix it up and hit the kitchen first. Where do you like it?"

I love a good double entendre but this man is well versed in the language of seduction, so as much as I want to react just like my body is, I stick to the business at hand. "Kitchens are the heart of the home. Let's start there."

He laughs under his breath, turns, and takes me into the kitchen. He pats the wall, and says, "It opens somewhat to the living room, but I'm wondering if we take down part of this wall if the kitchen, this breakfast area, and the living room can flow even better."

Standing in the middle of the breakfast area, I look behind me and into the kitchen. "I see what you mean. The breakfast area is really another living space and we can treat it as such. We can easily fit a table for ten in here. If we go smaller, then there's still enough room for a couch and chair, a coffee table and barstools at the bar. From the photos online, the space wasn't used effectively by the previous owners." I'm about to continue as I walk into the kitchen, stopping near the island, but I feel the weight of his gaze on me, coating my insides in ways that feel new and exciting. Slowly I glance over my shoulder and find his eyes directed on me, an indiscernible expression on his handsome features.

His phone rings, shattering the building intensity and I start breathing again. When he looks at the phone, he says, "I need to take this. Feel free to walk around. I'll catch up." He walks to the back door and answers his phone. "Hey, what's up?"

I take the opportunity to check out the rest of the first floor. The house really is stunning. It doesn't shout showy or celebrity. It's not a home most twenty-six-year-olds would choose when coming into a lot of money. It's large, but the perfect size to raise a family and have room to grow. I can see a lifetime spent in this home, changing with the different stages of life. *It's not just for show or to flaunt his wealth. Unlike some...* I'm impressed with his refined taste.

When I go upstairs, I start in the master bedroom. It's the most important room on this level and will need the most attention to detail. There are several large windows facing the backyard, which appears to be at least two acres, if not more. The view is spectacular. Downtown visible in the distance. Prime old Hollywood real estate.

"The house feels good, right?"

Staring out the window, I agree. "Very good. It's warm." I turn around and find him leaning against the doorframe. "It's a great home. I'm getting house envy."

He chuckles. "You're welcome here anytime." Moving to the en-suite, he asks, "Have you gotten the measurements you need?"

I haven't gotten any. I've been way too distracted. "Actually, I'll send Lane out to do that tomorrow if that's all right. He's my right-hand designer."

"That's fine." Running his hand through his hair, he questions, "What are you thinking construction wise? Much to remodel or do you like what you see?"

Looking him in the eyes, I reply, "I like what I see, and I also like the house." A perfectly imperfect smirk resides on his face. It's startling how disarming it is. I make a move to leave and pat his chest. "See? Two can play that flirtation game." I leave him in the bedroom with the sound of his laughter bouncing off the barren walls.

When the tour is complete, we end up in the living room. It's all good until my stomach decides to let the world know I'm hungry. "How about we eat?" he asks. "I brought salads and sandwiches, soups, crackers, some cheese and sausage, grapes, strawberries, and dessert."

"That's a lot of food."

"I didn't know what you'd want so I bought most of the menu." He takes my hand and leads me into the kitchen where the bags cover one of the countertops.

"You're very thoughtful. Thank you."

Kaz hops up on the counter and reaches into a bag. He pulls out a handful of grapes and pops one in his mouth. "Tell me how this works."

I hand him a strawberry while I hold on to another. "Usually you take it and touch it to your lips like this." The strawberry glides over my bottom lip. "Then you bite it." I take a bite, then lick the juice that's about to drip from my lip.

His mouth is hanging open before he says, "I meant working with a designer, but I like this a lot more. Continue..."

I laugh out loud. "Ohhhh. Well, since you know how to eat a strawberry, let's talk business. My designs depend on what the client wants. You have a Mediterranean home style wise but maybe you want a modern interior or maybe you want to match the home and bring out the home's unique features. Or maybe we can highlight what makes you so unique. Personalizing a space is always the best. You'll feel more comfortable when you're home. What do you want?"

"I want you."

"You've got me. I'm here. We're talking about the house just like we planned. I've already talked to Lane about the project and done a preliminary design board."

He hops off the counter and comes closer, trapping me between his arms. When he leans, he bends forward until he's eye level. "I meant what I said earlier. I couldn't get you off my mind."

"You didn't try hard enough." I gulp from the intensity as I drag my finger down the front of his shirt.

"I didn't want to try. I rather liked the memories, but seeing you here now..." he sucks in a rough breath, "I don't want to talk about the house." His lips meet mine and the two-day absence feels like a year when enjoying the bliss of this sweet pressure. I'm picked up and set on the counter. The surface is cold, the granite slick and expansive. A hard bulge teases between my legs as he pulls me to the edge, harder against him.

I lie back, my arms draped over my head. The top button of my jeans is opened, but he leaves that area, distracted by my exposed stomach. My shirt is pushed up as he slides his hands over my skin. Then I'm left alone. My head pops up and I anchor myself on my elbows to stare at him. "What happened?"

With an arrogance written across his face I know he can back up, he leans against the opposite counter, and says, "I think we should eat first."

My gaze darts to the erection in his jeans. "Really? 'Cause it looks to me like you'd rather do other things first." Then it hits me as I glance around. "Is this about respect? You know, you don't want to treat me bad and do it here on the counter or whatever?"

He scoffs. "Fuck, no. I have no problem disrespecting you on the counter, or anywhere else for that matter." His hand rubs over his cock. "I just thought I should at least feed you once before fucking you." He comes over and grabs my ankles. One swift pull and I'm face to face with him again with my feet on the ground. When I wrap my arms around his neck, he kisses me once on the lips and again on the neck. "Let's eat and then I'll be more than happy to disrespect you several times over."

He's addicting.

Body.

Mind.

Voice.

I'm head over feet completely addicted to him.

KAZ PROPERLY DISRESPECTED me twice before I drove home. I considered staying after being invited, but since he had no furniture we would have to go back to the place he shared with Derrick. If I had to see Derrick like that I'd feel like one of many and that's just not a self-esteem issue I was ready to deal with after leaving his house on a high.

The next day I'm back out at his house with Lane. Kaz and Tommy show up after we have measured the three rooms we're starting on first.

I try to remain professional, but why does Kaz have to have that dimple in his chin? Those eyes that seem to darken when his gaze lands on me? That damn shirt that fits like it was tailored to show off all his hard work in the gym? And I can't ignore the jeans that highlight his awesome ass. He makes it so hard to resist and resisting is exactly what I should be doing on a client call.

Tommy is asking questions, curious about my creative process. "Do designers have visions or is that something I got from TV?"

I lean down and drop the measuring tape into my bag.

"Sometimes I get visions and see a space's finished design in my head."

Kaz steps forward and with his hand pressed gently to my lower back, he says, "I can take you out back and show you the pool and hot tub."

"I love hot tubs." I admonish myself the second the words come from my mouth. "Sorry. That sounds so pervy." I shrug. "But I do despite the germ reports."

Smiling, his eyes light with laughter. "No worries. I'll have it thoroughly cleaned for you. Unless you want to live dangerously and take a dip."

I should almost feel ashamed for acting this way in front of Lane and Tommy. *Almost.* But I don't. I'm happy on the inside and that kind of happiness can't be contained on the outside. "I don't have a suit with me anyway and I'm not sure if I should be getting naked with a client." I wink as we open the pocket doors. They stick a bit. "I'll have someone check on these doors. They should glide smoother."

"Will they have to be replaced?"

"No, they're great quality. Just in need of an oil." I step outside and follow a path that leads to the pool. Just beyond the pool I see a cave-like area hidden by the waterfall feature. "What's back there?"

"The grotto with the hot tub."

"You have a grotto?" I ask, insinuating everything. "How very Hugh Hefner of you."

"The man is ninety and he's still got game—"

"So you're thinking the secret to his sexual success is his grotto?"

"Figure it won't hurt."

I can't help but smile, peeking back at him as I walk up the path. "Nope, it can't hurt. Have you ever been to the Playboy Mansion?"

"I've partied there a time or two."

"I went a few months ago. Apparently some of the Playmates are fans of my ex."

"I heard he plays pro baseball." He sits on a large rock near the grotto while I look inside. "How long did you date?"

"Six months or so."

"Not serious then?"

I'm flattered he's so interested in getting to know me better. Inside the grotto, I lean back on a short wall made of rock. Reflecting on that state of affairs. "I'm not sure what it was anymore."

Kaz sits down on the opposite side, the hot tub dividing us. His voice goes quieter when he asks, "Did you love him?"

I finally look up. "I think this conversation is too heavy for a Wednesday."

He nods, not saying anything else. Slowly he gets up and I watch him go inside. I stay a few minutes longer liking the solitude of the cave. No wonder Hefner always scored. Grottos are the way to go. Beyond the sex appeal of the intimate space, it's peaceful. I go inside to find Lane talking to Kaz and Tommy. They're getting along, which is good, but I know I'm going to hear more than an earful once we leave. I'm just wondering if that earful will be good or bad.

I grab my phone out of my bag to check emails and find I've missed two calls from Mark. *Ugh!* I really don't want to deal with him anymore, but I'm going to have to get my things sometime, and sooner is probably better than dragging it out and getting it later.

"Did you get the measurements, Lane?" I ask, joining the group in the kitchen.

"I did. And I got the two other spaces. Kaz said he wants to go ahead and get those done at the same time."

Kaz adds, "Makes sense to get it all done from the beginning." With his eyes on me, he leans against the counter, looking relaxed. "When do you think you'll have the preliminary designs Lane mentioned?"

"I sent you an email this morning with the questions. Once you fill it out, we can meet and go over your answers. The design part will begin after that."

"I'll work on it tonight. Unless, of course, I get caught up in something else."

Not subtle. *To anyone.*

I swear my body reacts like a whore to his voice. "Caught up happens sometimes."

Lane whispers so everyone can hear him, "I think he means you, Lara. I think he means caught up in you."

My eyes dart to Lane's, and I scowl. With a bop to his arm, my sarcasm drips with laughter. "Yeah, got it. Thanks."

Tommy rolls his eyes and heads for the door. "I'm gonna go. Your sexual innuendoes to each other aren't really innuendoes. I got the hint."

Kaz follows him. "Yeah, okay. We'll talk later."

Talking to me, Kaz asks, "Can you stay?"

Lane answers before I can reply, "Yes, we both can."

Kaz and I shoot Lane a surprised glare. He huffs. "Fine. I'll leave so you guys can get it on."

"Lane! We're not going to 'get it on.' We're discussing business." I'm not sure he believes me since my arms are waving around wildly. "And decorating stuff."

"Stuff?" Lane asks, his face contorting. "You never call it decorating *or stuff.*" When he looks at Kaz, he says, "You've done good, Fabian. You're the first man I've ever seen make her go loopy."

"There's always a first time. Glad I could be it," he says all suave and full of himself. He's hot like that. "Did you need any more measurements?"

Lane looks at Kaz's crotch and taps his chin. "Maybe your insea—"

"Okay. Okay," I interrupt before this goes even further south— literally and conversationally. I grab Lane's arm and start pulling him toward the door. "I'll see you back at the office later."

He smacks my hand on his arm. "Hands off my Vincent Vittori shirt. You know how protective I am."

Rubbing the fabric, I add, "It is very soft."

He leans in and whispers, "It's the material and the hand-sewn seams."

I can't stop from laughing and hit his backside. "It's fabulous. Now get your fabu-ass out of here."

With a hair flip that doesn't flip because it's styled to perfection on top of his head, he says, "I have to go out to Malibu. Calliope is having a dinner party and wants my input."

"With your help, I know it will be amazing." Just before he walks out the door, I bring him in for a hug. "Thanks for the help out here today."

"Always a pleasure."

The door shuts and I turn to face Kaz who's standing too far away for my liking. I start walking to him, but my phone rings and we both look at my bag, the moment slipping away just a bit. "I should get that. I like to be available to my clients during business hours."

"It's okay." He walks to the back and steps outside.

I reach for my phone, but see it's Mark, again, and hesitate. He can wait, but I have a feeling he won't, so I suck it up and take the call. "Mark, I'm with a client."

"I need to see you."

"You need to stop this."

"I can't."

With my patience gone, I speak directly and clearly into the phone. "I'm hanging up."

"Don't. *Please.* Just hear me out."

Kaz catches my eye when he walks back inside. Trying to act as professional as I can in front of him, I say, "I'll call you later."

"Okay. I love you."

I hang up and tuck my phone into my pocket. "I have a board in the car I can show you and get your initial thoughts on."

"I'd like to see it."

Leaving him, I go to my car and take it from the back of my

Rover, wondering again why Mark is so insistent. *Why?*

When I'm back in the kitchen, I set the board on the counter and back away to give Kaz space and to watch for his initial reaction.

He leans over the board on the counter, the muscles in his arm flexing as he rests his hands on the countertop, showing the gorgeous definition. I want to trace over them, but I look away instead, resisting the urges he brings out in me.

Because of the lack of furniture, I hop up on the other counter and wait.

Kaz turns, leaning against the cabinet. "I like what you've done."

"I made this from the photos I saw online."

"What about now, now that you've been in the house?"

"I want to bring emotion into play."

"What does that mean?"

"I want it to feel like you, like how you make me feel, how you want your guests to feel."

"How do I make you feel, Lara?" His words stroke my heart, coming in purrs when he says my name.

"I'm better with visuals than words."

"I'm better expressing myself through music."

"Seems we're both at a loss for what we want to say."

He smirks while crossing his arms over his chest. "How about we do what we know best and reconvene? Can I hang on to this for a few days?"

"It's yours." I get my bag in the living room and throw the strap over my shoulder. "Fill out the questionnaire when you have time."

"Okay."

"We can meet. We can go to dinner and discuss the direction of the project. My treat," I add with a goofy smile hoping to get the chance to have more time with him.

"I'm gonna hold you to that."

"I keep my promises."

"Good to hear," he says, following me to the door. "I was hoping you'd stay a while, but I know you're busy." *If only he knew how much I wish I could stay too.*

Turning around, I take him by the front of the shirt and pull him closer. "I want to, but I need to tie up some loose ends."

Wrapping his arms around me, he rubs my back. "Go take care of whatever it is you need to take care of and give me a call when you're free."

"Free is a frivolous notion."

"Free is what we all should be."

"How do relationships come into play if we're all free?"

He runs his index finger over my lips, then kisses me. "That topic feels too heavy for a Wednesday."

I laugh having my words used against me. "Very true. We should save all this heaviness for a Sunday or a Monday."

"How about Saturday? Dex is having a party."

"You want to take me on a date?"

"I do, but if your loose ends are tied up sooner, I'm free on Friday."

"Good to know." I lift up and kiss him quickly. "Very good to know." I twirl in his arms and head out the door. "See you soon."

"Goodbye, Lara," he says, admiring me with that look in his eyes that makes me want to stay. *And I want to stay. I want to feel. I want him.*

Sadly I can't. It's time. Time to tend to those loose ends...

10

THIS RELATIONSHIP WITH Mark has got to end once and for all. Not because of Kaz, but for me.

I find a Starbucks needing the energy to be on my toes for this confrontation. I want my things and a final conversation so we can end this once and for all. While waiting on my grande, I step off to the side and check Instagram. I scroll past the landscapes and beach pics, over the celebs puckering for the camera, but stop when I see a photo of Mark from last night. *You've got to be kidding me.* He has a girl in a bikini on his lap who's kissing him on the cheek while he's taking a selfie of them. Last. Night. The hot tub is his. I recognize it instantly. *The bastard.*

Anger takes over. I can't believe I fell for his lines. He doesn't care about me. These aren't the first pics to show up with him like this. It's the third or fourth in the last few months. *Does he think I'm a blind fool? He says he loves me, but how can snuggling up—and probably more—with other women indicate love? What's his game?* I don't understand the fake tears and begging me to stay. What part of *"We're so good together. I screwed up and I'm sorry. I promise I'll be better"* does he believe to be true?

My name is called and I grab my drink and rush out, furious.

While I drive over to his place, I know some could say I'm doing the same thing, but I haven't been begging him to stay in a relationship with me. This seals the deal... well, the deal was already sealed, but now it's super-glued.

When I arrive at his house, I punch the code to the gate in, but it doesn't open. I push it in again and still nothing. I call him on the phone, but there's no answer. "Damn it." *What the hell?*

"This is ridiculous." I'm not waiting. I am so done. Frustrated, I drive away, getting angrier each mile.

A PIERCING NOISE interrupts the bad dreams I'm having. It's louder and louder until it can't be ignored anymore. I peel apart the swollen lids of one eye with my fingers. Turning toward the noise, it's my landline. I forgot I even had that phone. I mentally add to my forever-growing checklist to cancel that service. In the meantime, I must change that annoying tone when I'm more awake.

My other eye finally opens though the sun coming in through the window is blinding and painful, making my eyes water. I grab my phone quickly and head under the covers where it's dark, just like my mood.

I answer, "What?"

A frantic voice says, "I need your help."

"Rochelle, why are you calling me so early and help with what?"

"The party. I need more liquor. And it's not that early. I can't believe you're sleeping in. You never do that."

I reach over and turn on my cell phone, hoping I don't regret that decision. "What time is it?"

"What's going on, Lara? First you don't answer your cell and now you don't sound like yourself."

"I've fallen behind on some projects so I worked 'til three in the morning. I'm just tired. And I turned my phone off to avoid any calls from Mark."

"Oh. I'm sorry. I feel bad for waking you."

"No. Don't worry about it."

"What's the deal with Mark?"

"I'm just stuck in this mess with him and I don't know how to get out. I went over last night to get my stuff but I was locked out of the gate. I called, but no one answered, so I came home and worked to take my mind off it."

"How about I bring you a coffee and something to eat and we can chat for a few. I have to run out for more food. I didn't buy enough."

"You'd do that for me?"

"Of course. I'll be over in twenty. I'll let myself in. Go back to sleep and I'll see you soon."

After we hang up, I roll over, twisting myself into the covers and try for some more shuteye.

Footsteps coming down the wood-floored hallway wake me. I open my eyes and push the covers away from my face. "I need you," I whine, holding my arms open for Rochelle.

The weight of a truck lands on top of me. "I need you too. I'm sorry."

I scream, scuttling out from under Mark. "What the hell? Get off me!"

"What's wrong?" Genuine shock is written on his face.

Jumping out of bed, I hurry to my bathroom and stand in the doorway for protection, similar to what I do when we have earthquakes. *He's* a force to be reckoned with and has caused me more damage than the threat of a natural disaster.

"What's wrong?"

"You're kidding me, right?" My voice sounds pitchy, but I don't care.

With his hands up as if he's the voice of reason now, he sits up and eyes me. "Calm down, Lara. I love you. Can't you see that?" When he stands, I back inside the bathroom. "Are you scared of me?" His eyes narrow as if he's approaching a wild and wounded animal. He is. "I don't deserve that. After all these months, you know I would never hurt you."

"You did hurt me. Look at my wrists." I hold up my arms for him to see the bruising, though it's fading fast.

"I didn't do that."

My gaze lands on him with a harsh scowl. "You did do this to me, again. You keep hurting me and you've been hurting me all along by your cheating."

"I didn—"

"Don't lie to me! I've seen so many pictures. They're all over the Internet. Even one from two nights ago. I trusted you, but I don't anymore. I was a fool for thinking you cared for me."

His tall frame is overbearing even in the best of situations, but he's flat-out intimidating and scary when we're fighting. I swallow hard, trying to stand my ground when all I want to do is lock myself in this bathroom until he leaves. He nods his head and lowers his voice as if he can convince me to change my mind. "We're not over. We're far from over, Lara. You're mine. You were always meant to be mine." I see his hands fist at his sides and the breath is knocked out of me, fear replacing it. "We're so good together."

I hate that my voice shakes, making me sound weak when I should feel strong. "We're over, Mark. I've been very clear and from the photos online from last night and every other night, you've moved on."

"You're not innocent, but I'm not throwing it in your face."

"You just did, but what did I do?" I challenge him. I know deep down that even if I had wanted to do something, I would have never cheated on him.

I see the change as something occurs to him. His eyes widen as some great revelation sets in. "It's two in the afternoon. Why were you in bed? You... you weren't expecting me, but you *were* expecting someone. Who is it, Lara? Who were you waiting in bed for?" His fists loosen and he reaches out and grabs me.

Just as I'm about to scream and fight my way to escape, we both hear a large gasp followed by, "What's going on?"

Behind Mark stands Rochelle. *Oh thank God.* "Rochelle—"

He yells, his voice both menacing and booming. "Leave us alone."

Her eyes meet mine as she scans me, making sure I'm okay. "No," she says to him with no fear in her voice. "You need to leave now, Mark, or I'll call the cops." Dialing 9-1-1, she holds her phone up in the air. "All I have to do is push one more button."

"And tell them what? Lara's boyfriend used the key she gave him to come in and climb into bed with his *girlfriend*? Call them. They'll find no case, so run along and play house with that loser. We all know he needs the supervision."

"Shut up, Mark," I say, gathering strength from my friend. I push past him into the bedroom. "I'm only going to tell you one more time. Leave." He stares at Rochelle, then turns to me and returns the same glare as I'm giving him. I have no patience for his bullshit anymore. "Get out of my place. Now!"

"You don't mean that," he says, but by the confusion written on his face, perhaps reality is hitting him square in the head.

"I do. I want you gone for good."

"Whatever," he says, walking toward the door. When he passes Rochelle, he hits the wall above the door. "Fuck this."

Rochelle looks worried, but she stands strong until he's gone. Eyeing me, she says, "You're shaking. Stay here and I'll make sure he leaves."

I nod, wrapping my arms around my body, then take my robe from the hook in the bathroom, I slip it on and sit on the edge of the bed, and wait. When she comes back, she sits next to me. "He's gone." My breath stutters as I inhale. I drop my head into my hands and cry. A comforting arm embraces me. "It's okay. You're okay."

Leaning my head on her shoulder, I continue to cry, the last few days finally overwhelming me. "What if you wouldn't have shown up when you did?" My voice trembles even more now I know it's safe to show my emotion. *What would he have done?*

"Why didn't you tell me? I could've helped you."

"It's not him. He's not been like thi—"

"Lara, wake up. You're making excuses for him. Why?"

I drop my head again. "I'm ashamed."

"You did nothing wrong. There's nothing to be ashamed of. Has he hurt you before?" *I can't tell her the truth.*

"No," I continue to lie, not even understanding why anymore. "I've seen a change in him. I've seen moments of his temper, but ignored my gut feeling that something was really wrong."

"I'm sorry this happened. I had no idea."

"It was only two times. I'm not trying to justify it, but it's since we broke up. He's always had mood swings. He says it's natural for pro-athletes. But the last few months they've gotten worse."

"Maybe he's taking drugs."

I shake my head. "He wouldn't. They test regularly and he works closely with a kids' foundation against drugs."

She hugs me tight. "I'm glad you're safe and I'm even more glad you're not with him. You need to steer clear."

"Yeah, good riddance." I flop back on the bed. "But I still need to get my stuff." *And get my locks changed.*

"Send someone to collect it. You don't go, okay?" She lies back next to me.

Wanting to change the subject, I nod. "You said something about liquor for the party?"

"Don't worry about it. You have enough to deal with."

"I'm happy to help. Anyway, I'll need the distraction. Tell me what you need and I'll bring it tonight."

We lie there—me trying to forget what happened—Rochelle showing her concern by taking my hand and holding it. "I'm here for you."

I give her hand a little squeeze. "I know you are. Thank you."

After many reassurances I'm fine, Rochelle leaves. She's planned a party because she's happy the guys are home, even if only for a short time. There's still a lot to do she says as she walks out the door with only a few hours left until show time.

I promise her I'm up to the task, then shut the door, making sure all the locks and the alarm are set. I make a cup of tea and heat up a bowl of soup from a can. Settling down on the couch, I set my food and drink on the coffee table and reach for my favorite swatch binder. It's my go-to binder for male clients. The colors, textures, and patterns tend to draw their eye. I flip through it this time with Kaz in mind, finding comfort in my work—my happy place.

Kaz exudes warmth, making everyone feel at home around him. It's not something he tries to do. It just comes naturally to him. He's open. His heart is welcoming. Maybe he's too trusting. I guess we share that trait.

A few swatches are pulled, then leather samples are set aside that coordinate. Picking up my phone, I text Kaz: *What time can you meet at the house on Monday? I want to lay some paper down to look at paint colors and arrangements.*

His response is quick: *What time do you need me to be there?*

I smile, then type: *How's ten?*

Kaz: *How about noon?*

He has a knack for mealtime. I type: *Noon works too.*

Kaz: *It's a date, but I'll still see you tonight?*

I'm quick to reply: *I'll see you tonight.*

I hold the phone to my chest, a huge smile on my face with hope in my heart. Then I realize how ridiculous I'm being and get back to work. I spend the next hour saving images on my iPad of furniture pieces I think will look amazing in his house before I start getting ready for the night.

My shower doesn't take long, but picking out the perfect outfit does, especially since I have a date with a hot rock star. I want him to find me as irresistible as I find him. I want to bring him home. I want to make love all night and sleep all day with him again. He seems to make me want so much. *Is it too early in our relationship to want the world?*

Do we have a relationship? Or am I just swept up in the moment?

I finally settle on black fitted jeans and a black blouse that has a gold pinstripe. It flows over the curves of my shoulders and breasts, but is tailored at the waist and gets tucked in. I leave the top two buttons open and add three dainty gold necklaces, a few bracelets though the sleeves are long, and gold stud earrings. With my gold strappy shoes, the outfit is chic, but sexy. Just the way I like to look and feel. And after the week I've had, I deserve to feel good and have an even better night.

11

THE ORDER WAS ready at the liquor store and the employees loaded the boxes into my car for me. The gate to Dex's drive is open already when I pull in and park next to him. He gets out of his car and comes around to my door just as I cut the engine. "Hey," he says to me. "What'd she send you to do?"

"Liquor pick up."

"Nice."

"You?"

"Haircut." He chuckles. "She likes it shaggy but not long."

He does look good with shorter hair. "Looking good there."

"Thanks. Go on inside. I'll carry the bottles in." He joins me at the back of the vehicle. When I open it, he smiles. "She ordered a lot."

"I think she knows her audience."

"Guess she does."

When I go inside, Rochelle is frantic, holding one open bottle of champagne in one hand and her phone in the other up to her ear. Her back is to me, her long brown hair enviously wavy, and her

95

figure in her shirt and jeans makes it easy to see why Dex is drawn to her. With all she's been through, I hope she can find happiness again.

"Hellooooo," I call out as to not startle her.

She spins around and sees me, a wide smile appearing. "Maybe around midnight," she says into the phone and nods for me to follow her. As soon as we reach the kitchen, Dex enters with the first box trailed by two valets carrying the others. "Thank you."

She hangs up and turns to the guys. "Make sure he tips well for doing his job for him."

Her teasing earns her a hug—Dex swoops in and grabs her. "Speaking of tips—"

"Not now," she says, laughing. She blushes and I turn away, the intimacy between them incredibly sweet.

Pushing the valets out, I tell them, "He'll be out shortly. Thank you for the help."

Rochelle catches me in the living room. "Thank you."

"You're welcome."

Her arm slips around mine and we walk to the guest room together. "How are you?"

"I'm fine. No need to worry." I set my purse down on the floor in the corner, and reassure her again. "Really. I'm fine."

"Okay." She doesn't push. "I'm glad you're here. Want to help get this party started?"

"I do indeed."

The first few guests arrive right after me. Rochelle is setting out the platters of food and I'm snacking on mini carrots she left in a bowl on the counter. I watch her and consider how much she's changed over the last few years. She's become herself again, but different in a way. She's a better version of the woman and friend she's always been. I envy her determination to be happy after the tragedy of losing herself along with her first love.

Breaking up with Mark hasn't been a tragedy by any means, but his turn is worrisome. Shaking it off, I decide to forget him for the night and have fun. It's the only thing that will help me forget the fear I felt earlier. "Did you make all of this?"

She smiles proudly with a tray of brownies in her hand. "I did. I started early this morning."

"Why not use a caterer? That would have been a lot easier."

After setting the tray down, she says, "I once had it all and it was taken away. I'm not afraid of hard work, so I don't need easy. If I did, I wouldn't be starting a relationship with Dex."

"I didn't mean—"

"No, no. It's okay. It's just being here—throwing this party—feels like a statement of sorts and I just want to show everyone that I care."

"You don't have to throw a party to do that. Everyone loves you and cares about you. You have the biggest heart of anyone I know." I look around at the table and at the bar being set up outside, and look back to Rochelle. "You are amazing in many ways. Make sure to enjoy the party."

"I will. And thanks."

"Can I do anything to help?"

Rochelle smiles. "Just have a good time."

"How about I get us a couple cocktails. Champagne?"

"I just opened one. Do you mind taking it to the bartender? It's a sparkling rosé, my fave."

She goes back to organizing the buffet and I head to the bar. The bartender leans forward on the marble top and asks, "What can I get you?"

"Rochelle said there's a bottle with her name on it. Two please."

"Coming right up," he replies with a wink. He removes the stopper and fills the glasses before setting them on the bar between us. "Friend of the hostess?"

"Yes."

He nods. "You gonna hang out awhile?"

"I'll be here all night."

He comes off as a cocky frat boy. Maybe he is. What he's not, is my type. "That's a coincidence. So am I."

"Thanks for the drinks. I should let you get back to your job."

"You're very welcome. Come see me again."

"I'm sure I will. You are the keeper of the liquor after all." I return to the kitchen, handing Rochelle her glass. "Cheers." We tap glasses and sip. Dex walks in, his eyes seeming to light up when he sees her. It's amazing to see a man look at a woman like that. They went from hiding their love away to sharing it with the world.

It makes me realize no one has ever looked at me like that. Envy fills my belly, mixing with the wine bubbles. "I'm gonna walk around." I slip off to the living room.

Sitting in a chair near the fireplace, I watch the orange and yellow flames as my thoughts drift back to Mark. It's a bad habit I need to break, but the stress of everything with him makes it hard. With imperfect timing, my phone buzzes in my pocket. I look down at the message on the screen: *I'm sorry. I miss you. I love you. I'll do anything to make this up to you. Anything.*

I won't reply. He doesn't deserve it and I don't know what to say anyway. What I do know is I *don't* want him back. But now I'm scared... scared *of* him. Deep down. I know he's hurting. Breakups are hard. He needs to move on. He needs to find his passion again and I'm not it. We're over and it's best if I remember the bad like today as a reminder when I'm feeling sorry for him.

Some of the band is gathered in the corner, but not Kaz. I look toward the back when I hear, "Who you looking for?"

His voice makes me smile, my body instantly on alert. I turn around, captivated by expressive eyes. My insides curl in on themselves. I'm well aware that an emotional attachment has already bridged the gap between us. "You."

He rubs his thumb over his bottom lip while looking at me with a wicked glint in the pupils of his eyes. "If it makes a difference, I was looking for you."

I touch him because I struggle not to, so I indulge my needs for this man, and give in. With my hand on his chest, I say, "It makes all the difference in the world."

Coming even closer, he whispers, "It makes all the difference to me too." A kiss follows, being placed so effortlessly on my cheek. I love his confidence and comfort in expressing how he feels. I love his openness to the world and his gentleness with me.

Giving in to my other needs, I lean in and close my eyes, ready to kiss him all night. My phone rings in my pocket, jolting us from the moment. *Damn it.* I pull it out and look down at the screen. *Mark.*

Kaz sees it. "I'm gonna get a drink and let you take that call." He walks away, taking all the ease and joy we were sharing with him.

Left standing in a bog of mixed emotions, I send the call to voicemail. My heart's not broken. He already destroyed that possibility. But I feel as though I should feel guilty. *Should I feel bad that I don't feel worse? That I don't feel heartbroken?* When I walked away from him, it was the best thing for me. *I know that's true.* Walking into the kitchen I find Rochelle refilling a tray of food. "You should have had it catered," I say, setting my glass down and helping her.

"I like to cook. It allows me to enjoy the process of planning for the party. Slows things down and I get to focus on the task at hand." She looks up with a smile. "This is the last tray anyway, so if you're hungry, you should eat now. As soon as the guys start eating, there will be nothing left." She laughs.

I sigh. "I've lost my appetite. I just sent Mark's call to voicemail."

"C'mon," she says, taking the tray and setting it on the table. She walks straight to the bar and grabs two more glasses of champagne and then makes her way outside. We stop just outside the door and she hands me one of the glasses. "Let's go over there." She points to two chairs at the other end of the pool.

We sit and she leans back, looking up at the stars starting to appear. It's that perfect part of the whole day, when day meets night, and twilight appears for a brief time. "A lot has changed over the years. Some for the worse. A lot for the better." When she looks at me, she says, "I've never had a man treat me how Mark has treated you. But I also understand how pliable, how resilient and strong the heart is. Forget what you're supposed to say, and tell me the truth. Do you still have feelings for him?"

"I have feelings but love isn't one of them."

"You and Mark were a whirlwind. It all happened so fast that I think you got caught up in the hurricane of his life."

"I often compare him to bad weather ironically."

"Maybe not so ironic. At the end of the day, it doesn't matter what I think, Lara. It's not my life. But from what I know, what I've seen the last couple of months, and seeing your happiness disappear, I think you're now heading toward a better emotional place." She looks beyond me, then back. "I like Kaz, but maybe you're heart needs some time to heal."

"I'm fine, Rochelle. I understand you're worried, but I really am fine."

"You have unfinished business with Mark. Wrap up the mess you're in the middle of and give yourself and Kaz the respect you deserve. He's a good guy. Don't make him a rebound."

I pause before I speak, surprised by the ferocity in her voice. "I won't. We're just getting to know each other, but I like him."

"I can tell. He likes you too. I've not seen him like this. His last girlfriend," she starts, "was a drama queen. He hated that. We all hated it."

"I can imagine. I know you and the band are very private. You mentioned respect. Respect seems to be a running theme lately when it comes to timing. Thinking about you and Dex, you took years, out of respect, to be together. I'm sure looking back you wish you could have some of that time back."

"I do in a way, but I wouldn't change the journey we took to be where we are now. We wouldn't be the same people if we skipped some of the steps along the way. Take your time now so no one gets hurt later."

"I hear what you're saying." Glancing over my shoulder, I see

Kaz through the open doors. He's talking to Derrick, but his eyes are on us. "I don't want him to be a rebound."

"Then don't put him in that position. Get your crap from Mark and end the phone calls and texts. End all contact. Finalize it." Leaning closer, she touches my arm, and adds, "You are a strong woman. Don't let him destroy who you are because he's weak." She stands and starts walking back toward the house, but stops and turns back to say, "Oh and I said nothing about sex. You should totally have all the sex you can get."

"Whore!" I laugh while teasing.

"Takes one to know one."

"God, I love you."

"Love you too," she says, smirking.

When she walks in, Derrick and Kaz walk out. They stop and talk to her a moment. All three look at me. She smiles, saying something else to them before she departs.

Derrick takes her chair, making himself at home in front of me. Kaz grabs a chair nearby, carries it over, and joins us. When he sits down, he leans forward on his knees. "I think I need a smoke."

"I've got weed," Derrick offers.

"Nah," he responds.

I watch their interaction. You can see how comfortable they are in their friendship. Derrick asks me, "You smoke?"

"No," I say, shaking my head.

"Do you care if I do?" Derrick waits for my response.

"No." I stand, locking eyes with Kaz. "I need to make a call anyway." Moving farther away from the guests, I try to figure out what I'm going to say.

"Hey, Lara?" Kaz calls me quietly, just the two of us around.

"Yeah?" When I turn back, he's close.

He's nervous by the way he shifts, turning us around so my back is to the party. "I came on too strong the other night. I know you said you aren't together, but it's new and considering he's sending you flowers and still calling you, I feel like I took advantage of the situation and it was selfish of me. I wasn't thinking about you. Well, I was thinking about you." He grins mischievously. "But I wasn't putting your needs first. I'm sorry about your breakup."

Reaching out, I touch his hand with my fingertips. "You don't have to apologize. I did what I wanted to do and don't regret anything if that's what you're worried about."

"I'm worried about you."

"I know you are, but you don't have to be." Then I tell him the first lie, "I'm fine. Everything's fine." To lighten things up, I prod for my own enjoyment. "Are you sorry for the flirting?"

"I said I felt bad and I shouldn't have done it." He leans closer, his hand taking hold of my arm gently. He's so close that I can smell the Jack and Coke on his breath. My eyes close, relaxing in the comfort of his touch. "But I'm not sorry."

When his lips touch my cheek, I lean into the kiss he's giving.

"Lara!"

My lids fly open, my body tense and shaken when I hear Mark over the music. Kaz's hand drops and he steps forward, shielding me with his body. His jaw is tense, contracting and tightening, his eyes set as he glares at the intruder to our conversation.

Hurrying around Kaz, I try to diffuse the scene that's building, and ask, "Mark, what are you doing here?"

Mark's eyes are locked on Kaz, his attention determined as he stares at him. I touch his chest, but he doesn't look at me until I tap him. "Weren't we both invited to this party?" I drop my hands to my side and I take a small step back, weary of his anxious demeanor. He's domineering and intimidating, his tone harsh, but threateningly low. "What are you doing with him?"

"Mark," I whisper. "I was invited. These are my friends. Why are *you* here?"

His pupils are small, little pinpoints, but like little daggers aimed at me. "No, no. We need to talk. You need to give me a second chance. I deserve that much. I deserve you."

My wrists prickle with pain, a harsh reminder of what he

actually deserves, and that's not me. "Go home and we'll talk tomorrow. Now is not the time and you are not welcome here."

"Because of him?" he asks, pointing over my shoulder at Kaz.

"This has nothing to do with him. Go home. You're making a scene in the middle of Rochelle's party."

He grabs my arm. "If I'm leaving you're leaving."

Kaz is suddenly there, his hand on Mark's arm. "Let go of her." He's not yelling, he's calm and in control. His gaze is a glare, solid and unblinking.

Mark's grip tightens, marking me as his property instead of allowing me to be my own person. I try to free myself, but if he holds me any harder, I'll be bruised. "Mark, you're hurting me."

Kaz grits, "This is your last warning."

His hand falls away instantly and his attention is back on me. "I'm sorry. I just want to talk to you, to sort through everything."

"Not here. Not now," I say, trying to stay calm, which is the exact opposite of how I feel. Kaz stands tall next to me, his arm pressed to mine. A lump forms in my throat, leaving me unable to speak as my eyes fill with tears.

"Please," Mark pleads, "talk to me. This is torture. I'm going out of my mind without you."

His eyes water, tears depicting the inconceivable emotion he wears on the inside for the rest of us to witness. Even I have a heart. When looking up at a six-foot-five professional baseball player with tears of desperation settling in, my stance on the matter falters and he takes advantage. "Please, Lara. Let's talk out front and I'll bring you right back to the party. Twenty minutes. That's all I'm asking for."

I don't even realize I've moved, my mind fogging from humiliation, until Kaz calls me, "Lara?" When I look back at him he's shaking his head. "Don't go."

"Please. Ten minutes," Mark bargains.

Knowing the relief I'll gain if I settle this tonight, I agree. "Ten minutes."

"Yes. Thank you." He takes my hand in his and turns for the door.

Just as I tear my hand free, I hear, "Lara?" and am pulled in another direction by Kaz's concerned voice. "Can I speak with you?"

Mark answers before I can. "I'll bring her right back."

"I'll be okay."

Kaz stands there with his arms crossed. "You sure?"

No. But I go anyway desperately needing this closure for Mark and me. I pass Rochelle. "I'll be back."

She eyes the two of us, worry creasing her forehead. "Are you okay?"

I nod while tucking my phone into my back pocket just as we reach the door. "Ten minutes, Mark. Not a second more."

He looks at me with a shit-eating grin on his face. "Nope, not a second more."

The door closes behind us and we walk to his large Hummer. As soon as we get in and the doors lock, I know I've made a fatal error.

12

Kaz Fabian

I SHOULD HAVE stopped Lara from leaving. My instincts told me to, but I didn't act on my instincts. I trust her even though I don't trust him. "I'll be back," I tell Derrick. He's sidetracked with the girl who's made herself at home on his lap anyway.

Working my way through the crowd, I look for Rochelle. I spy her in the kitchen with Dex, Johnny, and Holli. Dex has his arm around Rochelle's shoulders. Johnny and Holli are holding hands. I feel as though I'm intruding, but I need to speak with Ro. When I approach, everyone says hi in good spirits, but by the expression on Ro's face, something is weighing heavily on her, and I have a feeling it's the same thing weighing me down. Signaling over to an empty space nearby, I look at Rochelle. "Can I speak with you in private?"

She nods. "Sure."

Clearing my throat as we walk a few feet away from the others, I don't hide my feelings. "We shouldn't have let her go."

"I know. I was feeling uncomfortable about it, but they need to end this."

When she won't look at me, I ask, "What's going on?"

"I'm worried. I don't know why I didn't stop her."

"It's not your fault."

"She was so insistent and I know she wants this ended once and for all, but..." She looks up at me, but doesn't finish that sentence. "They left. I messaged her, but haven't heard back."

"I didn't know they were leaving. I thought they would talk outside."

"I didn't either. That's why I messaged. I don't know what to do." I see something change in her eyes. "If she's not back in ten like he promised, I'll text again."

Dex joins us. "What's up?"

Rochelle leans against him, her head falling back on his shoulder. "Nothing. Just chatting."

"About Lara?" he asks, wrapping his arm around her.

We both nod, but neither of us says anything. "Okay, can you guys be acting any weirder?"

Rochelle looks up at him and smiles. "C'mon, let's get a cupcake." She takes his hand and pulls him back toward the crowd, but when she glances back at me briefly, her eyes are sad, worrying me even more. Looking at my watch, it's been four minutes. Six more to go.

Ten minutes turns into twenty, and then I'm done waiting. I find Rochelle. "I can't sit here any longer. I've got to do something."

"We can't call the police. She went willingly."

"Do you know that for a fact?"

"She walked out of the house willingly."

Tommy knows everyone in this town. "I found out where Mark lives."

"I'll go with you."

She's feisty, and always been so strong, but she needs to be here. "Stay. Try to enjoy your party. I'll call you."

"Please, Kaz. I'm worried."

"I know you are. Stay here with Dex. I'll keep in contact."

She lifts up and kisses me on the cheek. "Call me."

"I'll have her call you."

Smiling, she says, "Thank you."

Slipping out of the party without saying goodbye to everyone isn't easy, but I'm swift enough to do it. I drive straight over to the baseball player's house, but it's gated. I should have had a plan, but the fucking security guard isn't budging and doesn't recognize me.

None of my texts or calls are returned, so I drive by her place. No lights are on and I don't hear any movement inside to make me stay. I call Rochelle on the way home and tell her, hoping she'll tell me Lara is back at the party, but she doesn't. I can hear the worry in her voice. She's gone from patiently waiting to shaking. "I should have told you, Kaz, but I know Lara doesn't want anyone to know."

"Know what? Tell me."

"He's gotten rough with he—"

"What the hell? Why didn't you tell me earlier? Why would she leave with him? We should have stopped—"

"I know her. She would have done it whether we wanted her to or not. She still feels she can get through to him and end this."

"Fuck." I rub my temple, a headache flaring on the right side. "What do we do?"

"We wait. I don't want to, but have to at this point."

My hands fly up and slam back down on the steering wheel. I'm frustrated and pissed the fuck off. "Call me if you hear from her."

"I will," she says, "I promise."

I cruise back to my new house. I can't be around Derrick as he fucks some girls in the other room while I'm worried about the one girl I care about. I had a mattress delivered with some things from the apartment. My wishful thinking that I might end up back here with Lara was a misplaced notion. Rochelle's right. She went willingly. I don't think she would have started something with me if she was still in love with him, but maybe she is. Maybe I'm so busy thinking the worst and she's fucking—No, that's not Lara. She knew what she was doing when she left. *She said she was fine, but now I'm thinking it was a front. Was she too scared to say anything?*

Shit. I need to wait and allow her to tell her side of the story.

There's a brand new bottle of Jack Daniels waiting for me when I walk in. Unfortunately there's no mixer or glasses, so I unscrew the top and tip it back, taking two good shots before releasing it from my lips. The burn feels good. The first half of the night was good, watching Lara mingling, seeing her in all her beautiful, sexy glory. The second half? Not so good. Not one I'm keen to remember. *Have I lost her before I really had the chance to have her?* I tip it back once more but lose interest in the idea of getting drunk and set it on the floor. I empty my front pockets and keys next to it, and then go into the bedroom and lie down on the mattress that's taking up space in the middle of the room.

MY PHONE RINGS, waking me. I look for the clock on the nightstand, but there's no nightstand or clock or furniture. Momentarily I'm stunned into confusion. *Where the fuck am I?*

The phone keeps ringing until I grab it from my back pocket, finally remembering I'm at my new place. "Hello?" My voice is gruff as I roll to my back and drape my free arm over my eyes. My ear is met with crying, causing me to sit up. "Hello?"

"Kaz, it's, it's... it's Lara. Can you... come? Get me?"

I'm on my feet heading for the keys. "I'm on my way. Where are you?"

"I screwed up, Kaz." Her sobs are getting the best of her and it's hard for me to understand her.

"Where are you, Lara? Tell me. I'm coming to get you."

"I... I'm not sure. I think I'm near the golf course in Calabasas."

"What do you mean you're not sure? Are you okay?"

Her breathing is broken, gasps between cries. "No. I... I... I stole his Hummer. He'll kill me. I have to leave it. I need to get out of here. I need a ride."

The area comes to mind. I've been there. I've been to that golf course. "There's a shopping strip near the country club. I'll pick you up in the parking lot in front of the market." I'm about to hang up, but add, "Keep your phone handy and call the police if he shows up."

The phone goes dead and my heart follows as anger courses through me, imagining the worst. It takes me too long to get to her. I lost track, her cries circulating in my head the entire time. I see the center on the right and pick up speed. At three thirty in the morning the parking lot is vacant except for a silver Hummer. I drive by slowly and see the driver's seat is empty. Looking around for any sight of her, I come to a stop and park. A woman comes from the shadows and makes her way toward me. I know it's her and jump out to meet her. "Lara?"

The light from a tall lamppost shines down as she hurries to me. Her head is down, her shirt ripped. Her body hits mine and her arms go around me. She buries her face into the crook of my arm and her body is trembling. I'm not sure if it's from sadness or fear, but I need to get her out of here and safe.

"We need to leave," she says. "Please. Can we leave?"

"Come on."

As soon as we get into my car, she slides down while locking the doors. Her seatbelt is fastened, but she turns away from me. I fasten my seatbelt and take off as soon as I can. I want to give her time, but I need to know what's going on and what to do, how I can help her. "Do you need to go to the hospital?"

"No."

"Do you want me to take you home?"

"No."

The darkness of her tone twists my insides, an unfamiliar fear coating each of her harsh breaths. I try to keep it cool and not push her to tell me what the fuck is going on, but I want answers. My shortness comes through breaths and I grip my steering wheel tighter. Steadying myself, I ask, "Do you want to come back to my house? The new one so we can be alone?"

I'm answered with only a nod, which is good enough for now in the confines of the car. Moments later, her voice is weak and quiet, when she says, "Can you stop by the store? I think I need ice."

My heart starts pounding as I pull into a store parking lot. "What do you need ice for?"

I park and there's enough light shining in from a Ralph's sign that when she turns, I stop breathing altogether.

"Please don't look at me, Kaz." Her voice is barely a whisper, her tears reflecting the light, her face swelling with red and purple coloring.

"Lara..." My words choke in my throat looking at what he did to her. Dried blood rims the right side of her mouth and her left nostril. It's light pink under her right eye and her cheekbone is starting to swell. He knew what he was doing to get away with this. Hard enough to hurt her, but just shy of long-term damage. "You need a hospital, and I need a fucking baseball bat."

"Don't. Please. Can we just get icepacks and go? I don't want this all over the news. I don't want to be all over the news like this." She reaches to touch me, but hesitates. As if warring with herself, her eyes close and she touches my arm with such care. It's the same care she deserves in return, so I cover hers with my hand.

"He deserves to go to jail for what he did. You need to think about pressing charges."

"We can take pictures if we need to, but I can't go tonight." Tears streak down her cheeks. "I can't. I'm sorry. I'm ashamed. Weak. I thought I was strong, but he showed me I'm not."

Anger forms, fueling me forward, wanting to kick his ass. "Lara, whatever he said to you, whatever he did to you, it's not because you're weak. It's because he is. You need to remember that." For her sake, I'll go get the ice, but I hate leaving her here. "Will you be all right by yourself?" She nods. "Hold on to your phone in case I need to call you. Don't answer any calls from him."

"I won't."

I get out, but duck back in, and say, "Lock the doors and don't open them for anybody but me."

She nods again and does as I say. I hurry into the store to the medical aisle. I grab several icepacks and some I can bend to make it go cold on the spot. The others I'll put in my freezer when I get home. I rush to the frozen aisle and grab some bags of peas and to the meat department for a small steak. At the register I get four bottles of water, grab a Vitamin Water for her, and take a small bottle of Ibuprofen next to the register. Tempted by the candy, I also buy some chocolate in hopes to see her smile.

When I get back to the car, the door is unlocked and I squeeze the bag behind my seat. I take a bag of peas out before getting in. "Put this on your face."

Leaning back in the seat, she closes her eyes, the bag of peas being held to her cheek. When I pull out onto the main street again, she whispers, "Thank you."

"I'm sorry this happened to you."

"I am too." She laughs lightly, but it's followed by an, "Ouch."

"Do you want to talk about it?"

Inhaling deeply, she then exhales slowly, bringing the peas down and holding them in her hand. "I know you probably have questions and rightly so since I dragged you into this whole mess, but can we talk later? I'm really tired."

"I have a mattress at the house now. Not much else, but at least you can get some rest."

"I'll feel safer than being at mine tonight."

How the fuck is she so calm when I'm shaking on the inside I'm so furious?

Once we get into my house, she heads for the bathroom and I unload the grocery bag. The last owners left the fridge and now I'm grateful as I place the icepacks in the freezer with the other bag of frozen peas. Noises echo around the empty house and I hear her nearing. When I turn, she's there, and that's when I get a good look at her. Oh, shit. With watering eyes and messed-up hair, she looks down, embarrassed in way a woman should never be. Her shirt is ripped more than I first noticed and her feet are bare.

"What did you do with his keys?" I ask, wanting to take them and destroy that motherfucking, gas-guzzling, piece-of-shit vehicle. Just like I want to destroy him. I'll make him pay for what he's done.

"I left them in the Hummer and locked the doors."

"Do you have shoes?" I ask, wondering if she took them off or I missed that detail earlier.

"I took them off upstairs."

I find some relief in her answer. The blood on her face is gone and she's cleaned up. Hating to have to ask this, I ask anyway because we need to have the evidence. I step forward wanting to be close but scared to touch her, to hurt her. "We should take photos. Just in case. Okay?"

"I don't want to take any photos." She wraps her arms around herself protectively.

"What can I do to make this better?

"You're here. That's enough. Thank you for picking me up."

"Don't thank me when I feel I've failed you."

"You didn't. You helped. So much more than you know." Delicate fingers touch her cheek.

"Are you in pain?"

"My whole body hurts."

"We need pictures. You need them. We can call Rochelle or Lane if you'll feel more comfortable with them."

"No, I don't want anyone else to see me like this." Looking down, she says, "Just you. Is this too much? I know it's a lot to take on when we're just getting to know each other."

"No. It's not too much." I cover her with my body. It's easy to do when she's so much smaller, but my anger surges again, knowing she's even smaller compared to *him*. "You need photos." I lean back and look at her, the top of her head as she keeps her eyes lowered. "I'm not letting this go and you shouldn't either. We can take them with your phone so you have control of them, and no one else, just in case you need them."

Contemplating the options, she finally looks up and says, "With my phone only, right?"

"Yes."

"Okay."

Each mark, each bruise, for every hit he put on her, he'll get three. I will kill Mark Renner. Trying to focus on getting the photos is doing my head in. Seeing her shame, watching the tears trail down her face, breaks one of mine free. I shake it off, making sure she doesn't see how my heart is breaking for her. Just take the pic. Just do this, for her. We spend the next five minutes taking photos of her body and close-ups of her face. When I give the phone back to her, I say, "Back these up and protect them."

"I will. Thank you," she replies shyly.

I raise her chin up, but it's still not any easier to see her like this. I tamp down the anger raging inside that could bury me knee-deep in my own pain and tears for her. I have to be strong. For her. "Don't let him touch your soul. No matter how he tries, he can't steal your beauty, who you are, or what makes you special. Protect yourself. Protect your soul." I kiss her cheek. "And go easy on yourself. There's nothing you could have done differently. This is on him. Promise me you'll keep the blame where it needs to stay—on him."

It's just a murmur, but I hear it. "I will."

I kiss her mouth gently. "Good girl. I bought a steak for your eye. The enzymes are good for healing."

That evokes an unexpected smile. "I think I'll pass on the raw meat for now and stick with the peas."

"I have whiskey."

"I definitely need a shot or two of that."

"No glasses, but a bottle."

"Perfect."

I retrieve the bottle, unscrew the cap, and offer it to her.

She comes to me, taking the bottle in hand. "I know I shouldn't drown my miseries in liquor, but I think tonight will be an exception." Putting the bottle to her lips, she keeps her eyes on me and takes a few large gulps of the liquid. "Ah! That burns."

"You're gonna need Ibuprofen and water before you go to sleep." She takes another gulp before handing the bottle back to me. I take a few gulps of my own before capping it. "I can get some for you now."

"Thank you."

With the bag in hand, we head to the bedroom together and stop just inside the door. "I can sleep out there." I hand her the bag.

"No. Please, Kaz, can you stay?"

"Are you sure?"

Looking me in the eyes, she says, "I want you to."

"What side do you like to sleep on?"

A smile is hidden in her expression. "Whichever. I don't mind. I usually end up in the middle."

Seeing her smile makes me glad she trusted me enough to call me. "Rochelle was worried about you."

"I'll text her." She picks her phone up from the floor next to her shoes and starts typing. "I'm going to tell her I'm all right so she doesn't worry." She looks to me for the promise she's seeking.

"I won't tell her tonight, but you need tell her tomorrow."

"I will." After setting her phone back down, she comes back and stands in front of me. "Is it okay if I take these clothes off? I don't want to make you uncomfortable or anything."

Make me uncomfortable? How could she think that? "You're safe here." That's a promise I can easily make. "I'm here however you need me."

"I knew I could trust you." While taking down her jeans, she says, "He's on steroids."

"Your ex?"

"Yes. I don't know how he passed the drug tests, but he did." She looks up at me and says, "I can almost pinpoint when he started. It was about three months ago. I left the party with him because I thought I could give us closure. He thought we were getting back together... or he hoped." I watch as she pulls her shirt overhead not bothering with the buttons. After all, it is ripped.

The bruising on her chest is worse when she's fully exposed. "He hit you here more than once..." Reaching forward she doesn't flinch or move when I touch her, which makes me realize how much she trusts me. I run my fingertips over her chest, right above her breasts. She bites her lip and closes her eyes. Stepping closer, I embrace her, stroking her back gently. And her tears start falling.

She must sense the change in me as anger fills every muscle of my being because she whispers, "Forget about him. Stay with me." Her hands touch my face and our eyes meet. "Stay for me. Please."

"I want to pummel him for what he's done. I want to obliterate him, but for you, only you, I'll stay."

"Promise not to leave me?"

"I promise," I say, leaning forward and kissing her forehead. "Come on, sleeping helps the body heal."

"And a bag of half-thawed peas," she says, taking the bag from the floor onto the bed with her. She settles under the covers, takes two Ibuprofen with a water chaser, and turns on her side to face away from me. "Hold me, Kaz?"

I hate hearing doubt in her voice. There is no way I wouldn't hold her. I take off my jeans and slip under the covers next to her. Leaving no space between us, I caress her hip as I slide my arm around her middle. Her breath catches, but settles. She puts the peas on her cheek as I move her hair away, letting it slide down her back. I place one kiss just at the curve of her neck, and then lean back. Neither of us says anything more. We don't need words. We'll speak through actions, caresses. This feels good... right. I just wish it were under different circumstances.

Lying in the dark with her, I listen intently to each of her breaths, hoping she finds sleep and knowing she needs the rest. Minutes later, the peas fall to the bed, letting me know she's asleep.

I stay still a while longer, then release her, rolling to my back. So many thoughts are running through my mind, rage in my veins, my heart weakened to the woman next to me.

The woman I've been dreaming about is finally in my bed. The one I've fantasized about for over a year and I've imagined when fucking others. She's here, lying next to me and I can't sleep.

Watching her, my chest hurts. She's the most beautiful woman I've ever seen and equally the most fascinating. She's so smart, teases, jokes, and flirts. And... trusts me. She trusts me with her life. That's what brought her here tonight. I would do anything for her and I think she knows it.

I sit up and scrub my face with my hands. She stirs beside me, making me want to stay. I really should, but I just can't stay here any longer...

A promise is a promise and all that. But some promises are worth breaking. *This is one of them.*

13

Lara

I WAKE UP to an empty bed and a wet spot where the peas have defrosted on the mattress in front of me. I'm not happy about either. My body aches in ways it never has before and I'm hoping never does again. *This is not good.*

After a few minutes, I force myself up, my neck just as stiff as my body. "Kaz?" I call, but no one answers. I slowly walk to the living room and call again, "Kaz? Are you here?" My heart starts racing from nerves and fear. It's barely dawn outside and he should be here. Looking out the front window, his car is in the driveway. He's in the driver's seat with his head down.

I run for the door and straight out to his side of the car and knock. He jumps when he hears me. Seeing the door is unlocked, I open it, but he just stares at me, a haze of emotions built up inside his normally happier eyes. His silence is frightening, so I shatter it with worried questions, "What are you doing? Why are you out here?"

"I couldn't sit by and do nothing."

My hand covers my mouth as I suck in a jagged breath.

"What did you do?"

"I went to see him—"

"Kaz, no." I lean into the vehicle and hug him. "Are you okay?"

When I stand back up, he says, "I couldn't get to him. I tried. I almost rammed the damn guard gate down."

I reach for his hand on the steering wheel. Resistant at first, he finally loosens his grip and allows me to tug gently. "Come inside." I'm hoping to coax him from the car. "Please. Come with me."

His eyes meet mine and our gazes hold an aching few seconds before he slowly unfolds from the car to stand in front me on the driveway. The moon is hidden behind clouds, the dark still fading away despite the pain evident in the lines carved across his forehead, marring his handsome face. He cups my face and holds my chin up. One kiss, and then another on the lips before he leans his forehead against mine. "I couldn't protect you or help you. Please forgive me."

There's intensity held between us as another kiss is placed on my forehead and his arms wrap around me, holding me as if I'll disappear if he lets me go. I slide my hands around him and hold him just as tight, until it starts to hurt my ribs. "Going after him doesn't help me, Kaz. Being here like you have does." I lift up until I'm looking into his eyes. "Thank you. Thank you for caring, but I'm relieved you didn't see him. He's..." I tuck my head against his chest and look down, shame filling my chest. "He's not himself right now."

"I know you want to see the good in him. I know you struggle inside against what you thought you knew and what he's revealed himself to be. But you don't have to fight this war. He doesn't fight fair anyway. A man should never hit a woman. *Ever*. A coward does." His soft strokes are comforting, his words firm in his belief. "You're stronger than him and he knows it. He's trying to intimidate you to get you back. You can't fall for it, Lara. Promise me you won't."

"I won't." The reply comes easily as the truth resides inside my heart. And then I confess too much. "I don't want to be with him. I want you."

"I know," he repeats as if reaffirming the first part, but not responding to the latter. Releasing me, he shuts the car door and then takes my hand. As we walk to the house, his body is stiff, the muscles in his arms tense. "My father hit my mother and my sister."

"What?" My heart pauses before picking up at the news he's just dropped. For a lack of anything else to say, I go with my gut. "I'm sorry."

"Don't be. No one should make apologies for him. He should own the damage he's caused. It's squarely on him." He waits at the door for me to pass and shuts it behind us.

"Do you mind if I ask what happened?" I have an idea, but I want to know everything about Kaz, even the darker side.

"Which time?"

My eyes go wide.

Kaz's chuckle is low, not like the lighthearted laugh I'm used to. He says, "It became the norm for them. I couldn't adapt."

"No one should adapt to abuse," I say shocked as we walk into the bedroom.

"I tried to tell them that. They wouldn't listen to me. I was a kid."

"Oh my God, Kaz. That's awful. Who broke it up?"

"His bodyguar—" He stops just as he seems to catch himself.

I climb into bed, but look at him before pulling the covers over me. His shirt comes off and his pants are removed. He slides in next to me and lies down, staring up at the ceiling. Turning to my side, I lay my head down on the pillow gently and watch him. "I've never heard you talk about your family. I don't know anything about you."

"My family is complicated."

"You said that last time."

"It's the truth every time. Nothing's changed."

"Do you see them?"

A wry grin spreads slowly across his face and he looks at me.

"It's almost six in the morning, get some rest."

I move my hand so it's on his chest and I can feel his heart pumping beneath. "Why won't you talk to me?"

"I do talk to you. I've already said way more than I intended to."

"You don't trust me."

Kissing my hand, he says, "This isn't about trust. I trust you, Lara. You wouldn't be here if I didn't."

"Then what is it? Why do you hold so tight to some things and are so open with others?"

Most guys would be irritated by now—all this talk about feelings and family—but not Kaz. His smile returns, the one that's most genuine. The backs of his fingers glide lightly over my cheek bringing me back to the reality of how I must look. "Go to sleep," he whispers. "We have plenty of daylight hours to learn every last thing about each other."

"Do we?" I ask, moving closer to him and placing a kiss on his shoulder.

He kisses the top of my head and slips his arm under me, holding me close. "We do." His body gives me peace, his words settle my mind, and I drift off... *hoping he won't leave me again.*

THE SUN HAS risen, his body silhouetted by the rays streaming in from the windows highlighting the strength of his muscles, his broad shoulders, and strong back. He's whole under the night sky, but the sunlight shines through his broken pieces. I move quietly from the bed and touch his back, gentle not to startle him.

The hardness of his body softens when he turns around and looks at me. Really looks at me, as if he's counting my bruises. "You're so damn beautiful and he tried to destroy that. What he didn't count on is your beauty goes deeper than your skin." His hand caresses my cheek. His touch is gentle, a caring gesture I wish could heal my outsides. He does in more ways than he knows for my insides. "No more swelling. That's good."

"Magic peas, I guess." I shrug unsure what to do in the light of day.

When I laugh with a softened tone, he leans in and kisses my cheek, moves to the edge of my lips and places another. His hand holds the curve of my neck, his touch more careful than I like. My eyes close, letting him cover me in his caring affection. "I've wanted to do that to you longer than you know." He stops the kisses and rests his forehead on my shoulder.

"You've kissed me before," I whisper.

"Not like this. Not with all the barriers gone and the obstacles out of our way. Free and easy like we have all day." His lips find mine and a passion ignites between us as our mouths open. My fingers weave into his hair, holding him to me. I want to enjoy this before the moment is burst by reality.

Our mouths part and he takes my hand. "Come with me."

We need to talk, but whether that is now or later, I'm game for either, weak to the man leading me back to bed. Kaz goes to shut the bedroom door though we both know no one will disturb us. I like the privacy, but I really like his thoughtfulness, or maybe it's a protectiveness he feels.

When he returns, he sits on the mattress and kisses me again. This kiss is not a solitary act, but one that leads to more. Our bodies fall back, entwining and sharing each breath we take and exhale. His knee parts my legs and he moves to position himself over me. The pressure elicits heavy breaths and quick whispers from him, "I want you... so much."

"Don't stop."

We lift and he takes my shirt over my head. I move forward to kiss him again, but when our lips meet, his are still. Kaz sits back and I look up at him, leaning back on my elbows. "What?" Following his gaze, I look down. The bruising has transformed into darkened abstract shapes. And my breath is taken away in the worst of ways.

My hands fly to cover myself, heat swarming my cheeks.

But before I can run, he covers my hands, gentle to the touch. "I won't hurt you."

"I don't want you to see me like this. I'd forgotten," I say, looking away, every little detail of plaster easier to stare at instead of the eyes that made me feel beautiful. *I don't want to close my eyes or I'll see Mark's disdain again as his punches landed on my skin.* Kaz's silence twists my insides, knotting my emotions, tears replacing the strength I thought I possessed.

He traces the bruising over my breast. The touch of his fingertips is cooling, and I look up when he asks, "What did he hit you with?"

His eyes stay focused on my body, when I reply, "I don't want to talk about that and ruin this, what we were doing."

"It's not ruined. I just don't understand how someone could hurt another person like he did you. *Until now.* Now I want to hurt him in ways that will destroy his career and rearrange his face for-fucking-ever."

"You're better than him, Kaz." I touch his chest, rubbing over his heart, that deep throb calming me. "I know you are. I see the good in you even when you pretend to be so bad."

"I have..." He turns away, but then leans down again and kisses me. "I don't want to talk about me." When he kisses me this time, it all changes from sweet caresses to a pressure that tells me his darkest desires. In a low voice that teeters on midnight, he asks, "Do you want to be with me?"

My lips feel abandoned, so I lift up, and press mine to his this time. "I do. So much. Make love to me, Kaz."

Running his hands over my shoulders, he says, "I don't want to hurt you."

"We'll take it slow."

With his mouth on my neck, his hot breath blankets my body in ways that make me want him more. "I don't know if I can with you."

I adjust beneath him until his eyes are over mine and our bodies are aligned. The feel of his erection through our underwear makes me squirm. The dreams I've had of being with him are becoming reality. Pushing my thoughts away, I go with feelings and act on instinct, succumbing to the fantasy, to the sensations, to the man himself.

His body taut, but gentle as he moves against me, pressing himself between my legs. Our kisses become a language spoken to each other, the words not needed. His body slides to the side, his breathing coming in pants like mine. Lying back, he covers his eyes with his arms, blocking the brightness of the room, blocking me out. "I don't know if I can do this."

My hands cover my chest as rejection trickles in. "What?" I ask, my voice weak, protecting my heart. "You don't want me?"

He turns to me, taking my hand and squeezing. "No, I'm sorry. That's not what I meant. I just don't know that I can be what you need right now."

"What do I need?"

"You need to be cared for and all I want to do is fuck you." He lies back with a groan. "See? I'm a fucking Neanderthal."

"Maybe I don't want care right now. Maybe I want to fuck too."

Levity invades the heavy space when an all-knowing grin appears. "I was afraid of that."

"Are you really afraid?" I tease.

"No, but it makes me so fucking hot for you."

My mouth drops open. "All I have to do is tell you I want to fuck and bam, just like that, we get to fuck?"

He nods with raised eyebrows. "I'm tired of us dancing around this," he says, waving between us. "This attraction, our chemistry. Whatever you want to call it. I want more than just sex with you. I..." His gaze lowers from my eyes to my hip where he traces over it with his hand. "I like you, Lara. I have since Rochelle started bringing you around a year ago. I thought that night at the beach might be our time, but our timing's been off. It's not now, and I'm not going to miss this opportunity. So if you want me to make love to you, I will. But if you'd rather take this slow and go out for breakfast, we can do that too."

My heart flutters to life, breaking free from the cocoon it's been sheltered in for months. I don't want breakfast. I just want him. "You won't break me, Kaz."

Deft fingers hook the sides of my undies and take them down, painfully slow as his eyes take me in. I want to squirm, to move from his view, but I stay still trying to fight against the humiliation Mark's attack has caused me. I liked my body and now I feel shame. I hate him for making me feel unworthy of affection.

"Open your eyes." His voice is low, but firm. I hadn't realized my eyes were closed, much less squeezed tight. When I see him, his are set on me. "Don't close your eyes when I'm touching you like that. I'll stop if you want me to, but if I'm hurting you, tell me."

"I'm sorry. You weren't hurting me. I like you touching me." I muster the courage to reveal my inner thoughts. "I feel embarrassed for you to see me like this. *He's* made me feel embarrassed to show my body."

"You have a beautiful body. These bruises will go away, but I'm worried he's scarred your beautiful mind."

"Me too. But I don't want you to stop. Help me through this. I want you to touch me, to feel me, to hold me, and to fuck me. Make me feel you, only you, Kaz." *Make me feel less battered and bruised.*

He kisses my chest, healing my soul as his hands caress my body. His fingers dig deeper into my hips, then his hand slides up and squeezes my breasts. "Tell me you want me to fuck you again."

I trail the tips of my fingers down his chest and lower until I'm holding his erection firmly in my hand. "Fuck me, Kaz."

As he licks his lips, his hands go to my waist. "*Fuuuck.* Are you sure?"

"I want you to make me forget. Replace all the bad with this. I want you." Just as he leans down to kiss me, my hands fly up to his chest to stop him. "Do you have a condom?"

"Shit!" He falls back heavily, his hands scrubbing over his face.

Then he jumps up abruptly, surprising me. "I don't have anything here. Maybe in my car?"

Sitting up quickly, I grab his arm before he takes off running naked out of the house. "I've got one."

He looks back at me, an impressed expression on his face. "You do?"

"I do," I reply with a little waggle of my eyebrows. "Ouch. Remind me not to do that again."

"You're not allowed to hurt yourself either. Where's the condom?"

"In the bathroom drawer. I left it there the other day, just in case." He's gone only a few seconds before he returns with the packet between his teeth and a smirk that could light up LA. Lying back on my elbows, I watch him and anticipation builds.

Kaz is just as hard as he was a minute ago and I take that as a compliment. He crawls up the bed. If crawling can be done with swag, he owns it. Cocky, confident, and totally hot. He rips the package open, sits back, and rolls it on. With a nod of his head, he asks, "You ready for me?"

"I don't know."

His smile falters. "You don't know?"

"No." Spreading my legs, I add, "I think you should take a closer look and find out for yourself... with your mouth."

His eyes go wide. "Damn, Lara."

I shrug. "I know what I like."

"You're fucking sexy as hell." Lowering down onto his stomach, he rests his upper body on his elbows. When his mouth is level with my vagina, he doesn't wait for permission. He's not gentle and doesn't ease into it. Kaz just plants his mouth on me, causing my breath to flee momentarily, and kisses me much like he kissed me earlier, and the fire deep inside is reignited.

I collapse onto the mattress, my body sinking into it as his tongue teases and his lips embrace. A moan too breathy for my liking escapes and I open my eyes and stare at the ceiling. I can't hold them open for long. His tongue swirls and I'm lost to the feeling again. My back arches until I grab the sheets on either side of my body to anchor me. A tornado forms, gathering strength on the inside and building into so much more until I can't hold back any longer. I hold his head, my fingers woven into his hair, as I fall apart beneath him.

Loud moans and soft sighs are given to the man who makes me feel everything too much. Heat covers my chest and he slips up my body and peppers kisses across it. When he reaches my mouth, his eyes meet mine just as he presses down, our lips parting and our tongues finding each other again.

I feel a different pressure as he pushes up to look down at me. "You lied."

"I did?"

"You're ready for me." A rough thrust forward and my head tilts back. I'm so full as a healthy stretch burns me in ecstasy.

When his chest meets mine, his head drops to my shoulder, and his body stops moving. His breath is heavy as if the whole world has weighed him down. I reach around and hold him, stroking the back of his hair, and whisper, "Hey there."

Turning his head into the nook of my neck, he replies, "One sec."

"Are you okay?"

He nods and starts moving again, slowly at first, then picks up the pace. Our bodies grind in love as we maneuver and relish each other. Pushing gently against his shoulders, I say, "I want to be on top."

Rolling us over, I'm situated and moving, using his chest as leverage. He struggles to hold his composure, and my hips are grabbed as he slams into me, grunting in a way that is sexual and such a turn on that I can't remain quiet. Sensations like these have to be expressed. "God, Kaz."

My body gives in just as he calls my name, "Lara, fuck!" His enunciation is dirty and the ending a hard K to go with the orgasm.

I lie forward, my own body depleted and worn out in the best of ways. With our bodies pressed together, I give him three kisses. He whispers lyrics in my ear while strumming along my spine, leaving goose bumps in the melody's wake. "He'll never hurt you again. I promise."

14

REGRET FILLS ME as I watch Kaz sleeping. I shouldn't have involved him in this mess that is my life, but he is just so damn irresistible.

It's early in the afternoon, the day not shot. I get up quietly and tiptoe to the bathroom, taking my clothes from the floor with me. I shut the door and get dressed. When I'm done, I peek out. Kaz is still sleeping and I feel guilty for leaving.

I should stay.

I want to stay, but I know Mark and this will be bad if I don't leave now. I walk out the door, then stop, tears filling my eyes. Everything about this moment. Everything I'm doing. It's all wrong. Entirely wrong. Every bone in my body tells me to stay with him. I take another step, but my heart remains behind.

His phone is nearby. I need to call a cab. There's cash in my jar at home. I can pay the driver when we get there. Taking another step, I stop again and look back at the door that divides me from something that feels like it could be more than just a few-night stands.

Kaz feels more like a forever. *Am I willing to walk away from my forever?*

Can I walk away?

Turning around, I go back into the bedroom and undress again. I slip under the covers and into his arms as he curls around me. "You okay?" he asks, his voice husky from sleep. *More than okay. This feels right.*

"I am now."

"WHAT ARE YOU gonna do?" Kaz asks.

The grass under my body tickles my hands. I sit up, looking around the backyard. "Go about life the best I can." Feeling like this conversation is going to need more than I can give at this time, I stand up. "I should get going."

He gets up, and with his hand on my lower back, he guides me inside. "I meant what I said. I want you to stay. At least for a few days."

My heart listens as I'm reminded that he wants me, as I do him. My head wages a war against the possibility. "I know, but I need to go to mine. I can't just disappear from my life as much as I want to right now." I reach to grab my purse out of habit, but I don't have anything here. "Do you mind driving me home?"

"Yes," he says, looking irritated. "Why are you going home alone?"

"Because I live alone."

"Does he have a key?"

He does. "He won't use it."

"How do you know?"

"I don't know. I don't think he meant—"

"What the fuck, Lara?" His voice is raised, but the anger isn't directed at me. "Come home with me. Or let me get you a hotel for a few days, a week, enough time until you're safe and have changed the locks."

"I don't want to live in fear."

"Look where your bravery got you."

"Stop," I warn, my head starting to hurt again as I climb into the car. "I'm going home." Then tears start to come again. When he gets in the car, I look at him, letting them fall. "I need to do this. I need to prove to myself, and to you, that I can be strong. I'm not this person. He's made me into someone I don't want to be."

"You don't have to prove anything. You don't have to change for me. You don't have to be anything but who you are with me. But you do need to be safe and I'm not as confident as you when it comes to that."

"I can't just stay away forever, Kaz."

"Stay away another night."

Looking down at my lap, I wish I could, but I don't want us to be about him. Our time is precious. It matters in ways I can't tell him yet. I won't taint it any longer with my burdens. "I have to work."

He watches me. Kaz sees everything and he knows I'm not giving in, so he shifts the car into gear and nods. "Okay." Reaching over he rubs my leg. "I'll buy you a coffee on the way."

"Deal."

After getting a large cafe mocha, I'm anxious to get home and shower. I'm sure Kaz is as well since the new house doesn't have towels, soap, or clean clothes. After texting Lane to stop by and leave his key for me under the mat, I sit back. Kaz's hand finds its way between mine and our fingers intertwine. His eyes are focused forward, the air in the car changing with the emotion that burdens us. "When will I see you again?" he asks.

"I'm not sure." I glance out the window before saying, "I'm not sure about anything right now. I don't know how to feel. I'm sorry. I know *what* I feel, but that seems to be all." I take a deep breath and release it before finishing. "Obviously I have some stuff to sort out.

But I can't even think clearly until I clean up and assess the damage."

"How does your face feel?"

"Tender to the touch, but I'm okay. A lot of it I can hide with heavy makeup. But I'll work from home for a few days to make sure all the swelling is down. I don't want this getting out."

His words aren't harsh, but there's an underlying fury hiding in the question. "Why are you protecting him?"

"I'm protecting myself. I don't want to answer questions about what happened. I just want it to go away."

"Will *he* go away that easily?

Resting my arm under the window, I whisper, "I hope so."

"I'm struggling not to go over and kick his ass for what he did. I need you to be angry as well."

"I am. My head's just crazed, my thoughts scattered. I can't believe he did this to me, to be honest. I need time to think, to process what's happened, and to make sure nothing else does."

"Okay." He pulls up to the front of my townhome. Before I can stop him, he's out of the car and headed to my side. When the door opens, he says, "I'll walk you up." I won't argue with him. He needs to do this and I like that he wants to.

My front porch is filled with vases of roses in the deepest shades of red. I pause when I see them. *Oh God. What will Kaz think?* There are at least ten vases with a dozen or more roses in each. My hold of the railing tightens and I look back, catching a glimpse of Kaz's troubled face.

I try to pretend I'm not scared, try to pretend that my heart hasn't dropped to the pit of my stomach, try to fool Kaz into believing that I'm fine. Moving forward, I step through the vases, leaving them there to rot outside. I don't have to guess who they're from. I know, and I want them gone, out of my sight, but I don't want to worry Kaz though I have a feeling from his expression it's too late for that. When we reach the door, I turn, put on a wide smile, and say, "Thank you."

With his brows cinched together, he looks past me to the door. "Do you mind if I have a look around before I go?"

"You don't have to do that," I say nonchalantly.

"Lara."

His tone is enough to cause me to step aside. He opens the door with the key we find just where Lane left it, and walks in, looking around. His gaze darts around the room and I follow him inside. Maybe he's pretending like me because he asks, "You'll call or text me?"

Each door is opened, but he's not intrusive, just glancing around each room quickly.

"I will."

He seems satisfied and heads for the door. "The offer still stands. You can stay with me or I'll get you a hotel."

"As you can see, I'll be fine. But thank you. That doesn't feel adequate for all you did for me last night, but it's sincere."

"Anytime. If you ever need me, I'll be here for you."

I nod, then lean closer to kiss him. I whisper against his lips, "Thank you," then step back again. Neither of us says goodbye and I'm glad. I can't handle the permanency of that, not with what I still have to face. He does say, "Change the locks right away."

"I will."

He shuts the door behind him and I lock it, then lean against it and take a deep breath. When I exhale, I push off and go into my bedroom.

I'm not home even ten minutes when a ring of the doorbell sounds throughout the townhome. I look through the peephole, but it's the flower guy. Well aware of the routine at this stage, he sets them down and leaves.

I go into my bedroom and straight for the bathroom to start the shower. While taking off my clothes, I get a glimpse of myself in the mirror, something I'd been avoiding. My mouth drops open, breath catching, and the color in my face drains away in an instant as reality sets in. Kaz had taken my mind off things, allowed me the time to forget. But here it is in all its purplish glory, now perhaps Mark's bragging rights to his steroid-using buddies. He's not the first pro-athlete to hit a woman. In time, his paychecks will rise even higher and I'll become locker-room fodder.

Covering my cheeks with my hands, I step closer. I'm hideous in blues, purples, grays, and hints of yellow. A little scab has formed at the corner of my mouth and my eye still has a little swelling around the lid, but I never would have known around Kaz. He treated me like he always does—like I'm beautiful.

I'm not. Mark took that away. He stole it without so much as an apology.

He's not going to let me ride off into the sunset with Kaz. He won't be happy until I'm as miserable as he is, and he's come close already. I just don't understand why. A knot in my stomach tightens, pulling my heartstrings attached to Kaz in with it.

I don't want Kaz dragged under in the process of settling things with Mark.

In the shower, the water flows over my body, drowning the negative away and leaving me clean with the memories of being with Kaz. There's something about him that exposes my heart in ways I've been so careful to protect in the past, an openness that I trust, and an honesty I need. He doesn't have a hidden agenda or want something from me. And he wants me.

Once I'm out and dressed, I go into the kitchen. With a hot mug of tea in my hands, my subconscious braces for what lies ahead. My hands begin to shake, my thoughts well aware of the inevitable confrontation with Mark. He said I was his. *Only his*. He said I will stay willingly or he'll make me. All the things he said come flashing back like the ringing in my ear. Hot liquid and shards of glass hit my feet making me jump, my scream deafening on the inside, but outwardly silent. I teeter on shaky legs as I slide down the cabinetry. The shattered mug and tea-covered floor beneath my feet. A throbbing draws me to look down and blood swirls with the dark liquid.

A lump forms in my throat stifling the need to call for help. There's no one to help even if I could vocalize my need. Grappling for the edge of the counter, I secure my hand on the side, and pull myself up, careful not to press down on the balls of my feet.

I step out from the mess and hobble to the sink. Hopping up on the counter, I inspect the bottom of my foot. The cut is small, but the shard remains. The irony of Mark and the broken glass not lost on me. I pull the glass out and run it under water a second to clean it. Getting back down, I look at the mess as I pull a roll of paper towel from the holder. I kneel down on my hands and knees and with a huge wad of towels, clean the mess. This chaos of browns and reds on the paper, purples, blues, blacks on me, this is my life. Somehow in the span of a couple months, my better senses turned against me allowing me to let the little signs slide. This is what happens when you lose sight of the reason you started in the first place. This is what happens when you witness horrible things and brush them under the rug, or worse, don't do anything at all.

Mark Renner was a ticking time bomb in our relationship. It started out good and somewhere during the fun, he twisted it into a game of control, obsession, and possession. *How did I not see that?*

I shouldn't have confronted him about the drugs. Not alone anyway. I had no choice. I was just turning a blind eye to what deep down I already knew, as the changes in him were evident. I grew up in LA. I know the signs. I've dated guys who did drugs. But Mark was different. He was a master of disguise. *Don't the major leagues drug test?* I know they do, but they didn't catch him. Or they turned a blind eye in exchange for a title win. Maybe I relied on what I assumed instead of what I knew.

My doorbell rings. *Again.* I know it's more flowers, as it seems that's his "thing" when he's done something wrong. By the onslaught of deliveries, he knows it's bad between us. I've told him. He knows. Why is he so desperate to hold on to something that he can't? I heat my kettle to make another tea, not bothering with the door, but then I hear it open and freeze. *Damn it!* The deadbolt.

Shit. I forgot to latch it. I reach into a drawer and pull out a knife.

"Lara?" Mark calls.

My hold on the knife tightens, my legs shaking as much as my hands. I stay still and silent, hoping he doesn't find me.

When he rounds the corner a smile covers his face. "Hey there."

The knife shivers in my hands as I hold it up. Despite wanting to drop into a ball on the floor, I steady myself, and force myself to speak. "Get out of here."

The smirk on his face sends anger shooting through my veins. He shrugs. "Babe, c'mon. I came over to apologize." With his hands up in surrender, he looks at me like I'm the crazy one, and chuckles. "No need for violence."

I choke on his words. "No need for violence? Look what you did to me."

"No. No." Now that asshole grin disappears. "I didn't do that."

My eyebrows shoot to the ceiling in astonishment. "What are you talking about? Look at me." My phone is nowhere near and my landline closer to him, but I square my shoulders. "Leave or I'll call the police."

He steps closer and my breath catches in terror. I swing the knife in front of me, my thoughts unclear if I am strong enough to take him on if it comes to it. "Don't come any closer, Mark. I mean it."

"You don't look that bad. You're always beautiful. You'll always be my pretty woman. I screwed up, but I did not do that to you. You must have fallen and hurt yourself. You're clumsy."

"No, I'm not. I'm not weak and I'm not clumsy. I did not fall. You hurt me," I spew through gritted teeth. "Leave. Now!" I step forward, stomping down the fear that leaves tremors along with my words. With my life on the line, my grip firms, and the knife is solid in front of me as my body steels itself for a fight.

"I can leave, babe. But we're not over."

"You're a delusional drug addict. Get out!"

He pulls something from his pocket and I flinch. When he opens his hand, I see a flash drive. He sets it on the counter and backs up, giving me space.

My gaze flickers between it and him. "What is that?"

"It's us, babe."

My brow furrows, causing pain to shoot across my battered forehead. "What do you mean?"

"I screwed up. I apologize. But despite everything, I still want to be with you. You're successful and smart. You're not a gold digger, and I can bring you home to my parents. Basically, you look good on my arm and I look better for it. You're what every successful athlete needs standing behind him: a woman who believes in him; a woman who can take care of him. That's you. You're that woman for me."

I'm dumbstruck by his audacity to plead his case as if he has a chance in hell with me. "You're lucky I don't press charges, Mark."

"Just watch this," he says, pointing to the flash drive on the counter. "I'll give you tonight alone. I expect you back at mine by tomorrow night."

"You're fucking crazy. I will never return to you or your house. Now get out!"

He leaves without another word and I follow him with the knife held in front of me until he's out the front door. I bolt the locks this time. His key doesn't work on the bolt, so I'm safe for the time being.

My heart races as I lean against the door, exhausted from the unexpected confrontation. I'll call to have the locks changed tomorrow. That's easier than trying to get my key back from him. I go back into the kitchen and grab the flash drive. My curiosity has gotten the best of me. When my computer comes to life, I plug it in, and wait to see what pops up. There's only one file—a video.

I pause as dread fills my limbs. With the knife set next to the mouse, I click play.

My heart stops.

My breath stops.

My world stops.

Both hands cover my mouth just as a loud gasp startles me. Then I realize that sound came from me. I stare at the screen in horror. Mark is naked on top of me as he grunts my name for the camera. *My* body is exposed.

Mortified, I turn it off, not able to watch anymore. I run to grab my phone and dial his number.

"Hello?" he answers from his car, sounding so fucking full of himself.

"What have you done?"

"Nothing yet, babe."

"Why do you have this?"

"Originally, because I liked watching it, but now I've found a new use."

The fight leaves my body as dread sets in, knowing what he's going to say next. "And what is that?"

"That's up to you, Lara."

"Just say it, Mark," I cry. "What do you want?"

He sighs, and if I know him at all, he's shaking his head. "Have I not made myself clear?"

"You're as clear as mud." I wrap my arm around my stomach, worried of losing its contents. "What do you want?"

"You. It's that simple."

"You can't have me. I don't want to be with you."

"I've been nice—"

My anger battles with fear and my words and accusations come barreling out. "You beat the shit out of me and then say you didn't. Are you psycho?"

"Lara, I remember us fighting, but I don't believe I did that to you. I love you. I wouldn't do that. I've never hit a girl before." He pauses, then says, "Maybe I blacked out—"

"You knew exactly what you were doing." I look down in disgust while readjusting the phone in my trembling hand. I want to throw it across the room, but I don't, knowing this has to be finished. "You make me sick. I will never be with you again."

"That video says otherwise. It's my insurance policy. It's awards season and I want you by my side."

"No."

"Yes, or I'll send a copy of that video to every publication in California. And then I'll send the other twenty-six videos I've made over the months to all the tabloids in the world, as well as hire the most successful porn directors to release it as my compilation."

"You wouldn't." I hit him where I know it will hurt his ego. "You would lose sponsors."

"When was the last time an athlete looked bad while having sex with his girlfriend? And," he says, and I can tell by his tone, he's smirking, "I look damn good in them. But as you know, the public doesn't look well upon the women in sex tapes. This would destroy your career and make you the talk of the town in the worst of ways. God, I love public opinion."

"You're sick and need help."

"But I'm also right. And you're smart enough to know it."

I'm too angry to cry, the hate I feel for him comes in a wave of venom.

"I'll go to the police and show them what you did to me. No one likes an out-of-control steroid-using athlete. You'll be ruined."

"You know what people don't like?"

He pauses, toying with me. The words held hostage until I play his sick game. "What?"

"A druggy rocker who beat up a groupie after a sex-filled rager."

"What are you talking about?" My words barely make it out, my heart sinking to the pit of my stomach.

"Your boy on the side. What do you think is more believable? An all-American hometown hero or a replacement guitarist who can't handle his drugs and liquor? The more likely conclusion isn't me, sweetheart."

Kaz.

I can't be with Kaz. Not with Mark like this. I can't. The tears finally fall over the lids and down my cheeks. "I won't," I whisper. "I won't hurt him. I won't let you either."

"You sound so convincing right now, babe. I'm almost tempted to turn around and make sure you understand what choice you're making." My head jolts back as I listen to his threat, his tone menacing. "Maybe it was a blackout. Or maybe it wasn't."

He's going to kill me. I can feel it in my bones. Resolve is starting to fill my veins. He's never going to let me walk away, not without a fight for my life.

"Why are you so quiet, babe? Reconsidering?" His tone is back to normal as if he's just asked if I want kung pao chicken or beef and broccoli for dinner. *He's not delusional. He's dangerous. But why me?* He could and does get any bimbo he wants.

"Why do you want a girlfriend? You were cheating on me. Be single. Play the dating field. It's what you do best."

"How about this? We go out a few more times when your face looks pretty again and I catch you hitting on another guy at a bar. I kick his ass. Of course. And then you and I have a big fight in front of the paparazzi. We break up and I hit the talk show circuit to talk about how heartbroken I am and win the sympathy of America, which in turn, makes me look good going into mid-season."

"And makes me look bad, right?"

"All's fair in love—"

"And war. You'd be wise to remember that."

"You'd be wise to look like the arm candy you are and remember your place."

"Fuck you!"

"Fuck you, babe. I'll see you tomorrow with a smile on your face, or else. And bring dinner. It might be a long night while we plan the big event." He hangs up and just like the mug that broke, I'm left with shards, destroyed in an instant by the man I once thought I had a future with. *It's not love.*

KAZ CALLS AROUND nine that night. I had fallen asleep on my couch watching an old black and white movie. I answer, but I shouldn't have. Not in the state I'm in and not when I know what I have to do, and how it will hurt him. It's a domino effect of the tragedy that has become my life. Better now than later before love is involved. *Because he is a man I could love.*

"Hi," I whisper into the receiver.

"Sorry for disturbing you. Were you sleeping?" he asks.

"I was, but it's okay."

"I wanted to check on you, see how you're doing."

I hide under the throw, wanting to disappear wholly. But reality keeps me grounded right here in heartbreak. "Kaz, we need to talk."

"That doesn't sound good."

"It's not," I say, my true emotions bleeding through. "I like you so much, but there's this stuff I have to deal with that you shouldn't have to suffer through."

"I like you too, Lara, that's why I'll be here for you, however you need. Just name it and I'll be it, for you."

"Be my friend. Be my client. But we can't be more. Not right now."

"What's going on? Don't shut me out. Be honest with me. What has changed?"

"Kaz, I'm sorry. I am. More than you know. You're good. You're amazing, but I can't do this with you. I can't be anything for you right now. My life is just full of complications that I can't drag you into any deeper." I hate the hitch in my voice, but I need to get this out. He needs to be free of me, and any threat to his career... his life. I take a deep breath. "I'm not even sure we should work together."

"I'm not the groveling type, so if you don't want to be with me, we won't do this. But what the fuck happened in the last five hours?" His words are short. His voice is tight and controlled.

"Kaz—"

"Stop saying my name like that! *Fuck.* I thought you were different."

And there it is. There is my out, and even though my heart will splinter into a thousand pieces, I take it. "No," I say, barely getting the single syllable out. "I'm not." Save him the trouble of getting involved with me. Save him from this disaster. He's silent for a moment, and I hold back the sob so desperate to escape. I add, "I don't think it's wise for us to work together either."

"Fine. We won't work together. Then it's okay? Right?"

"I can't—"

"Did last night mean so little to you?"

"No, last night meant everything to me. But today, I have to live in reality."

"Don't do this, Lara. I can come over. We can talk."

"I can't. I can't talk to you anymore. It's too hard. Please don't try to convince me. This is just no good for either of us."

"We're good. We're so good, Lara. Don't do this. Whatever has happened, we can talk through this, we can—"

"Kaz, stop." I close my eyes, but I lower my voice until I'm whispering, "It was good while it las—"

"You're giving up."

"I have no choice. It's too much, too complicated right now. You need to be happy and that can't be with me."

"I don't know why you're doing this, but I really hate you for it."

The word hate is a dagger to the heart and I start to cry. He says, "I've dragged this out long enough, I guess." He stops and I hear his rough breath before he steadies his tone. "Have a good life, Lara." Then he hangs up on me before I have a chance to say goodbye. I don't know if I could anyway, but this time, I wanted the chance.

I'll trade my heart to protect his. The pain now is far less than it will be down the road. He'll see I saved him the trouble. *I just hope one day he forgives me and knows I only did this for the best.*

Even if my heart died in the process.

15

I ANSWER MY phone on the third ring. "Hello?"

"Open the door, Lara." Rochelle sounds irritated.

Dragging myself out of bed, I don't bother with my robe, and go. When I crack the door open, I keep my head down, not wanting her to see my face. She stands on the other side of the field of delivered roses, all still looking beautiful despite the intention behind them. "What is this?" she asks.

"Flowers."

"Obviously. Who are they from and why are they still out here?"

"One guess."

"Mark?"

"You got it."

"Man, he spent thousands on these. Guess you've talked then." I hear the glass vases grinding against the cement as she rearranges. I peek out, but she catches me. "Can I come in?"

"I'm sleeping. I was—"

"Sorry about that. Since you're up, wanna brunch?"

"I can't." I fake yawn, hoping to convince her how tired I am with my bad acting. "I'm just gonna lie in bed all day."

"What's going on? Why aren't you opening the door? And since when do you do nothing all day? You don't know how to relax."

"I'm tired."

Her hand reaches the door and she presses, but I hold firm, only one eye still revealed to her. But she's onto me, and I'm a shitty liar. I've got to get her to leave. After everything she's been through, I don't want to be another burden when she's finally found peace, so I say, "Thanks for stopping by. I'll call you later." I shut the door and lean against it, guilt covering me from head to toe. I run to my phone and call her, trying to assuage my emotional turmoil. When she answers, the words come rushing out. "I'm sorry. I just, I can't do this today, Ro. I want to tell you everything, but I need some time."

"You're scaring me, Lara. Open the door."

"Don't worry about me. I'll be fine. I'm just dealing with stuff I can't talk about right now."

"What is going on?"

"Please trust me. I'm fine."

Her frustration is heard. "Are you sure? I'm seriously worried by this conversation."

"I'm sure. I'm gonna go back to bed and rest. We'll talk soon."

"I'm going to trust you, but if you ever need anything, call me."

"I will. Thank you again."

I don't like to lie, especially to my friends, so keeping it vague keeps us all safe for now. I look down at the time on my phone. Seven hours to figure out what I'm going to do or show up at Mark's with a smile and dinner ready.

THE STREET IS quiet. If all the people only knew what I was about to do; if they only knew how far their neighbor has fallen from his shiny pedestal. If they only knew what he was making me do.

I know. And I feel worthless for doing it.

I feel despicable.

Disgust.

Shame.

I hate myself for doing this, but it's a necessary evil. The man is unstable, so this is for the greater good. Until I figure out a way to end this forever, I'll do what I have to, to survive, and to protect Kaz, who I already miss so much.

The gate code has been restored to the one I know and I'm let in. Once inside, the large bag of takeout is set on the kitchen counter and I start unpacking the food. After pulling the plates from the cabinet, I serve the food and set the table just the way I know he likes it. Stupidly, I once thought we were just getting to know each other when he'd comment on domestic things I did around his home, like setting the table, doing his laundry, and straightening up despite him having a maid once a week. Now I realize I was the one set-up. He wanted me barefoot and pregnant, his little stereotypical Stepford wife.

I stop my inner tirade and my fingers begin to shake.

He's home.

I can sense him near, my emotions curling in on themselves out of fear. He's chosen to torture me, to use this "insurance" to his complete advantage, and here I am a pawn in his sick game.

Satan himself enters the room. I move quickly behind my chair, hoping he just sits and eats, and doesn't expect more from me. But I'm foolish to think he'd want any less.

"Sit down, Lara," he says from the head of the table. "You know I don't like to eat alone."

"I thought that was why you pay the hookers," I reply, inwardly berating myself for speaking out.

"Silly woman." He laughs, but there's no amusement in his eyes, sinking fear right back into me. "I pay hookers for deviant sexual acts that you wouldn't do. Oh, but maybe you'll reconsider now."

The smarmy smile that crosses his lips makes me lose my appetite, as if I had one. "Now sit down."

I sit and take my napkin, folding it across my lap. After a few sips of wine, I gather my thoughts together before raising my chin. "What are you doing?"

"What do you mean?" He sets his fork down, as if my very voice annoys him.

"You don't have to do this. You can have a million women. You're famous, rich, and Mark Renner for crying out loud. Why are you doing this?"

"I told you. But I also told my parents about you. I said you were the one."

"If I was the one, you wouldn't have been fucking all the others."

His hand slams down on the table. "Are you dense?"

I jump and the saltshaker tips over. My breathing picks up, so rough in my chest that I reach for my water to quench my throat that's gone dry. "Do not touch that glass," he warns. I look up, our eyes meeting across the table. "You were supposed to be different." He makes it sound so easy, so obvious. "And now you know too much. You could destroy me in one leak to the press. I can't have that. I'd lose everything. Now eat."

"I won't say anything. I promise," I beg. "I'll sign anything you want and be silent, never speak a word of it to anyone."

He stands so abruptly that his chair falls back, causing me to jump. His plate hits the kitchen cabinets, making me scream. All the visions of him hitting me come flashing back as he yells, "Clean that mess up!" His heavy footsteps are heard as he walks out of the room, leaving me in the middle of his disaster.

I swallow hard, wiping away the tears that flood my eyes. My body ceases to rock and I stand up, holding on to the table for support. I don't understand how life can change so dramatically in a few days. I don't know if I should clean up or leave or try some other tactic. Fighting against everything I want to do, I take a deep breath, a large gulp of wine, and go into the game room. He practically lives in there when he's home.

When I open the door, the projector is on, the reel from last season playing on the large screen. Any other time, this would be normal for him. He watches playbacks regularly, but this isn't a playback reel to see what went wrong and to correct it. This is a highlights reel. He sits in the center recliner and stares at the player like he doesn't recognize him.

I don't anymore. Scanning the room for a laptop, I don't see one, so I say, "Please erase the videos, Mark." He doesn't move, not even an inch. "Please."

"I feel like you haven't been listening to me, Lara."

"I have." My voice quivers. Damn it.

"Bring me that black box on the bar and make me a drink."

Since dinner didn't go as I planned, I do as I'm told, trying a new angle. "Mark, it doesn't need to be like this. Women love you. Men envy you. You should be with someone who celebrates you, not fears you." After dropping the ice in the glass, I fill it to the halfway mark with Scotch. I grab the box and take both to him.

"Do you fear me?" There's sincerity in his tone that brings me to look his way. The handsome man I was first attracted to gazes back at me in curiosity. Then confusion clouds his eyes, as if he genuinely doesn't understand why I would be afraid of him.

"Yes." The ugly truth—plain and simple.

He closes his eyes and I stand there waiting. Waiting on a reaction, realization of what he's done, for him to do anything to make this right and hoping it doesn't get worse.

When he opens his eyes again, he takes the drink and downs it, and then hands the glass back to me. Looking right into my eyes, he says, "Fear is a strange emotion. We fear love sometimes or the act of falling in love. We fear death. We fear losing. Sometimes we fear winning. Winning isn't always easy to accept because we start to fear never winning again after tasting victory." Taking the black box from me, he opens it on the wide arm of the leather chair.

I thought I knew fear.

I didn't.

I don't move a muscle, not even to breathe when I see the needles and vials inside the dark blue velvet-lined box. "So fear," he says, preparing the needle, "is not always a bad thing." He loads a vial and I watch though I should probably be running for my life. Tapping the needle twice, he looks up at me and squirts a little, testing it. "Fear drives us to do things we wouldn't normally do."

"So do drugs," I add, wishing I had my phone to record this so I have my own insurance policy.

He nods, and then slowly repeats, "So do drugs."

He injects himself right in front of me, my body tensing even more as if that was possible. Acting calm, cool, collected, I can tell by the intensity of his tone that this isn't just a casual conversation. This is a confession and I'm going to be held liable to keep the secret. "We pay a lot of hush money to keep this secret, but I'm not paid millions for fun. I have to perform and my team looks the other way. Do you think I'm the only one? They love to win as much as I do. You don't get to our level by playing fair. This isn't little league. This is the Majors."

Leaning back in the plush chair, he asks, "What else do you fear, Lara?"

His lids blink, the action not smooth, then he hits me with his gaze again. "Do you really fear those videos being leaked? You fear that people will find out that you have sex, that you enjoy sex? Most people have sex. It's nothing to fear for them to find out, so I'm thinking it's not the videos that you worry about." His hands are balled, fisted until the knuckles are white. "What do you really fear?"

When I don't answer, he stands, grabs the back of my hair and twists down. I scream. My defenses kick in and I slam my fist into his stomach. His hand tightens until I'm bended on my knees in pain, sobbing for his mercy.

His hold on me stays firm while he sits back down. Hatred fills his eyes, his lips contorted in disgust. "You *should* fear me. I can end you. I can end him."

Him—Kaz.

End both of us. My heart lurches into my throat.

"I can make it so he never plays that fucking guitar again. So I'll ask you again. What do you fear, Lara?"

Through pained breaths, I answer, "You."

I'm released and pushed to the ground. "Good."

He clicks play on the remote, and with his eyes glued to the screen, he says, "The Entertainers of the Year Awards are in ten days. I'm nominated in two categories—MVP and Homerun Hottie. Be ready. You're going."

Scrambling to my feet, I trip and land on my hands and knees just behind his chair. Pain shoots through my kneecaps and up my thighs and that's when I realize there is no escaping this. He doesn't hurt me where it can be seen this time because of next week. *Bastard.* There is no escaping him, much less time to search his computer for the videos.

Nice doesn't work.

Fighting back doesn't work.

He's right. The sex tapes don't matter at the end of the day. I might lose clients, and I'd definitely lose respect. One day though, someone else's scandal will bury mine.

But Kaz... I don't know that I can save him when I can't even save myself, but I'm willing to do anything to try.

I don't run this time. I get to my feet and look at the screen. There's a man running bases with a huge smile on his face and the taste of victory on his tongue. That's not the same man sitting in the La-Z-Boy.

No, they're not the same at all.

The man on the screen used to be charming with an award-winning smile. He had a contagious laugh and caring touch.

The man in the chair would hurt someone just because he feels threatened, because he feels little inside. The man who used to play the game because it made him smile is lost. He traded his soul for a paycheck and his greed may kill me in the process.

My heart goes numb, the beats quiet to the slight ringing in my ears. Walking out of the room, I grab my car keys and leave. The night air is thin and I shiver from the chill.

I'm not the woman I was in that house. I'm not weak. *Normally.* He wants me to be. He wants me weak and under his thumb. What length is he willing to go to make that happen? What length will he go to not just control me, but to hurt Kaz?

Mark is a drug addict. That much is clear. Will it be an intervention or a drug test that takes him down? I'm willing to stage both. This is not about my safety or me.

I have to do something to end this once and for all.

I MANAGE TO avoid most everyone the next week, especially Kaz. He had two out-of-town shows, which helped me to stay away. But his words have played over and over in my mind. *There's no point dragging this out then. Have a good life, Lara.* I have almost texted him so many times, wishing I could replay our last conversation and tell him how I wish things were different. My life is in shambles though. I can't—*won't*—drag him down with me, so I try to remain strong most of the time. Despite what we decided, my heart hasn't gotten the memo.

My office down the hall is busy this morning. Lane comes into my bathroom while I'm putting makeup on and sets a coffee down in front of me. "Late start?" he asks.

"Tired." I've covered the remains of the bruising, which is light at worst and gone for the most part. Hopefully no one can tell.

"Oh God, me too. This guy at the club was a mess last night at disco night, and I had to rescue a friend, dragging his cute ass home, after they got in a kerfuffle." Kerfuffle makes me smile. Lane makes me smile. He's resilient, troubles rolling right off his back. It's a quality I've always admired in him. I take things to heart and carry my troubles around like a mass that can't be amputated.

He sits on a bench near the tub and starts scrolling on his iPad. "I have Calliope's this morning. The samples came in from France for the toile we ordered. You need to approve two before we can take them to show her. You have Kaz's this afternoon and," he says, smiling to himself, "maybe into dinner, if all goes well. Hubba hubba."

"The Fabian project has been cancelled. Take it off the books please. What time do you leave for Calliope's?" I ask while swiping on mascara. "I'll work from the studio today and I have four ca—"

"Whoa. Whoa. Whoa! Hold up there, cowgirl. I know he's been traveling, but what do you mean the Fabian project has been cancelled?"

I dig through my makeup tray, keeping my eyes lowered. "It's been cancelled. No big deal. Just changed his mind is all."

"No."

My eyes meet his in the reflection of the mirror. "What do you mean, no?"

"I mean that no one cancels on us and especially not someone I know for a fact, after much pressuring from Rochelle, admitted that he likes you. So try again. What's the real story?"

"Don't go all Sherlock on me. Sometimes it is what it is. There's no hidden conspiracy here, so move along, Watson."

"Oooh, nice work in with the Sherlock reference. Gives me an idea for Halloween." He comes over and leans his ass against the counter next to me. "That's another conversation though. Now tell me the truth, woman."

I drop the mascara into the tray. "We decided to stay friends and with that, not work together. It would put undue stress on our friendship that neither of us wants right now."

"Since we're sharing truths and all—"

"I don't remember you sharing any truths other than you think your friend has a cute ass," I reply.

"When I say we, it's the royal we, meaning you, honey." His eyes search mine, his happiness showing in the smoothness of skin around his eyes. He Botoxes way too much to actually see the happiness, so I pretend it's there. "Anyway, you know everything about me—"

I laugh. "And I still choose to work with you."

"Why are you wearing so much makeup? That's not like you. Special client?"

"No, just got some freebies and trying them out."

His non-response grabs my attention. When I look at him, he asks, "What did you do to your eye?"

My hand flies up in response and I cover it and turn away. "Nicked myself with the damn flat iron. Don't you have work to do?" I sidetrack him and walk into the closet.

"Going. Going."

The quiet of the room signals it's safe to exit. Lane's gone, but he leaves a message written on the mirror in red lipstick. There's a heart and the word "you." Although he can't hear me, I smile and say, "Heart you too, my friend." And I do. Especially. On a daily basis, he provides color in my very dark world.

Today I will try to avoid everyone as much as I can. I'll either be caught or a pro by the end of the day. Burying myself in my work will be nothing new. My team understands my passion and supports it, so I become a professional by the time six o'clock rolls around.

TWO HOURS OF lying in bed with a raw steak on my face, three different creams promising to reduce bruising, and a day later, I'm almost ready for the awards. They've been working. Thank goodness. I couldn't have a makeup artist do my makeup for the awards or they would see. So I spend the afternoon doing it myself.

By the time I'm done, nothing is visible.

The strapless blue dress I choose to wear is fitted with a mermaid bottom. I wear a single strand of diamonds around my neck. Simple, but beautiful.

I dread tonight. The cameras. The attention. Mark. *The Resistance.* Kaz. I dread it all. I will go only because I have to. Sleep was replaced with thoughts whirling like a dervish last night. I know what I have to do to get the much-needed leverage back, but I also need to earn Mark's trust back in the process.

Mark shows up on time. When I open the door, he looks me over disapprovingly. "I want you in black and something short. Go change."

"This is a designer dress, Mark. It's perfect for the red carpet."

"I said go change. Make it fast or we'll be late."

Closing my eyes, I try to calm the anger that's awakened inside, and take a deep breath while turning to go upstairs. To my back, he says, "Snap. Snap. Chop. Chop."

"Don't talk to me like that," I snap before I think. The glare I send over my shoulder is instantly reduced by the fury burning in his eyes. My knees weaken, but I reach for the railing to steady myself in front of him.

The change in him is physical, all his anger dissipating before my eyes. His shoulders ease and a small smile appears. "Please change. Black always looks good on you."

I'm not sure how to handle him, or his mood swings. Wordlessly I go to my bedroom and walk into the closet. I have at least five little black dresses and three of them are formal enough to work for the night, so I pick the prettiest since I'll be photographed, and slip it on. My shoes are exchanged for Louboutins, and my handbag is a black beaded clutch. I spend a few extra minutes putting concealer on my knees. It will hold for a while, hiding the damage, but I bring it with me when I hurry back out. Surprisingly, I'm greeted with a big smile. "You look beautiful, Lara."

Ignoring him and his worthless compliments, I walk past him

and out the door. When he comes out, I lock it and follow him to the car waiting to drive us. The ride is quiet. Mark plays on his phone. At one point he gets engrossed in a text conversation that I notice he purposely hides from me. A stupid grin is on his face as he reads the messages. He's definitely still fucking someone else or plans to soon. Another reason why I'm so confused that he wants me by his side. It's humiliating. *She* knows about me, but is happy to fuck him anyway. It's the first time I've ever regretted making an effort when it came to becoming who I am. I had convinced myself otherwise, but he's proved I'm weak. I'm practically a bull's eye for his target practice. I can't live like this. I won't. He has to be stopped. Somehow. Some way. I will play along until I have enough information to bury him. One opportunity is all I need to destroy his computer and back-up Cloud.

On the red carpet, I wait in the wings while he has his photo taken over and over. Some photos are taken of us together. I have a hard time smiling when my emotions are getting the better of me, but I manage for the most part.

The fans in the stands scream loudly letting us know someone big has arrived. Mark turns to see over the crowded red carpet. I know he loves being famous and just below the surface his jealousy bubbles. He hates when others steal his thunder. When he turns back, he says, "Your little friends are here."

I don't have to see above the sea of bodies to know who he's talking about. My heart races and I lift up to catch a glimpse of *The Resistance*. Even in platforms I'm not tall enough to see over everyone. Sharpness slices through my side and I grab hold with both my hands. Mark places his hand on my back. "What's wrong?"

"I don't know. I need to sit down. You finish here and I'll meet you inside."

Before he can weigh in with his thoughts, I hurry toward the hotel where the awards are being held. Once I'm inside, I frantically search for a bathroom. When I spot a restroom sign across the busy lobby, I walk fast, hoping no one notices me beelining it. The door is pushed open and I'm leaning against the sinks heaving for breath by the time I'm alone. My heart hurts so badly that I wonder if I'm experiencing the early signs of a heart attack.

The door opens again and an older woman walks in. "Are you all right?" she asks when she sees me.

I stand up, trying to appear as normal as I can. "I'm fine. I just overheated out there."

She smiles kindly. "I hate these events and crowds, but my husband is nominated, so I come for him."

"Congratulations to him. That's quite an honor."

She touches up her lipstick, then turns to me. "Thank you." She smiles. "You're looking much better now. You've got some color in your face again."

I turn toward the mirror, something I'd been avoiding as much as I could. If it didn't involve applying makeup, I wanted no part in seeing myself. "Yes. That's good," I reply, humoring her as I walk out, but stop to say, "Thank you and good luck to your husband."

"Good luck to you," she replies as if she sees right through me, sees the bruising on the inside.

Back in the lobby, the crowd has grown as more celebrities have made their way inside. I stand off to the side and look around. Mark is tall with broad shoulders and stands out in a crowd, but I don't see him. He must be on the red carpet still doing interviews. I head to the bar and take a glass of champagne. I finish half before I lean against the wood bar top.

"Hi." *That voice.* My heart begins to ache in ways it only does for one man.

I peek to my right and see Kaz's eyes with their comforting warmth. Kaleidoscopes of chocolate make up their uniqueness, and as he looks at me, I feel his comfort, as though he's wrapping me in his leather jacket like he did once before, warming me with his nearness. *He shouldn't show me such gentleness, not after our phone call.* As if I hadn't cruelly pushed him away, he reaches up and strokes his finger down my cheek. I wish I could lean into his touch, but I can't. "You shouldn't be here." *I don't deserve your kindness any more.*

"The band was nominated."

Daring to look at him though I know I'll struggle to leave once I do, I correct myself. "I don't mean at the event. I mean talking to me."

His eyes narrow, so I turn away quickly. I look for Mark, making sure he doesn't see us.

Kaz states, "I'm not scared of him."

"I am." I walk away, easily slipping through groups of people and escaping before I'm caught by Kaz again. I can't have him involved in this mess.

I'm grabbed from behind and abruptly taken aback. Mark nods to the doors to the ballroom, and says, "Let's go in."

I nod and follow. His hand is wrapped tightly around mine until I'm at his side. He keeps his arm stiff so I can't stray until we reach our table. Pulling my chair out for me, he's the appearance of the perfect gentleman, but I know the monster lurking beneath. If only I'd seen the real him sooner.

Glasses of champagne are served and more drink orders placed. I don't allow myself to look around the large room though it's all I really want to do. I want to see him again. Breathe him in. Touch him. Be with Kaz. But there's no use indulging in what can never be.

The lights go down just as the first course is served. The comedian should be funny, but this charade is drowning me. Mark touches my arm, and normally I would consider it gentle, but I don't like him touching me at all so my skin crawls beneath his fingertips.

"My first award is up next. Wish me luck."

I look at him, hating the man before me. If only the daggers I want to shoot him in my glare were lethal. "Good luck." My reply is dry and as heartless as I can manage, the champagne letting my real emotions loose in the moment. But I calm, saving the stronger emotions for when I need the physical strength to handle him.

Over Mark's shoulder, I see Kaz, the band, Rochelle, and Holli two tables away from ours. Kaz's eyes are fixed on me. I want to look away. I really should, but I'm captivated by the man, entranced by the emotions he wears for me on his sleeve.

I shake my head and look away. At this point, Mark is winning his game, and until I can end this, I'm stuck. *I know too much. He could destroy me in one leak to the press.* Would Kaz be there after the fallout, after leaked tapes spread?

Mark wins his category and like a doting girlfriend, I play my part. There should really be an Oscar for this performance—showing my support while controlling my gag reflex. As soon as Mark's on stage, I glance toward Kaz, but he's gone from his seat. I see Rochelle instead. Her expression shows her sadness, which is understandable. In her eyes, I've returned to Mark. I wish I could tell her more, tell her the whole truth. I look away, not able to handle that right now. When Mark leaves the stage, I escape to the bathroom. Once inside, I stare at the reflection, staring at someone I barely recognize, someone I'm ashamed to be.

"You can't say things like that then disappear on me."

My eyes meet Kaz's in the mirror. "Please go, Kaz."

"What if I say no?"

I turn around just as he leans forward, trapping me between his arms. "I know you're scared of him, but you don't have to be scared of what you're feeling for me, what I feel for you, or of us." His lips almost touch mine, teasing me in ways I won't be able to resist for long. "I see how you look at me. I see that same desire I feel inside for you in your eyes for me. You're conflicted and guarded, but you don't have to be. You can always trust me."

"But you said—"

"Forget what I said the other day. I want you, Lara."

17

"I WANT YOU any way I can have you. I want you in my bed. I want to make love to you and then fuck you so you never forget me."

I sigh, dropping my gaze to his chest. "I could never forget you."

"Why are you doing this then? Why are you with him?"

"Because I have to be."

"That makes no sense. I want you. You want me. I can tell."

With his fingertip, he raises my chin until I look into his eyes again. My knees weaken just by the sincerity I find there. He whispers, "Whatever you need, I'll be. Just give me a chance to show you, to prove to you how much I care about you."

A tear teeters on the edge of my bottom lid before falling, which reveals to him my true feelings. I push him away and leave the confines of his arms. I start to run, but I can't, my traitorous feet remaining planted near him. I turn back and say, "Kaz, you can't. You don't understand—"

"I'm trying to, but you won't tell me anything. I know he beat the shit out of you and for some reason you feel the need to stay with him. I don't get why. Leave with me."

"It's not that simple."

"Fuck, Lara." He turns his back to me, his hand running over his head, agitated. "You make this so goddamn difficult." When he faces me again, his frustration is heard. "Is he threatening you? This makes no sense. If you don't want to be with me, just say so, but I can't promise to leave you alone."

My mouth remains empty of what I know I need to say. I bring my lower lip under my teeth and scrape. This was awful over the phone, but saying these words to him in person, where I can see his gorgeous face, is torture. "We're done, Kaz."

I repeat the lies—the heartless words—but there's no passion in them, no truth to be found.

Thunderous applause from the ballroom fills the doorway when a woman enters the bathroom. Her eyes go wide, but then she smiles, recognizing Kaz instantly. "You just won."

He glances to me. "Not even close, baby." Then he rushes past her. I'm left unsure what to say, so I start to leave, but she practically swoons in front of me. "You're so lucky you got to talk to him. He's so hot."

"Yes, he's amazing." I walk out and back to the ballroom, entering in time to see the band on stage accepting their award. I know he can't see me from up there, but deep down, I wish he could. He would see the smile I save for him, the one only he can evoke.

When Mark's large paw of a hand rests on my thigh, I'm glad Kaz can't see me. He won't have to bear witness to my weakness, my waning strength.

Sitting through the rest of the show, I barely touch my food. Mark doesn't win the second award, and he's been restless since. My mind starts to wonder what that means for me later. I peek at Kaz several times throughout the show, but make sure to look away before he sees me. The lights brighten the room and we get up to leave. Kaz is already long gone. Mark takes my hand and kisses the top. "You ready to go to the after-party?"

I've resolved not to bother with speaking to him. It's pointless.

My anger can't be contained and I don't want to make a scene in public. I tried that once and I was shown who is more powerful between us...

"You act like six months is six years, Mark. Don't be ridiculous."

"Don't call me ridiculous."

"Then stop acting like—" My arm is grabbed hard, jerking me to a standstill, and cutting off my words.

"Ow!"

I try to pull away, but his fingers tighten around my upper arm, and I'm yanked against him. "Shut your mouth," he warns, his voice gruesome and terrifying.

The shock of it stiffens my body. Every red flag flies up, putting my muscles on alert.

Fight or flight?

He's my boyfriend... was my boyfriend. He won't hurt me. Until his nails dig into my skin. Then I reminded he will.

Fight or flight?

"Mark, please. Let go of me."

"No. You won't embarrass me like this."

"I don't love you. You can't possibly love me when you can't even be faithful to me."

"I do. I love you."

"If you love me, let me go."

"I can't. Don't you see?" he asks, shaking me. "I need you."

Fight or Flight?

Trying to remain calm, to not show weakness to this hulking figure of a man, I ask, "For what?"

"To love me." Darkness is etched into the soul of his eyes, something I never noticed before. It's not sadness. Disdain? Power? Desperation?

Fight or flight?

My gut knows. No good is going to come of this. He's not the man I dated.

And I can't trust him.

Fight!

Swinging with all my might, my hand goes for his face. He blocks my arm, grabs, and twists it behind my back. An excruciating pain heats my shoulder and I cry out, "Stop. Stop. Stop!"

"Will you stop?" He tightens, my shoulder feeling close to broken. Pain overpowers my thoughts.

From the corner of my eyes, I see them. Strangers in the distance, but close enough to see what is happening. And they do nothing. So I do what I have to. "Yes," I reply through tears running down my face.

Fight!

As soon as I'm released, I kick him in the balls as hard as I can. Mark keels over and I run...

We begin walking up the aisle toward the ballroom doors. I'm pulled aside and in the dark of the corner near the exit, he asks, "Can you not muster any enthusiasm, Lara? Tonight has not exactly been torture. Do you know how many women would like to be you tonight?"

"I assume many by all of the whores who were willing to fuck you knowing you had a girlfriend."

"You're always so fucking sarcastic." He gives up his energy on me. "And *had*?"

"Had," I reply definitively.

"Try *have*. And I'm being nice. Can you be nice?"

"Nice? Why would I be nice to you?"

"Because I've asked one favor. We can plan the breakup for our next date, but give me tonight."

"Are you psychotic? You do realize you forced me to come here tonight, right?"

"I didn't force you. You freely got in the car. So when did I force you?"

"You beat me, Mark. When you accept that responsibility, I'll be nice." I walk past him and out the door to where our car is waiting.

He joins my side, and opens the back door. "Get in the fucking car."

Every ounce of my sanity tells me to run, but I can't. My feet feel like lead, heavy, making it impossible to move. I know the outcome. I've been here before. So I make a choice that I'll be judged for later, but that saves me now.

I get in the car.

The after-party is at a popular restaurant nearby. We walk the shorter red carpet, smiling for the cameras, then I make my way toward the head of the line like I'm directed and give Mark his shining moment. A man with a clipboard hurries Mark along, announcing *The Resistance's* arrival.

Perking up, I look past Mark just as he grabs my upper arm and squeezes. My eyes catch Kaz's gaze locked on me and I watch it play out before I have a chance to react.

The rest is a blur of commotion.

Kaz closes the gap in a few long strides, his arm raising as he closes in on his target. One perfectly executed right hook lands squarely across Mark's jaw, sending the giant to his ass and me wobbling. And the feeding frenzy begins.

The photographers raid the red carpet, encircling the two. Kaz is pumped, light on his feet, fists up in defense. "Motherfucker! If you ever come near her again, I will kill you."

I was already running, but I'm grabbed by a security guard and held back. "No, Kaz. No! Don't."

Struggling to break free, I bear witness to the horror before me. Mark is on his feet and lands a straight hit to Kaz, and I scream, "No, Mark! Please. Don't hurt him."

Kaz is swinging again, but is grabbed, each arm restrained. Johnny and Dex pull Kaz back. Mark with his huge ego smiles as if he's won. Blood covers his teeth and he laughs, but a fist to the face stops him cold.

"Don't fuck with my friends!" Derrick stands proud to have ended the fight.

Security takes hold of Mark, trying their best to hold him back.

Kaz's arms are behind him as he lunges forward, fighting through what must be pain from the expression on his face. But is he in pain from the guys or because of me? He shouts, "I will hurt you five times worse than you hurt her, asshole." His eyes remain focused on Mark as he struggles to get free, adrenaline coursing through him. "Let me go. You don't know what he's done."

Bodyguards surround the band members, but Kaz still fights for his freedom. Chaos surrounds us. Johnny's yelling for Kaz to stop and walk away. Derrick is fully invested in the fight. Dex is working with the bodyguards to pull Kaz from the scene. Paparazzi engulf us, making it hard to move anywhere.

Their security detail gets them to safety at the beginning of the carpet and whisks them to their black SUVs. A strong hand embraces my arm, guiding me through the cameras. Tommy is in front of me, protecting my space while we walk. "Get in the car. We need to get you out of here." The door to one of the vehicles is opened and he lifts me up to the running-board.

"Lara!" Mark's voice booms from behind me, rattling my insides, but I don't look back.

My world lights up when I see Kaz inside the car. His fists hit the seat and he yells, "Fuck!"

Tommy gets in behind me as I slide across the leather and cling to Kaz. "Oh my God, Kaz! Are you okay?"

The Suburban starts moving. Kaz's arms come around me, his breath heavy in his chest under my cheek. When I look up, he says, "That's what I should have done the other night. I'm sorry I didn't."

"No. No. You don't need to do this for me. I'm not worth the trouble."

"He hurt you."

Tommy sits next to me and leans forward to stare at Kaz. "What the fuck? You realize you just attacked Mark Renner, *the* Mark Renner, in front of fifty journalists?"

"Paparazzi aren't journalists," Kaz says sarcastically.

"You know what I mean." Tommy shakes his head. "I don't understand what just went through your head."

Kaz warns, "Tommy, stop."

"He's a fucking major league baseball player. You play guitar for a living." He glances down at Kaz's hands, which causes me to do the same. *Oh no.*

His knuckles are bloodied, the skin ripped apart across the top. I shield them from view, careful not to hurt him more by touching them. "I'll take care of you when we get home." The word home rolls off my tongue so naturally with him.

Kaz directs his eyes back to Tommy. "I have my reasons." Then he takes my hand and brings it to his lips and kisses.

"Leave it to a woman," Tommy says with an eye-roll. "This is a PR fucking nightmare." Tommy leans away from us, his arm against the window.

"I'll take the heat, Tommy. Don't worry. I'll make sure the band isn't dragged into this mess."

He sits up abruptly, anger getting the better of him. "Too late, Kaz. What were you thinking?"

I remain quiet, the side effects of my actions sinking in. "I left him."

"Good," Kaz adds.

"You don't understand. I left him. *I* left *him*. In front of the press."

My hand starts shaking. Kaz now covers mine with his and gently squeezes. "It will be okay. I'll take care of you. I promise."

"I don't want you to take care of me. I want to take care of myself." The rage in Mark's voice. I feel sick hearing him call my name over and over on a loop in my mind. Grabbing my head, I close my eyes. "What have I done?" I turn to Tommy as desperation sets in. "I need to go home. Please take me home."

"Lara—" Kaz starts but I whip to my other side to face him and beg. I'm not above it for him. "Please. Please, Kaz. You have to take me home."

After a long hard look at me, he doesn't argue. He turns to the driver and gives him my address. The next fifteen minutes of listening to Tommy tap away on his phone are painful. The lack of a kind touch, the absence of his comforting words, the tension that never existed before wedges between us like a tangible emotion, hurts—my heart, my head, and my soul. I feel the wound caused by Mark's scheme gaping open. *I know what he is going to do next.* My blood runs cold from the thought of the violation I will endure. No one wants what was sanctioned in the bedroom thrust into the limelight for all to see. And of course, there is no way I can be with Kaz. Any way I look at it, there's no winner in this nasty game.

Only pain.

The car stops and Tommy's door swings open. He gets out first and as I'm maneuvering to exit, Kaz catches me. "Tell me," he says, coming to terms with our situation. "Tell me why you can't be with me. Give me something, Lara, I've got nothing left to lose."

"Kaz," I start, feeling horrible, the door that leads to my heart already closing. I can dance around the truth all I want but that's not going to fix this mess. It's not going to heal his heart. Not when I have to put distance between us now more than ever. Mark will seek his revenge. I just need him to take it out on me and not Kaz. "Please understand this is for the best." I lean back over and kiss him. Surprisingly he lets me and kisses me back. My mind swirls with all the feelings he evokes, sensations I want to grab hold of and keep. But I know to keep him safe I must give him up. I reach up and move the hair that's fallen over his eyes to the side and kiss him gently on the cheek. I don't know what possesses me, or what inspires me, but with my lips lingering on his skin, I don't say goodbye. "Live a great story. And share it. Share it through your music, your lyrics, your notes." Turning away, I slip my feet to the ground, landing solidly on my high heels. I glance back just long enough to see his eyes, to see something wild blooming inside... wild with possibility.

With my head down, I close the door, and walk away. Like his eyes, my heart beats wildly in my chest. Terror of what's to come, or what could be ahead: if he's in my home, or *if if if* rumbles through my body and I swallow hard, pretending everything is A-okay as I leave Kaz. With my finger on a lit-up phone, I'm ready to call the cops if needed. While knowing I need to fear what's right in front of me, my thoughts are on all the different outcomes when I walk inside my home. The *what ifs* run free.

What if I choose Kaz?

What if I take the chance?

What if Mark releases a video or more?

What if Mark hits me again for leaving him or... kills me?

What if I die on my terms instead of his?

What if I choose love?

What if Kaz ignores my pleas and comes after me?

I've got to form a solid plan that can succeed this time. How do I do that? What do I do? What if—A knock breaks the vicious what-if cycle and I swing open the door before common sense kicks in. Kaz is standing there. Like too often lately, tears fill my eyes. "What are you doing?"

"Choosing to live my story with you."

My body crashes into his and we kiss as if *what ifs* never existed.

The threat of Mark's retribution.

The ominous knowledge of broad-spectrum humiliation.

The fear I've lived in, the fear of Mark, the fear of losing Kaz forever.

It's all replaced with warmth, hope, and love.

Kaz's warm lips feel like heaven compared to the hell I've been living. I pull back and look him in his glorious, loving eyes. "I'm going to pay for this, but I need and want you so much." I kiss him again, wanting to wipe away all thoughts of Mark and his threats, to live a new story.

THE SUV DRIVES off just as Kaz pulls back from me this time. "What do you mean, you're going to pay for this?"

"It's about Mark. You must know—"

He stops me. "Let's go inside."

After we're safely in and the door is locked, I lead him to the kitchen. "Drink?"

"Yes, but tell me what you mean?"

"You're gonna need peas too. Fortunately, I have a few bags in the freezer." I grab a bag and go to him. Holding it to his cheek, I place my other hand on his chest. "Stay calm. I need you to know what might happen if you're choosing to be with me."

"I'm here and I plan to stay."

"Kaz, the other day I wanted to see you. It was all I wanted, but he turned up here. He's made videos of us." Hoping he understands without me going into great detail, I leave it open-ended.

"Videos? Of you having sex?"

"Yes." I turn my back to him, feeling ashamed as if I did something wrong, as if I should be embarrassed. *Again.* Another

S. L. SCOTT

moment Mark has tainted.

"You knew, or you didn't know he was filming?"

When I turn, I plead, wanting him to know I wouldn't have made them with him. "I didn't know. I didn't know about any of them, but he says he has a lot and he'll release them if I leave him."

"He's blackmailing you into dating him?"

"Only until he can break up with me. Publicly. He wants to win the hearts of America by playing the *Poor Me* role of the heartbroken golden boy to the media."

His brow furrows. "Why?"

"Ego," I reply, the only word needed to explain. "I couldn't let those videos get out. I couldn't let him drag you through the media."

Fingers flex at his side. "What do you mean *me*?"

"We should clean and bandage your hand." I reach out offering mine, relieved when he takes it. I lead him down the hall and into my master bathroom. He sits down on the bench while I dig out the first-aid kit.

When I sit next to him, I start cleaning his wounds with hydrogen peroxide. He never flinches, but asks, "How can he drag me through the media?"

"He said he would." I take a closer look to make sure the blood is gone and his knuckles are ready to be bandaged.

"And?" He chuckles, seemingly amused by what I'm saying when my heart is still firmly planted at the bottom of my stomach.

"What do you mean *and*?" I start wrapping the bandage tape around his hand. "I don't want to hurt your image, the band, your brand. I know how Hollywood works."

He laughs, a laugh that's hardy and deep. "A sex tape being released of my girlfriend and her ex doesn't hurt my image." He caresses my cheek. "You can't hurt my image. You can only make me look better, baby."

A bunch of words are coming from his mouth, but I only hear one. "Your girlfriend?"

"Yeah," he says. "I'm not letting you go this time. We've been playing at this tug of war for too long." The caress of his hand soothes my soul and he leans in to kiss me. "I don't want to be one of those couples who loses sight of what's important because of bad communication or misunderstandings. Like I told you before, I want you. I want to be with you. What do you want?"

"I want you." There's no hesitation in my voice.

"I'm so damn glad you said that." Nose to nose, he breathes me in, closing his eyes, and licking his lips. My own breathing deepens and I close my eyes as his hands hold my face to his. "I'm going to kiss you again. And again."

I move his now-bandaged hand to my lips and kiss, hoping to heal it quicker. "I want more than a kiss." My voice is breathy and desperate, but that's how I feel whenever he is near.

Turning my hand in his so he's holding me, he says, "Come with me." We only make it as far as the door. "Take off your dress, though I'd like to add that you look amazing in it."

My eyes go wide from surprise because his are deviating from polite to determined to demanding in an instant. "Thank you. You look amazing yourself."

I lift my leg up to take off my heel, but he kneels down in front of me and takes my ankle between his hands. Looking up at me, he rubs his hands up the back of my legs and under the hem of my dress. "You wanna play truth?"

"Not dare?"

"No dare needed. Just truths."

It's so easy to forget the world outside these walls when we're together. So easy. And wonderful. "Tell me all your truths, Kaz."

Encouraging me, he guides me closer, pressing his face against the fabric at the apex of my thighs, and he inhales. Hot breath strikes and I inhale sharply. I stand before him, watching him, allowing my fingertips to rest on his shoulders. He inhales me again, moaning from pleasure. The sound is vulgar and raw, his voice husky when he looks up. "I'll tell you a secret if you tell me one."

"You go first." His lust-filled expression engages the very core of my being and gives me confidence.

Hiking the bottom of my dress higher, he takes one of my legs and lifts it over his shoulder, and confesses, "I've gotten off more than a few times imagining your legs wrapped around my neck, and your heels digging into my back while I fuck you with my mouth."

Just take me now.

But he asked if I wanted to play along, and I intend to. Feeling sassy and very flirty, I set both my feet back on the ground and take a step back. With his eyes glued to me, I bend over, sliding my hands down the front of my legs until I reach my ankles. All those years of yoga have paid off when it comes to my flexibility. While bent over, I look up and ask, "Shoes like these?"

"Shoes exactly fucking like those."

I lift up, curving my back in the most seductive way I know how. "Then I'll leave them on for you." I turn my back to him and move my hair to one side, and over my shoulder. But I look back while I do. "Maybe you can help me with this dress."

"I've wanted to do that all night." His fingers take to the top of the gold zipper and he slides it down slowly as his breath blankets the back of my neck.

I drop my head forward and close my eyes. The troubles of the day drift away. Kaz's touch consumes me. His lips against my skin cause me to sigh in pleasure, his sentiments intoxicating. "I missed you." The sweetest of kisses is placed along my spine, followed by another even lower.

"I missed you." His hands slip into the open back of the dress and around to my chest. He takes my breasts in hand, taking what he wants, making me feel sexy and desired. His erection is steel against my back, and my body reacts, molding my softness against his hardness.

He kisses the curve of my neck and my head rolls to the side as he lets the dress fall to the floor. "Lara," he whispers, then kisses my shoulder while caressing my breasts. "You pushed me away, wanting me to hate you, to feel used by you. But I know you. I know you would never do that. It's not in you. That's why I came for you. It's why I can't leave. You're the most beautiful woman, the only woman I've ever dreamed about. I want to be yours. And I want you to be mine. *Mine.* Promise me you'll be mine."

Turning around in his arms, I look up. It doesn't matter that my body is bare, or that he's fully clothed. We're equals together. *I want you to be mine. I want to be yours.* It's not a demand. It's a request. This is not about ownership but a relationship. It's about us. "Yes, with all my heart."

Kaz makes me feel special, sexy, and intelligent. I don't need to hear a promise in return. I can feel what I mean to him and that's a heady combination. "Kaz," is all I manage to say before he takes me quickly, backing us onto the bed behind me.

His belt is undone. His jacket comes off. The buttons on the front of his shirt are popped off as he pulls it open across his chest. After settling between my legs, he hovers over me, his words a bond. "All I need is you. Only you."

"You say that as if you can predict the future," I whisper, searching his eyes for his truth.

"I say that knowing that what I feel for you has never been felt before. Our love is unique, Lara. Our love is a world of undiscovered prisms fighting to be seen for the first time. Together, there is only good."

"I need to know all of you. Your good. Your bad. What I feel for you is new and different. It scares me, exposing me as a fraud in every relationship before now. How is that possible after such a short time?" *What bad have you known, Kaz?*

"We can't see the future, but we can change it. Your past doesn't matter just as mine doesn't. Right now I need to kiss you, and I want to make love to you."

"I want to make love to you." I whisper, "Just us. Nothing between us. Just us."

"Are you on the pil—"

"Yes."

Divine lips take mine as if he's owned them all along. He enters me, my mouth falling open with a light gasp from the delicious pressure. Tilting my head back, I leave my neck exposed. Kaz sucks gently, moving along my throat, and down lower. I tighten my legs around him and run my fingers through his hair. His movements have a purpose, a mission to please me. He does, feeling so good. Our bodies heat as our breaths pick up. "I want on top," I say, my desires getting the best of me, wanting any control I can muster to help take my mind to otherworldly places only Kaz takes me to.

The bed feels too small for something that feels so amazing, so explosive in my chest. The blinds are open and the moonlight streaks across the bed. Messed dark hair, alluring eyes, and hands that know my body—he's magnetic.

I climb over him and sink down, take a deep breath, and embrace the fullness that could easily overwhelm if I let it. My head lulls back as I begin to rock forward, the sounds of our sex slick as moans fill the air.

When I look down, his eyes are open and fixed where our bodies are joined together. My hands land on his chest and I gather the control to slow things down. I want to remember everything—everything between us—about him, and this moment when ecstasy overrides everything else.

I'm flipped in a drastic turn of events, and he says, "You're teasing. Turn over."

With a devilish smile, I admit, "I might have been, but I was enjoying you."

When I roll over, he takes my hips and lifts them up, angling me before he touches me between my legs and thrusts his cock deep inside. With each push, my breath is forced out and I close my eyes, loving his strength. I drop my head forward just as my orgasm hits, taking over.

His chest covers my back as his body falls into the same blazing bliss. Kisses are placed on the back of my neck and down my spine, bringing the romance back full circle. He falls to the side. My body is stiff, betraying me after such an amazing high. I straighten my legs, falling flat on my chest. When I turn to look at him, my hair sticks to my face, but Kaz carefully pushes it away until I can see him. He watches my mouth, then leans down and kisses me. "You're worth the trouble."

"You say that now, when everything feels good, when we feel invincible."

"No, I say that always. So I gotta warn you now, you might be stuck with me."

I kiss him, then with my eyes closed, I lean my forehead against his, appreciating the peace I feel with him. "That sounds like an offer I can't refuse."

19

I TOLD MYSELF I would never rush into another relationship ever again, but that was before I was with Kaz. He makes me want to free-fall from the clouds, like that is an actual possibility. He gave me hope when I was at my lowest, swooping in and giving me strength when I struggled to find it.

But as I watch him in the hours just before dawn, Mark's threats replay in my mind. Good and evil. Kaz and Mark. Kaz is reliable and caring, everything Mark is not. Mark is unpredictable, and the drugs are making him rage. How he'll react to the red carpet incident is worrisome. I know him too well. He won't let this go. His plan didn't play out how he wanted and he'll make us pay. How? When? Where? I feel edgy from the questions that linger in the air.

I kiss Kaz on the cheek. I don't want to give him up. My like... my *love* for him runs too deep. Our relationship has been on a fast track and reckless, but it's true and wild, and free. Mark can't destroy us. He may hinder, but he won't win in the end. My faith in the man next to me is too strong.

Slipping out of bed, I tiptoe into the bathroom, wanting to

freshen up. I turn on the shower and brush my teeth while the water warms. Removing my makeup will show the little bruising that remains, but I'm not worried about exposing my flaws to Kaz. He's seen me at my worst physically and emotionally, and been at the receiving end when I pushed him away. I don't have a fear of him leaving me now. He's done more than he ever needed for me to believe he plans on sticking around. I just hope he'll see I'm willing to do the same for him.

The water is the perfect temperature when I walk into the shower. I close my eyes and let it rain down over me. It feels good to wash away the night, especially knowing I get a fresh start with the man in the next room.

The door is opened, and cool hands caress my breasts from behind. The bridge of his nose glides behind the shell of my ear before he whispers in it, "You snuck off."

"I wanted to get clean for you."

His hands go lower, one moving between my legs. "I like you dirty."

Curious, I ask, "How dirty do you like it?"

"However dirty you're willing to go?"

"Can I be honest with you?"

My body is left bare and he moves in front of me. His voice remains relatively calm when he replies, "Always be honest with me." Despite looking into Kaz's open and warm eyes, I hear Mark's bitter and snide remarks as if he was here in the room. *I pay hookers for deviant sexual acts that you wouldn't do.*

"I'm boring. I've not really done anything sexually adventurous."

"I like that."

"But you're a rock star. You'll get bored." *I don't want to see photos of him with other women too. I think that would break me.*

"Hey," he says, his tone changing as worry creases his brow. "We're not just sex, Lara. We're more than that."

"Are we?"

"Yes." He taps my chin. "It's you, Lara. Only you."

"I feel the same for you, Kaz."

"There's shit to sort out and consequences. I may be a rock star, but I'm also just a man. With us, it's not just about who has been more sexually adventurous. Sex between us is amazing because it's you and me. Okay?"

My smile for him is soft as I touch his cheek with one hand and hold his hand with the other. "Okay." Words can be toxic when spewed from a narcissistic, controlling drugged asshole. But Kaz's words heal, a soothing balm to my battered and bruised heart.

"I still need to know that you're okay."

"I might have some bad times, but right here with you, I'm more than okay."

"Since we're opening up—"

I grab the shampoo and pour some in both of our hands. "Are we opening up? I don't seem to know much about you. Still."

Instead of scrubbing his own hair, his hands come to my head and he rubs the shampoo on top before massaging my scalp. "I'm weak to a head massage."

"I'm hoping you're weak to me in general."

I look up at him. "I am. Can't you tell?"

"We're on equal footing then."

I love that he considers us partners, both all in with the same stakes on the line. I reach for his head and say, "Bend a little." He cocks an eyebrow and bends. I clean his hair, rubbing it together to make it stand in a sudsy Mohawk. "Tell me the craziest thing you've ever done."

Laughter echoes in the space as a smile appears, fond memories surfacing in his eyes. "The craziest *and* stupidest thing I ever did was standing on the hood of a car on the Autobahn while it was going forty miles an hour. I lost to a guy who made it up to fifty."

Slowly blinking in disbelief, I ask, "You mean you fell at forty miles an hour?"

"No. I stomped, which meant stop the car."

"That is crazy stupid."

"That was the last time I did molly. That drug made me brave in ways that would eventually kill me if I kept doing it."

"It made me feel sexual the one time I did it in college."

He dips his head under the water and rinses, his gaze firmly on me. "I like you sexual."

"I don't need drugs with you."

Spinning me around so I'm under the water, he kisses my neck as I rinse my hair. "You could very much make me do crazy and stupid things."

"Like a drug."

"I'm already addicted to you."

I kiss his lips, and then say, "Me too. And I think enough happened yesterday to satisfy those checkboxes. How about we try happy and calm things?"

"Right after this." He lifts me until his hard cock is between my legs. With my back to the cold marble wall, I hold tight around his neck, my body wrapped around his, and I slowly slide down until he's inside me. The feel of his slick erection feels too good, but I don't stop him. I trust him and what he's told me.

I don't close my eyes this time, wanting to see his face, his reactions, his pleasure while embracing our connection.

Kaz's head is tilted back, his lids heavy, a reflection of how I feel. His lips are parted and I get a glimpse of his tongue when the tip touches the front of his teeth. His hips move making my body slippery against the wall. With a quick adjustment, I'm pinned in place as he thrusts. Wet kisses fall away as he leans down to tackle my neck with sweetness and lust combined. He doesn't whisper. He states his needs, the words emblazing themselves like a tattoo on my skin. "I want you so fucking badly."

My fingers tangle into his hair. "You've got me."

"I want more. So much more. Give me everything, baby. You feel so good. So, so good."

I understand his needs. "You make me want to rush because this feels so good."

"More. And faster."

"Faster. And harder."

He pumps in and out of me harder, listening to my cravings. "Fuck!" he yells against my chest as he comes, his body erratic. A deep inhale of breath, then exhaled in frustration as his fist slams to the wall. "I'm sorry. That was too fast."

"It's okay. I like when you lose control because it feels too good."

"I wanted you to come first, but you felt too good."

"I'll come next," I say, running my hands over his shoulders.

He sets my legs down and steadies me. "I'll make you feel so good, baby." He lowers to his knees and leans forward kissing up the length of my thigh before making me come twice with his hands and mouth. I can get used to coming last if it's this good every time.

I sleep another three hours before I feel stirring next to me and hear Kaz's groggy voice. "Your phone."

Rolling onto my back, I open one eye and look up at the ceiling. "Huh?" I ask half asleep.

"Your phone is ringing."

As I come to, his words start to make sense. "Oh." I look around, but it's nowhere to be found. I can hear it though. I hurry from bed and into the living room where I find my purse on the chair. I dig in and pull the phone out. Mark's name flashes once before it goes to voicemail. Reality pops my peaceful bubble. I know I have to face my problems but I was hoping to do it after lunch.

Quietly padding back into the bedroom, I slip under the covers and close my eyes pretending that call never happened and trying for sweet dreams with Kaz again. He asks, "Was it him?"

I roll onto my side to face his direction and sigh. "Yes."

"Did you want to answer?"

I'm not going to lie anymore. "It went to voicemail."

"I don't want you to see him again. I shouldn't say things like that, but it's how I feel and I'm not going to hide how I feel. I have to hide enough in my life, so I don't want to do it with you."

"I like that you told me how you feel." I scoot closer to him. "If it makes a difference, I don't want to see him again either. Everything I need to say can be said over the phone."

"What is left to say?"

"He will get revenge. He's not going to let yesterday just go. Neither will the press. He believes he holds the power by having those videos. But maybe there's something I can say that will convince him not to release them."

"Maybe there's not. Then you're just wasting your breath."

I nod with my hands on his chest. "Kaz, I need you to trust me and let me do what I think is best."

"I do trust you, but I don't trust him. I don't want you to see him again. He's not safe." He gets out of bed and walks into the bathroom. His shoulders are tense, his body agitated.

Sitting up, I wait with my back to the headboard and the sheet held over my chest. When he comes out, he leans against the doorframe, looking a little tired, but still so sexy. He's not shy or embarrassed being naked like that. He's just comfortable and all Kaz. "This situation could get nasty in the press. I don't want to pull the band into a tabloid mess, but I'll stand by you. I care about you and that's what we do for people we care about."

"It's just that easy? You'll risk being annihilated by the paparazzi because you care about me?" I look down, feeling terrible. "I don't want that for you or the band. I don't want that for us. That's why I tried to push you away."

His phone rings interrupting us. "That's Tommy's ringtone, so I should answer it. He doesn't call before two if it's not important."

I wait on the bed as he runs to the living room to retrieve it. I hear him talking, a muffled voice that becomes louder and clearer. "What do you mean?" *Silence.* "No." *Silence.* "Fuck!"

As much as I want to rush to his side, I know he'll tell me when he hangs up, so I give him time and wait. He comes in and grabs his clothes. "I've got to go."

"What's happening?"

Dressed in jeans and a tee, he sits on the bed and starts to put on his socks and shoes. "I fucked up." I stare at the back of his head, and he turns, our eyes catching. "And I'm about to pay the price for it."

When he stands, he comes around the bed and sits down next to me. I take his hand, not wanting him to go. "Stay. Please." I hate the wobble in my voice. It makes me feel weak.

Touching my cheek, his voice is not his own, but one that seems to carry burdens beyond since I've known him. "I can't." His smile is not big, but it makes me smile. "You're so fucking beautiful, Lara." His hand falls from my cheek and he says, "I'll call you later."

Sitting back, I watch him leave the room, eventually hearing the front door open and close. I go to lock it behind him and peek out the side window. Tommy is parked at the curb and Kaz is sitting in the passenger's seat. He looks upset. Tommy looks like he's in shock. I start to worry about what's happening and am about to go out the door, the sheet wrapped around me be damned. But they drive away before I have the chance.

My phone rings and I go to turn it off, but it's a number I don't recognize. It might be a client, so I answer it. "Hello?"

"Lara Kessler?"

"Yes."

"I'm David with *Caught Magazine*." My heart starts to race as he continues, "The great missing prodigy has been discovered fighting for your honor. Do you have a comment?"

Great missing prodigy? *What?* "I think you have the wrong Lara Kessler."

"You're the right one. Designer to the stars. Mark Renner's girlfriend. Oh, I'll need to correct that. Are you and Kaz Fabian dating? Did you leave Mark for Kaz?"

"I don't know what you're talking about."

"So no comment on leaving Mark Renner for Kazimir Petrowski?"

"No comment," I mumble and quickly hang up.

Kazimir Petrowski.

Missing.

Kazimir Petrowski.

Prodigy.

Kazimir.

Kaz.

I run to my laptop and type the name into the search box. An image of Kaz hitting Mark at the awards banquet pops up as the most recent results. I scan down the page to a link to Kazimir Petrowski and click.

Kazimir Fabian Petrowski—world famous pianist. A prodigy at age fourteen who won the world over with his talent and playful, but dramatic style. At fifteen, Petrowski, descended from Russian royalty, was touring Europe and playing for sold-out crowds that included royalty anxious to see a legend in the making.

In shock, I stare at a picture of a youthful Kaz. I've heard of the mysterious missing Petrowski, but I never put two and two together. No one did. Until now. *Oh no.* I did this. I'm responsible for this getting out. Kaz held this secret so tight that even his closest friends didn't know and now because of me, the world knows who and where he is. *But how? How did this get out?* Surely Mark didn't know about Kaz? The damn paparazzi. The punch that took him from the back of the stage to front and center spotlight is the downfall for my mysterious rocker. The paps are better than the CIA when it comes to digging up dirt.

Looking at the ceiling, I feel terrible for being the cause of this exposé, and exhale. When I look down again, I continue to read the article. *Petrowski skipped two concerts from reports of him being ill, but he finally showed in Luxembourg to another sold-out venue. The audience waited forty-five minutes for him to begin before the show was cancelled. He did his last interview after that performance in the dressing room. He reportedly said, "I played the entire show in my head. I just couldn't get my fingers to cooperate."*

He left that night and disappeared. At age sixteen, his career was over. The greatest pianist of his time walked away from that stage determined to disappear into anonymity and he succeeded.

Rumors have spread with alleged sightings over the years, but with no photographic proof, the rumors have remained just that— rumors.

One of the greatest pianists of our time was hiding in plain sight, right under a spotlight. With the incident on the...

I take a minute to absorb the information before picking up my phone and calling him.

20

Kaz

FUCK!

It was one punch.

Fine, two.

And then Derrick's. But what a pussy for filing restraining orders against us. What a fucking coward.

My life is so fucked. My life was coming together. Finally. Did I really think no one would discover my secrets? No. I'm not naïve. But I had hoped. Life had been going great for the last ten years, and even better in the last few weeks.

Two punches.

That's all it took to take down a baseball legend. Technically the first landed him on his ass. But now, I'm a wanted man—by the press. Correction: wanted even *more* by the paps and fans. My life took center stage overnight. Everything I've worked so hard to hide is now headline news because of the interest in the man who took down the baseball All-Star. Literally. It's a lead topic on the news channel.

Missing Pianist Prodigy Found!

As I scroll through the headlines on my phone, Tommy cuts into my racing thoughts, "Why did you have to go after Renner's girl? Lara Kessler is a hot piece of ass and sweet as pie, but, man, she wasn't just taken, she was off limits."

I shoot him a look. "Don't call her that."

"You're awful touchy over a girl you barely know."

"I know her."

"Fuck me, Kaz. What are you talking about? Rochelle brought her around a few times and you're acting like a love-sick groupie."

The reference makes me smile. "I would be a groupie for her."

He takes a turn sharply, jerking me to the side, and pulls over, stopping in front of a house. Shifting the car into park, Tommy's eyes narrow in disbelief. "You're knee-deep in a whole lot of media mess all because of a girl. You hitting Renner drew all the attention to you. Did you think they wouldn't dig into your past?"

"I wasn't thinking about me when I hit him."

Sighing loudly, he says, "Truth. I need it. I need you to tell me everything, Kaz. I can help. I'll cover. I'll lie for you guys, but tell me what I'm dealing with."

I rest my elbow on the door and lean against it, debating with myself. How much do I want the world to know? Tommy won't tell, but I'm not sure I'm ready to share.

"With one blow to Renner's face you became the target of the media. Once they show interest, they'll dig every dark secret out of your past. So how the hell did we not know you were a pianist? By the way, that's really fucking close to penis. What jerkoff thought that was a good name? And if you're this so-called prodigy, why the fuck aren't you on keys?"

Chuckling lightly, I sit up. I know he means well and is trying to make me feel better the only way he knows how. But I'm not in a good mood and his humor is lost right now. "You need to know I don't like to talk about it, so I don't. This isn't easy having my skeletons scattered across gossip sites like there are no victims. There are. A whole slew of them. Myself included. I hide my life for a reason and now it is dragged out for entertainment purposes." I would still hit that asshole even at the expense of my past being exposed.

"Is it worth it? This thing with Lara?"

"I don't regret hitting him. Maybe I'm supposed to because of where it's landed me, but I don't. And I'd do it again."

"You said he hurt her."

"He beat the shit out of her two weeks ago. He's six foot five. I don't know if she reaches five foot four. He could've killed her. That sick fuck knew what he was doing. He slapped her across the face, but hurt her the most on her body so no one would see."

"Shit." His eyes close tight and he rubs the bridge of his nose. He finally looks back at me and asks, "Did you see?"

"She called me to pick her up after it happened."

"And why would she call you, Kaz?" *Because she knew I would be there for her. Because she trusted me. Because I had given her my heart. Because she wanted to give me hers.*

After a hard long stare, I just say it, "Because we love each other."

The back of his head hits the headrest. "I was afraid of that." He shifts the car into drive and says, "I'll help take care of this, but you need to let me know what you want out there and what you don't."

"I want that fucker to pay for what he did, but I don't want to hurt her in the process."

"Are you willing to sacrifice yourself to save her?"

"Yes," I reply instantly.

"Don't answer me now. Think about this. Really think about it. Everything you've kept hidden for a reason is about to be exposed and on a large scale. If the information about Renner gets out, it will take the heat off you. No one's going to attack her in the media. She's the victim, but to be on the safe side, does she have proof?"

"There are photos."

"She needs to file against him immediately." He pulls up to Johnny Outlaw's estate gate and punches in a code. We drive up the long driveway and park. Tommy looks over the hood at me when I get out. "This isn't just about you. It's about the band."

"It's about Lara. She's the victim here. Everything I did I'll own, but I won't throw her under the bus to protect myself. I won't."

"Okay. Then I'll stand by you. A band meeting has been called. Let's go inside and figure out what to do next."

"Thanks, man," I say following him to the door.

"Don't thank me yet. I'm good, but I can't work miracles."

Grabbing his shoulder and giving it a squeeze, I say, "You've been known to pull off a few, so I rest my faith in you, Tommy."

"*Fuuuck.* We're going down with this ship then."

I laugh and open the door. Inside the band isn't around. Holli peeks around the corner from the kitchen and says, "They're in the studio."

"Thanks," I reply. "All good with you?"

Tommy smiles and waves. "Hi, Holli, I'm heading downstairs."

She smiles at him. "Okay." When she looks at me the smile remains. "I'm good. How are you holding up?"

I lie. "Like I have no problems in the world."

That makes her laugh as she comes around and leans on the corner of the wall and crosses her arms. "Hold on to that feeling, Mr. Petrowski."

"Not you, too?"

"I can't let the boys have all the fun."

"Well, you could, but it's fine. There are worse things to be called than your birth name."

"Very true."

"How's Lara?"

"Worried about me."

"Women tend to do that."

"I'm worried about her."

"Do you need to be?"

Such a simple question. I should be able to answer it easily, but when asked, I pause. "I want to protect her."

Her smile is soft, sympathy seen in her eyes. "I have no doubt you will." She takes a step forward and hugs me. We've known each other for a while, and Holli's always treated me like I belong. She whispers, "Take care of yourself too. The band needs you."

"I will."

We part and she says, "The guys are waiting for you. I'll bring some snacks down later."

"Thanks, Holli."

"You're welcome."

WHEN I ENTER the recording studio, everyone is in their prospective places: Derrick on the far side, Dex on drums, Johnny in a chair up front, and Tommy off to the side. This is where we rehearse and record. Each section of the large soundproof room has designated space that we've taken over, staked claim as our area. "Hey," I say dropping down into a large beanbag near my amp.

Johnny's expression is tense, his eyes holding a million questions that his tongue holds on to. Tommy starts, "The label's publicist is handling the media, but she wants to know if you're willing to go on record with your story—the family drama."

"Do I have to?"

"I think it will settle the rumors quicker and quiet a lot of the press," Tommy answers.

I look to Johnny. He's had to deal with a shit-ton of press—good and bad. "What do you think?"

"I don't know your story, man." He sits back. "We're a band. That makes us family. We'll do whatever you need us to do."

I was on my own for years. This band saved me in many ways and here they are saving me again. They're my family and it feels good to be a part of theirs. They're my brothers, Rochelle and Holli sisters to me. "My name's out there. It's only a matter of time before my family is found."

Dex cuts in, "If they haven't already. Russian royalty? Really?"

I nod and shift, never comfortable with my title.

"Shit," Derrick says, "this whole time I've been rooming with Russian royalty. You were late with rent a couple times. What the hell, dude?"

Knowing he's teasing me, I say, "I lost all my inheritance when I didn't walk out on that stage in Luxembourg."

Rochelle appears in the doorway, and asks, "Why'd you leave?"

"Because my mother and sister chose to stay."

Tommy says, "Less riddles. We don't have much time to make a decision."

"My dad was violent and hit them. Everyone respected him because of his name, his family, his job. He ran a successful investment firm out of Moscow. I was the pride of his eye, the boy he bragged about, the one who would inherit the legacy. The only problem was that he drank too much and he liked to take out his problems with his fists. He particularly liked if they were weaker— my mom and eventually my sister. Anyone who crossed him was fired. Anyone who tried to stop him never came back to work. He didn't scare me. I saw who he really was underneath his suits and furs, and his money."

Rochelle sits on a stool nearby and says, "You were sixteen?"

"Yes."

"Your quote said you couldn't get your fingers to cooperate." And with that comment, she leads me back into a time I want to forget.

"I hit him. And then I hit him again and again until his bull of a body hit me again and again. My mother screamed and my sister cried. But he was finally taking his disappointment in his life out on someone closer to his size. I sprained my wrist, which caused damage to the tendons running down two fingers." I drag my finger over my right hand. "I couldn't play, so the family counsel lied, saying I was sick. Then continued to lie because I wasn't healing fast enough to keep the concert dates."

"That's when you left?" asks Tommy.

"No, I left two months later when I got in a fight with him while touring. He backhanded my mother when she asked if I wanted tea. Her mistake? She didn't ask him if he wanted one first. So fucked up. I lost it. Saw red. Her knees hit the floor and I was on my feet to stand between them. He pushed me. I pushed him. He punched me. I punched him. That's when I realized my injuries hadn't healed. Something in my wrist snapped and he laughed. My mother and sister ran to help me, but he gave them an ultimatum. *Yesli vy vybirayete Kazimira, vy vybirayete golodatz.* They had to choose either me and starvation or him. In the middle of a palace in Luxembourg, I stood with an injured wrist and bloody knuckles and they chose him." I can still see their faces, their broken, desolate faces. But in the end, their inexplicable loyalty made my decision easy. *I don't even know where they are. How they are. If they're still alive. How did I let so much time go by without checking on them? I used to do it, secretly, every couple months, but once I joined the band life got hectic.*

Comforting arms wrap around my neck from behind. Rochelle cradles against my back like the sister I should have had, comforting me in that familial way I've missed. My hands cover her forearms when she whispers, "You have us. We're your family."

"Thanks."

Johnny looks as troubled as I feel. "Where did you go? What did you do about your wrist?"

Rochelle sits down and then looks up. I follow her gaze and see Lara in the doorway. Standing, I go to her. Tears glistens in her blue eyes, her hair a beautiful mess, a wrinkled plaid shirt over ripped jeans. Fuck, she's stunning.

"I had twenty-four hours before they cut off access to my credit cards," I answer him, so I can talk to my girl in private. "I went to the hospital, got my wrist wrapped, and then took out two thousand dollars and flew to Amsterdam."

The guys laugh. Derrick says, "I would have done the same, but probably skipped the hospital. Just get me to the hashish."

"Of course you would," I joke.

Lara's not joking though when she asks, "What happened after that?"

I touch her cheek to ease the lines that show her concern. "Got odd jobs and bought an instrument I could take anywhere I went. Pianos are a real bitch to carry around." I turn my wrist several times. "I'm all healed. Don't worry about me."

"Of course I worry."

Taking her by the waist, I turn her around. "Come with me." Over her shoulder, I tell the band, "I'll be right back."

Around the corner, the door shuts, giving us privacy in the dark hall. Before she has a chance to speak, I bring her chin up until our lips meet. *This.* This is what I need. All I need. *Her.*

Her heels lower her back down and she leans her forehead against my lips. I happily kiss her head. Looking back at me, a tear falls down her cheek. "You're a guardian angel on earth. You're built from strength and compassion, goodness. I'll be here for you like you were there for me. But I need to ask you something first."

"Okay." My heart braces from the unknown.

"Do you love me because of this situation we've found ourselves in?"

The strength of this woman astounds me. *With all she is going through, she came here. She came to find me, to see if I was okay.* "I love you because my heart bleeds for you. I love you because the sun rises in the east and sets in the west. I love you, Lara, because without you breathing becomes useless. I'm in love with you because you're as beautiful on the inside as you are on outside."

She wraps around me, holding me tight. I close my eyes holding her tighter. "I love you, Kaz Fabian. Petrowski, Kazimir. Whatever you want me to call you, I will, because I love your soul."

I kiss the top of her head. "Kaz Fabian is good. I left Petrowski behind a long time ago."

"Why didn't you tell me about your family? About the abuse?"

"Because my world ended that night. I no longer had a family to talk about. As for the abuse, it started when I was younger and when I was old enough to know it would never change, I left."

Derrick opens the door and says, "Come back in."

We walk in hand and hand and take a seat on the couch along the closest wall.

Tommy asks, "Where do we go from here? Do you apologize to the fucker to make it right in the media? To get them to back off?"

"I won't. I told you. I don't regret hitting him, so I'm not going to back down. I'll take the consequences that come along with it."

He leans forward resting his arms on his legs. His brow is creased, his mouth twisted. "What about your family?"

"I stand by what I did. I wouldn't change it. I know in my heart what I did was right. They chose him for money, for worldly comforts. They chose to live in fear instead of stand by me and fight. That was *their* choice. I couldn't stay and watch the destruction he was causing, so I left."

"And now the great pianist is back," Johnny says with a smile. "Why the fuck do we not have you on keys? Get to work on some melodies. We need new material."

Relieved by the support, I joke, "Happily, but don't kick me off guitar yet."

Dex says, "We can't. Derrick still screws up too much."

"Fuck you," Derrick snaps, laughing while nailing Dex in the head with a pillow.

While the guys sling cheap shots at each other, I chuckle. Lara's hand squeezes mine, and she smiles. "So what are you going to do?"

"Guess it's time to face my demons."

21

Lara

I HEARD IT takes twenty-one days to break a habit or replace it with a different behavior. I wish I had reached that goal already, but some things take time to heal.

It's only been a few weeks, but Rochelle referred me to her therapist who helps patients who have gone through traumatic events. I've been seeing her four days a week and with her help, I already know Mark was never a habit. The sessions have shown me that he was a distraction, someone I once had fun with. That I didn't spend every night with him, or even see him every day during our relationship, nor miss him during our times apart, should have been a clue. He was fun. All those memories reveal who he really was. I was too blind to see, but I see clearly now.

Walking out of my therapist's office, Kaz is leaning against the car, head down, looking at his phone. His gaze lifts to mine and my heart speeds up, my steps lighten, my burdens lift.

His smile makes me weak in the knees and the way he looks at me—I'm gone to this man. He didn't take twenty-one days to takeover my heart. He's a habit I've happily taken on. I even talk about him to my therapist. She tells me to take it slow.

But I know.

There's no slow when it comes to *Kaz*. And there's no in-between when it comes to *us*.

He pushes off the car and meets me in the middle of the parking lot. With his hands cradling my jaw, I lift up and kiss him. Heat-sweltering, heart-singeing passion ignites my whole body, an inferno in my chest that only burns for him.

"My therapist confirmed it. You're dangerous for my heart."

A smirk quickly takes over—the cocky one that often appears alongside his ego. "And what do you think?"

"I *know* you are."

He kisses me again.

LANE IS BACK on the Fabian project, helping me, much to his delight today.

Tonight, I'm back on Kaz, much to mine. "Oh God! Yes!"

Kaz rolls me off him. "From behind." His eyes are alight with a fiery lust as he looks into mine.

Coming down from that blissful space between heaven and hell, I roll onto my hands and knees and brace myself. Large hands take hold of my hips as he taunts with his cock between my legs. "You're teasing."

"Just making sure you're ready."

"I'm ready." The words are more a plea than statement. *He always makes me so hot, so ready for him.*

One of his hands disappears and I'm surprised when rough fingers dip deep inside between my legs. "You're so wet. You're so ready, baby."

My fingers fist the sheets when the tip of his cock presses against me. His chest covers my back, our bodies covered in sweat.

Lifting up, his tongue glides over my shoulder blade as he pushes into me. My head falls forward, the top of it pushed into a pillow as he fucks another orgasm right out of me. I rest my cheek against the mattress until his fitful movements cease, his bliss captured.

Both of us are sated after the second round tonight. I'm lucky to have this man in my life, both physically and emotionally. With his forearm over his eyes, his breathing is hard as he exhales, exhaustion taking hold of him. I know he is burdened, but in the last week he's only told me portions of his history. I want more. I want him to feel free. Lying on my side facing him, I reach over and rest my hand on his chest as it rises. I whisper, "Talk to me."

"I can't."

"Please."

His voice is low, eerily so despite the intimacy of our bodies. "I've been thinking about my family. I'm all over headlines here and in Russia. They're gonna know where I am and who I am. What if they try to contact me? Am I a bad person if I don't want to see my family?"

I rub my hand softly over the shield of his body that protects his beating heart. "No. You did nothing wrong. They forced your hand and you took the offer. You made a life, Kaz. Now that life has been spun around. But you don't owe them anything. Nothing. Not even another chance if you don't want to give them one."

"But you said it—my life has been spun upside down. Things were easier, more black and white. The feelings I held for them were buried. On purpose. Now the lines are gray and I'm expected to push my pain away like it never happened. Just open my arms as if we're the same people we once were."

Moving, I mold against his side. His arm comes around and holds me close. "The world's not gray, black, or white. It's whatever color you want it to be."

"Red, for how I feel about you." He kisses my head. "I worry."

"About?" I whisper.

"Us."

"Why?"

"Because you're dangerous for my heart too."

"Red seems fitting then."

"I love you, Lara."

"I love you too, Kaz."

My eyes grow heavy, and I'm lulled to sleep from the sound of his heartbeat.

I awake to the sound of dishes clanging around in the kitchen. A smile makes its way quickly across my face. *Kaz.* The night was too fleeting. My time with Kaz feels much the same. Only a few weeks together and then our world has crumbled again. I want more time. I want easy and relaxed. I want Kaz in the morning just as the sun rises playing his guitar at the edge of the bed. Coffee in hand and the scent of us all around. I want late-night chats on the patio and grilling outside as if we're a normal couple, as if we didn't overcome huge obstacles to be together, or have more to face. I get up and walk down the hall, thrill to see him again coursing through me.

When I enter the living room, I'm not sure who screams first, but Lane's is louder and about ten octaves higher than mine. Jumping back, my arms go to cover my body. My knees knock together. "Oh my God." I turn and run back to the bedroom.

His voice trails behind me though I can hear the distance growing between. "Oh my God, is right."

I grab my robe from the bathroom and swing it around my shoulders. My heart is still racing when I return to the kitchen. Laughter greets me first and then Lane says, "Good morning, sunshine."

"Oh good Lord, let's pretend that never happened. Okay?"

"It will be hard to forget. I may not be attracted to women, but your perky boobies are so cute. I almost want to dress them in little pink nipple bows and throw some lipstick on them."

"Ugh." I roll my eyes, wishing this morning could start over. My head drops down. "Please don't talk about my boobs. My humiliation level is already at an all-time high after that incident in there."

Kaz grabs the belt of my robe and pulls me to him where he stands in front of the stove. "I like your perky boobies if that makes a difference." *My sweet, man.*

"It does indeed make a difference. A huge one," I say, rubbing up against the front of him.

He leans down and whispers into my ear, "They're the best tits I've ever seen, tasted, touched, licked, and I plan to do that again later. Do you want me to do that to you, Lara?"

Kaz's words are aphrodisiacs and my body reacts, pressing against him, and closing my eyes.

"I'm still here, just in case you forgot," Lane says from behind me.

I smile, and then open my eyes. "I could never forget about you, Lane. Why are you here so early though?" Kaz hands me a mug of coffee, just the way I like it—two sugars, two creamers—and I take a hot sip. "Thank you."

He smiles. "You're welcome. Hungry?"

"Starved." Kaz turns back to the eggs he's scrambling while I steal a piece of bacon cooling on the paper towels on the counter. "So hungry."

Lane takes two pieces and goes to the barstools at the counter and sits. "Are we really doing this whole love-bird thing? I'm not griping. It's good to see this lady so happy. She's practically floating. Whatever you're doing, Kaz, keep it up."

"I'll keep it up. No worries there," he replies so casually, so comfortable in the kitchen. I love it.

Lane's palms land down on the marble. "Okay, on that note, I've got work to do."

Kaz turns and asks, "Not staying for breakfast?"

Walking into the living room, he replies, "I'm not sure I can handle the ooey-gooey sexy sweetness. You know what they say. If you can't handle the heat, get out of the kitchen. Tootles. I'll see you in the office in a bit, missy."

"I'll be in shortly."

Kaz yells, "Maybe an hour or so. I have plans."

"I don't need to hear about those plans," Lane calls over his shoulder, "or any screaming from the bedroom, so keep it down. Or better yet, I'll go visit Calliope today."

Laughing, I say, "Probably best."

When the office door closes, Kaz puts the eggs onto a platter, then turns to me and says, "C'mere."

"It might be safer to keep this bar between us."

"It definitely is, but c'mere anyway." Then he gives me that look. The one that says all the things we don't say out loud, one that communicates the hunger inside that craves me in ways I'm willing to give in to. I walk into his arms and we stand there wrapped in each other's arms. "I fly out for a few shows on the East Coast tomorrow." I try to lean back and look at him, but his arms tighten around me. "I don't want you here alone. Will you come with me?"

"Only because you don't want me here alone?"

"No, because I'm a selfish bastard and want you with me."

"And?"

"And yes, I don't want to worry about your safety."

Closing my eyes and with my cheek pressed to him, I take in his shower-fresh skin mixed with his musky cologne. The depth of the musical notes make me take in another inhale, wanting to take him all in and hold him close to my heart. "I can't."

"You can't or won't?"

This time I lean back and he lets me until our eyes connect. His hands lower down my back while still holding on to me. "I can't. I would if I could. I have three projects in the final phase of completion, so I need to be here for them. How long will you be gone?"

"A week. I can fly back between shows. It's just tiring to do that."

I run the tip of my finger over his bottom lip and then lift up and kiss the dip in his chin. "Don't do that. I need you rested when you come back." I follow the kiss with a gentle little bite.

Grabbing hold of my ass, he lifts me until we're eye level. "Don't you worry about me, baby. I'll have plenty of energy for you." We kiss good and hard.

The tips of my toes touch the ground and my feet roll the rest of the way down. "I'm still starved, but now I'm not sure if it's for the food or you."

"Not sure, huh? I think I need to swing things in my favor." Scooping me up, he says, "The eggs can wait. You're all I want to eat for breakfast."

"What about the bacon?"

"You're right." He bends us down and I grab the bacon. "We definitely need to bacon in bed."

I burst out laughing. "I love that bacon has become a verb." Taking a piece, I feed it to him as he takes us back into the bedroom.

With the door shut and locked, he sets me on the bed. "Question."

"Okay," I answer.

"Lane is working. Are you going to be able to keep it down?"

"Pfft. Me? *You* are the problem." My robe falls open on one side.

"Oh really?" His gaze is otherwise occupied when my chest is exposed.

I like his eyes on me, so I don't move. "Yeah, really, noisy pants. I can be quiet, but I have a feeling you're going to be yelling the f-word before I even get off."

"God, you're so fucking cute with your f-word and perky tits."

"Perky. Perky. Perky. One day they won't be so perky. What then?"

His gaze slides up to mine. Maneuvering over me, his hips dip down to meet mine. "Then we live happily ever after."

My breath quietly catches in my chest and my heart stops. "Kaz," I say half warning, half worried, "don't say things like that."

"I can say how I feel. You should too."

"I don't want to be hurt."

"I will never hurt you."

"How do you know? How can you say that when we've been together a month."

His weight settles on top of me when he kisses my cheek. Then my mouth. And then my nose. "I can say that because I knew the minute I saw you that everything I've been through, the life I've lived, has led me straight to you."

I want to live in his words, his confidence, and that world. But my life has been shaken, my once strong beliefs turned inside out. Finding faith has been hard, but I've been doing it every day. Some days I need a little more reassurance. I rub over his shoulders and up his neck. "How can you be so sure?"

"I was born from royalty and destined for greatness." He speaks with such confidence and I'm completely captivated. "My family raised me to believe in destiny. I thought it was playing piano. I thought it was coming to America and planting roots. I thought it was when I joined the band. It wasn't."

"When was it?"

"It's been almost a year to the day since we first met. You didn't notice me—"

"I noticed."

He smiles gentle like his expression. "You were in and out of my life for too long, our timing off. Six weeks ago, you were wearing a purple shirt and tight dark blue jeans. Your sunglasses were on your head and Rochelle had told you she'd be in the car." He whispers the rest. "Tell me, Lara, why didn't you leave with her that day at sound check? Why were you still standing there as if waiting for your own destiny to arrive?"

"Because I was." The admission sends my thoughts to relive every stolen moment we shared before I knew that my soul mate was right in front of me all along.

I HATED EVERY minute of our goodbye. I'd prefer a *see ya around* much better. But after the death of a band member, goodbyes are always said just in case there's not another chance.

Sitting across from Rochelle and Holli with an empty pitcher of Sangria between us, I wait for someone to say something. They've been too quiet for too long. "We should do something," I suggest. "To take our minds off the guys."

Holli smiles and holds up her glass. "I thought we were."

"It's not working," I reply.

"You've got it bad."

"No worse than you, my friend." Rochelle elbows her playfully.

She sits up and sighs. "We've been spoiled by them being home."

Rochelle says, "I have the night. Why don't we go dancing or somewhere else with some atmosphere?"

Holli replies, "Somewhere not so paparazzi ridden."

Rochelle agrees.

I say, "Somewhere where we can have fun but still talk."

THIRTY MINUTES LATER we're sitting at a table in the back of The Hotel Café, a singer is on stage playing guitar with two band mates—a drummer and a guitarist. The music varies from Frank Sinatra to *The Church*. They're good and not so loud we can't talk.

"They're halfway through the set. They should be on the seventh song," Holli says, her eyes on the band, her fingers tapping the table lightly.

Rochelle adds, "*Beautiful Deathly.*"

I ask, "How do you guys know that? I've never heard this band before."

Two sets of eyes land on me and then they burst out laughing. Holli says, "*The Resistance*. We've got the set schedule down. It's weird, but I like to know when they have their break before the encore and be ready. Johnny calls me, even if it's a quick call."

"That's so sweet," I say, wondering if Kaz and I will be *that* kind of couple, the kind that sneaks time together when apart or if we'll have a family. Wow, a family. My mind struggles to wrap my head around having a family. I take a quick gulp of my cosmopolitan.

Holli adds, "Dex does the same. It's so sweet."

If there was more light I might be able to prove it, but I swear Rochelle is blushing. She's also waving her hand frantically in front of her as if that will brush us off so easily. "Uh-uh. Let's talk about anything, anything but me. How about Kaz being of royal descent?"

Leaning forward, I rest my elbows on the table and move in closer to whisper. "He hasn't told me the details. He hates talking about it because of how it all played out with his family. The few things he has told me break my heart for him. He basically left that night of the concert and disappeared. I don't know how he survived, but I know it hurts to see the pain in his eyes when he thinks back on that time."

Rochelle looks around to make sure no one's listening to our conversation. "He's agreed to an interview next week when they're back. I've been working on the details. It will be at a secret location so there's no chance of leaks before it airs. But he agrees that this is the only way it's going to be put to rest. He's been thrust even more into the spotlight that he didn't ask for. He has a fascinating story to tell though, so the media's going to hound him until they get it."

"It's good he has this opportunity," Holli adds. "Some of us aren't so lucky. He has a better chance of keeping it contained this way, making sure the truth is out instead of the blatant lies."

The thought still weighs on my heart. "I worry about him. He's a private person."

Rochelle asks, "Would you like to come with us? You can be there for him. It might help. When you agree to these types of interviews, you can dictate what is off limits, but that doesn't mean they stick to the script. Reporters have a way of working in a curveball or two. He might like the extra support."

I love the thought of being there for him how he needs, but I worry about being intrusive. "I should wait to talk to him. Make sure it's something he wants."

She smiles. "I can ask him so it's not awkward."

"Thank you."

We watch the band play a few songs and I let my mind wander to last night and how good, how natural, how at peace I feel with him.

"How's the house coming along?" Holli asks, breaking into my thoughts.

"I love it there. It has such a great energy about it. It's actually been a dream to work on. It has a style that defines the structure, but with Kaz, everything is lighter. Lots of light streaming in. Whites, soft beige, blues, and navy are playing a strong role in the design."

"Sounds beautiful," Holli says. "Can't wait to see."

Rochelle smiles. "Sounds like Kaz is finally becoming an adult. First he gave up the hard partying, then he bought a house. You're having a great effect on him."

"He did that before I was in the picture."

"You were in the picture, Lara. You just didn't know the role you were already playing in his life. I knew you were good for him."

The thought of Kaz putting the stepping-stones in place for a relationship is romantic, but then I remember the hard time Rochelle gave me for showing interest in him and laugh. "Then why did you tease me relentlessly?" The answer pops into my head as soon as I ask her the question, and our smiles and good times are gone. She doesn't answer. She doesn't have to.

My stomach twists as the name taunts my mind.

Mark.

Mark.

Mark.

I stand. "I'll be back."

Rochelle grabs my hand before I can escape to the bathroom. "Do you want me to go with you?"

"I'm fine." I put on a fake smile and leave the table. Fortunately there's no line when I reach the restroom. I go to the mirror and check for blood, swelling, and bruises. They went away weeks ago, but they're still there on the inside. With my hands on my cheeks I stare at the woman reflected back at me. She's not who I want to be. She deserves happiness and love.

I've not taken any of Mark's calls and not opened any of his emails. The threat of filing a restraining order against him has kept him at a distance, but I wonder for how long. Forever? For another few months, weeks, or days? Hours?

Kaz's story has overshadowed Mark and my relationship troubles. Royalty is intriguing to everyone, especially when it's a member of a popular band.

My heart starts to race and I wish Kaz were here to help calm it. I reach for my phone but remember I left it at the table. *Shit.* He's doing a show. Panic starts to rise, the pit of my stomach reaches my chest, and each breath becomes harder to grasp until I'm gasping.

My head drops down as I press my palms into the cold, tile countertop.

"Lara?" Rochelle calls, but I can't open my eyes. I can't speak. "Lara, breathe. In through the nose. Out through the mouth. Do you hear me?"

A jagged breath works its way in my mouth, but I lose it when she tells me, "Nose. Breathe in through the nose. Listen to my voice, Lara. In the nose, out the mouth."

I focus on her words and take a slow breath into my nose, my grip on the counter loosening. When I exhale, I open my eyes, the tightening in my chest, the viselike squeeze on my lungs releases, and I look up.

"It's okay, honey. You're safe."

I take in another deep breath and release slowly. "I'm safe," I repeat. "I'm safe."

"Come here." She hugs me lightly. "You're safe, Lara."

Wrapping my arms around her, I rest my head down on her shoulder. "I'm safe. I'm okay."

Her arms tighten around me. "You are." She leans back. "Are you really okay?"

Rubbing my hands through the ends of my hair, I manage a small smile. "I am. Thanks." I release another breath feeling the heaviness lighten under my ribcage. "I don't know what happened."

"You had a panic attack."

My head goes back in disbelief. "No, I don't have panic attacks." Rochelle remains quiet as my mind starts to process this information. "I'm happy." But as much as I try to convince myself, it's clear I'm not convincing her. "You have panic attacks when..." I can't seem to finish the sentence and feel a different kind of panic take over. "When does someone have panic attacks?"

Rochelle takes my hand. "It's okay. All kinds of people have panic attacks, even happy ones. It's your body feeling overwhelmed with emotions, sensory overload, or other stimulus. I used to get them."

"What? But…" *Cory.* "But why would I get one? I'm in a good place."

"You weren't when you left the table. It's okay though. Now you know what you need to do when that—"

"It's not going to happen again," I state defiantly. I take a step back, pulling my hand away in the process.

If I've hurt her feelings, she doesn't show it. Her kind soul is exceptional, and I'm lucky to count her as one of my dear friends. "Okay, but if it does, remind yourself to breathe through it." Reaching for the door, she says, "There's nothing to be ashamed of."

"Rochelle?"

"Yeah?"

"Thank you."

Her expression lifts. "You're welcome. Come out when you're ready."

"I'm ready now." I follow her back not wanting to be alone, still so confused by what happened. *What did happen exactly?*

When we reach the table, Holli announces excitedly, "It's almost time."

Rochelle checks her watch. "The break before the encore." Her phone is placed next to Holli's on the table, and they stare in anticipation.

When mine rings, all eyes land on me. Looking down, Kaz's photo is on the screen and I smile, like a seriously goofy big grin. When I meet their eyes both of them are smiling too. With a twinkle in Holli's, she says, "I think it's more serious than you thought."

Rochelle excitedly says, "Answer it."

I grab the phone. "Hello?"

"Hey there." Kaz's smooth dulcet tone comforts me and I release a breath that felt like it was trapped in my throat. *Until now.*

"Hi. How's it going?"

Both Rochelle's and Holli's phones ring.

I plug my free ear so I can hear him better. "Good," Kaz says. "We're taking a quick break and then heading back out."

"I heard it was sold out."

"I'm not sure. I miss you. How are you doing?"

This time I smile, but I want to hide it away and keep it safe for his eyes alone. "I'm doing okay," I reply, not worrying him with small details like panic attacks in bar bathrooms. He has enough to worry about without me adding more to the load than I already have. "I miss you, too. Six days."

"Six days." He pauses and the quiet makes me nervous. "So, I've been thinking."

"About what?"

"You and me."

Fluttering emotions swarm my belly. "Yes?"

"I was thinking maybe since you have a key and all, you might be at mine when I get home." How am I meant to resist that? *Resist him?*

"You want me to wait for you at yours?"

"Yeah, like I've said, I've been thinking about you and me. When I do, it's at my place."

Smiling ear to ear, his sweet nervousness entirely charms me. "I'll be there."

"We get back late."

"I'll wait up."

There's a commotion on the other end of the phone. "I have to go."

"Yeah, there are about thirty thousand people waiting for you."

"You're the only one I care about waiting on me."

I lower my head for a bit more privacy. "Kaz?"

"Yeah?"

"Thank you for calling me."

"I love you."

And there it is without any obligations or requirements, without anything expected in return. Love. *True love.* "I love you, too."

"I'll call you later."

"All right. Break a leg."

"Goodbye, Lara."

"Goodbye, Kaz," I singsong, and then we hang up.

Rochelle stands with her glass in the air. "I love *love*."

Holli stands. "To being in love and to being loved."

When I join them, I raise my glass. "To love and all the happy side effects that come along with it."

"To love," we say in unison. *And I realize I feel happy. Content, something I haven't felt for a long time. How did I get so lucky?*

We all finish our drinks. I head to the bathroom to use it this time and they stay to order another round.

When I'm finished washing and drying my hands, I open the door and practically walk into a wall.

My feet stop and I look up and right into my biggest fear.

23

Kaz

"HEY, IT'S ME. Give me a call back when you can." I hang up the phone after leaving a message for Lara.

My back is slapped and I'm dragged forward under Derrick's arm. "Man, we fucking rock. It's pussy time."

Wrangling out from under him, I say, "Yeah, you go do that."

With his arms out wide, he stops walking. "What happened to my boy? I need my wingman back, brah."

I laugh him off and keep walking. "I'm off the market, brah."

"For now."

"Might be for good."

"Ugh! You're killin' me. Not you too."

Walking backward, I shrug. "What can I say? I've got feelings for the woman."

"Fuck," Derrick replies just as Tommy walks by. Derrick grabs him by the neck. "Come out with me. You're not fuckin' ball and chainin' it up yet, are you?"

"Not yet, but I'm not going out with you. I'm tired."

"C'mon guys."

Jimmy, one of the roadies, says, "I'll go."

"Fuck, man. I'll take whatever I can get."

"Never mind," Jimmy says and walks off.

Tommy and I laugh at Derrick. We turn and go to the dressing room. Taking a seat on the opposite end to Dex, I settle in for our usual after-gig wrap-up. Dex is banging his sticks on the arm of the couch. Johnny tosses his tee that's been ripped from fans and grabs a clean shirt from a hanger when he says, "Good show." He glances at me. "What do you think?"

I look behind me and then realize he's asking my opinion. Wow, this is new. "It was good. We missed the bass kick in during the encore and one of the left amps blew during *Beautiful Deathly*."

Dex stops his drumming and stares at me. "Awe, our little boy is all grown up."

Johnny stands there with his arms crossed over his chest and nods. "Holy shit, you're like a real member of this band now." Sticking out his hand, he says, "Welcome to *The Resistance*."

I shake it, but I also roll my eyes and laugh at my expense. "What the fuck ever. I won't mention shit next time."

"You're supposed to so it doesn't happen again," Johnny says, laying down the law. He grabs a bottle of water, downs half of it, and then looks right at me. "You did good, Fabian."

Here's the thing. When one of the greatest singers and musicians of our time gives you a compliment, you take it. He doesn't dole them out freely and he's not one for idle chitchat. He says what he means and getting his respect is not easy. I've done several things in my life that I'm proud of: played piano for kings and queens, performed in front of sold-out shows before I was fourteen, got hired to join one of the greatest rock bands that ever existed, and now earned Johnny Outlaw's respect. Yep, it ranks right up there for me. "Thanks, man."

Dex stands, tucks his sticks in the back of his jeans, and holds his hand out to me. "You did good. 'Bout time."

When I shake his, Derrick pipes in. "What about me?"

Dex laughs. "You're lazy as fuck. A damn good bassist, but lazy. Now fix the bass kick in. I never heard it either."

As the teasing continues, I check my phone, wondering why I haven't heard back from Lara. The guys go about their business, but Tommy yells, "Pack your shit and get on the bus. We hit the road in thirty."

"How long is the drive?" Derrick asks.

"Four or five hours. You'll get to the hotel around three, but sound check isn't until five, so you'll be able to get some sleep."

I grab my jacket from the couch and walk to the door with my phone in hand. Looking back, I ask, "Is security in place? I want to go to the bus." I want to find somewhere quiet I can call her again.

Tommy answers, "They're outside the door. Take two with you. The crowds are huge out back. We'll wait until they return."

Nodding, I open the door and make eye contact with a guy twice my weight with a good five inches on me. I'm not a small guy, but this guy is a monster. When I start walking, he and another guy flank my sides. I hate this part. The attention sucks. Everyone stares. Everyone. Most are looking for Johnny or Dex, some for Derrick. I've got my fair share of fans and more attention than I care for or ever need. I'm called sexy, hot. My name is shouted like a thunderstorms heartbeat—throbbing all around, a pulse that puts your body on alert. They shout things at me—*number-one fan, pick me, fuck me, take me home.* It gets vulgar from there.

My phone vibrates just as we reach the doors. The double doors are swung open and I'm squeezed between the bodyguards—one in front, one in back. I keep my head down, watching their steps as they lead me to the bus. The phone buzzes again, but I can't answer until I'm on the bus. Lara's pretty face graces the screen.

I push forward and take the steps by two. The bus door closes tight behind me and I rush to the back, pressing the answer button as I walk. "Hey."

She doesn't respond.

"Lara, can you hear me?"

Nothing. *Fuck.*

I call her right back, but am sent right to voicemail. *Shit.* I scroll contacts and call Rochelle. She answers on the second ring. "Hey, it's Kaz."

"Hey," she shouts.

"Damn." I hold the phone away from my ear. Bar. She's out. But is she out with Lara? "Is Lara with you?"

"Yes. She's in the bathroom."

"Can you tell her to call me right away?"

"Sure." Just before I hang up, she says, "Shit."

"Ro?"

"I should have checked on her. I think she's been gone a while.

"What do you mean a while? How long?"

"Let me call you back."

"No, Rochelle. Don't hang—" Fuck. Fuck. Fuck. I immediately call Lara again.

"Hi," she answers. The background is quiet and she sounds normal. *Too normal.*

"Where are you?"

"Home."

"Home?" I ask, baffled. "Aren't you supposed to be with Rochelle and Holli?" There's a pause that drags. "Where are you?"

"Home, Kaz. I'm home." Her voice trembles on home.

"Are you okay?"

"I'm fine. I'll call you soon."

"Soon? What is going on?"

"I'm tired," she says. "I'm going to bed. We'll talk tomorrow. Okay? Later gator."

Later gator? Something's wrong. "You're home, right?"

"Don't worry about me. Later gator."

No goodbye... "Later gator."

We hang up and I call Rochelle back. "Kaz, I can't find her. She's gone."

"Find her right now. Go to her home. I'm calling nine-one-one."

"What's happening?"

"I don't know but I could tell she was trying to get me off that call. I think that sick fuck is there."

Rochelle sounds out of breath and the noise from the bar is going in and out of the background. "Holli and I will go right over. Do you think she'll be there?"

"I don't know. She kept saying she was there. You've got to get over there as fast as you can. I'll call the police."

"Kaz?"

"What?"

"Her purse is still with us. I thought she was going to the bathroom. Are you sure she's at home?"

"No. I'm not." I admit the thing I was trying to avoid, feeling sicker by the second. "I'm across the country, Ro. I can't help her. I can't save her. I can't even fucking protect her from here. You've got to find her."

"We will. I'm sure she just went home. Didn't want to deal with the crowds here. The place is packed."

"How would she get home without her purse?"

She can't answer that, so she says, "We're catching a cab now."

"Call me back."

"I will."

The call only rings once. "Nine-one-one. What's the emergency?"

"I need the police. I think my girlfriend has been kidnapped."

"Sir, slow down. How long has she been missing?"

"I don't know. Twenty, thirty minutes. She was with her friends at a club. She went to the bathroom and never returned. Her purse was left behind."

"I'll need more information to move this case forward."

"I don't have to wait?" My fear.

"Not in California. Some departments may choose to wait twenty-four hours, but you can file if you want to go down to the department."

"I can't. I'm in Georgia right now."

"Okay, can you answer a few questions for me?"

"Yes."

"When did you last speak to the missing person?"

"Maybe ten minutes or fifteen minutes ago."

"Sirrr," this time the operator sounds sympathetic, but I can tell this isn't going to go anywhere. "Do you know it's illegal to file a false report?"

I hate the way my fear turns to panic. It summons memories I had successfully buried. "It's her ex. He's hurt her. I'm afraid he's got her right now, taken her against her will."

"And why do think that if you just spoke to her?"

"She left her friends at the club. She left her purse there. How'd she get home? And she said 'Later gator' to me. She never says that."

"Later gator? That's not compounding evidence even added together. Sir, if you want to file a report you will need to go to a local police station. I can't file a missing report or send police to a home when you just spoke to the missing person or because they used a term she doesn't normally say."

"Please."

"Sir, would she have gone home with someone she met, someone you're not familiar with, or someone she didn't want you to know about?"

Now my frustration turns to anger. "She wouldn't cheat on me if that's what you're implying."

"We have other calls, emergencies that need immediate attention. I'm sorry, sir. Please file a report at your local department for further assistance."

I'm hung up on.

I want to throw my fucking phone, but I can't because I need to call Lara and Rochelle. I try Lara, but get voicemail. Next is Rochelle. When she answers, I ask, "Are you there?"

"Not yet. I tried her phone, but she didn't answer."

"I'm telling you. I know something is wrong."

"Calm down, Kaz. We'll be there soon. Try to breathe. It may all be a misunderstanding."

"A misunderstanding that she took off and not only didn't tell you but left her purse?"

"I'm freaking out too, Kaz. Please just wait until I call you back to freak out. Okay?"

"Sorry."

"You don't have to be. I'm nervous like you, but I'm trying to stay calm."

"Call me back."

"I will."

The bus door opens at the front and the screaming infiltrates the quiet that was occupying the space. All four of the guys load on. The door shuts and Dex and Derrick flip onto the couch. Tommy tells the driver to take off. Johnny leans against the wall and looks at me. "What's up?"

There's a good possibility I could be freaking out for nothing. I hope that's the case. But I don't want to lay it on the guys without having more information. I stand and brush past him and climb onto a bunk. "Nothing."

"Okay," he replies. I know he won't delve into it. He's good at giving others their privacy.

Dex on the other hand... "Why is Rochelle upset?"

I poke my head out and his glare hits me. "Just give her a few. She's checking on Lara."

Johnny asks, "With Holliday?"

Nodding, I lie my head back down and close my eyes. I know he's not going to let it go when it involves her, but I'm about to lose my shit, and can't deal with his concern right now. "Call her. She's okay."

"She fucking better be." He takes his phone and calls her. "You okay?" While she talks to him, I wait with my phone in my hand.

When it rings, I sit up and hit my head. "Fuck." I manage to still answer it but I'm going to have a knot on my head. "Are you there?"

Rochelle says, "She's not here."

"Are you sure?"

"Positive. There are no sounds coming from inside and from the windows no lights are on. What do we do?"

"I don't know. I feel so helpless."

"Did you call the police?"

"Yes, after they practically laughed at me, they hung up." I stand up and pass the guys, and step down a step at the door. The world is moving at least sixty miles an hour outside and I have no fucking clue what to do. "Tell me what to do, Rochelle? I'll do it. I'll fly back."

"No. Don't worry yet. We'll find her. Get some rest. You'll need it for tomorrow night."

"I can't sleep. Not knowing, I can't."

"Unfortunately, I think you'll have to."

I can't lose her. She's my air. My sun. My light. I can't lose her.

Lara

THERE ARE TIMES when you sit and reflect on what went wrong and how to learn from your mistakes.

This is not one of those times.

I know exactly what went wrong and no matter how many times Mark says we're good together, he won't convince me. I can't forget what he's done, although he acts like he's forgotten, which makes it more disconcerting being here now. I'm the one who paid the price, and I continue to. I don't know if he was stalking me, but I don't believe it was a "happy accident" we ran into each other like he claims. As if the physical damage he caused wasn't enough, he is determined to destroy everything good that remains—like Kaz.

The threat has always been there. I just didn't know Mark could stoop lower than he already had. He showed me an email that had the photos Kaz took of me attached. Every bruise and bump in its full glory with implications of Kaz Fabian as the abuser from some anonymous account Mark created.

Mark Renner worked out a plan while I was stuck in this closet. I should have cleared my phone, but I thought I might need the evidence handy. Now the photos are in the wrong hands and Kaz and I will both pay the price for my carelessness.

Over and over again he's repeated his mantra: If he can't have me, neither will Kaz. Pacing in front of me like a caged animal, he holds all the cards, but seems close to losing it all. His anxiety rolls off him and right onto me when he asks, "Who took those pictures? Did he? Did you let another man look at you, touch you, be with you?"

When I don't respond, he slams his fist against the door, sending it to hit the wall. He's trying to break it like he wants to break me. He may have stolen the pictures off my phone, but he won't take anything else away from me. My hands haven't stopped shaking since I ran into him at the bar, but I refuse to go down without a fight though. "What are you doing, Mark?"

Bloodshot eyes hit me and my breath stops. His demeanor has become more crazed the longer we stay here. I was shoved into my closet and told to sit on the floor. All the lights are out, but the door is open and the blinds let a little light in from outside. He stops in front of the door, his fingers flexing, an action that should scare me, but doesn't. It's more concerning. Unpredictable. Something tells me he's looking for something other than to hurt me. He finally replies, "I don't know anymore."

I refuse to be afraid of him. "What happened?"

His head drops and he says, "My teammates turned me in. They got me hooked and then fingers started pointing when Coach was onto them."

"What does that mean?"

"It means I'm suspended indefinitely because I failed the drug test."

The gasp is caught in my chest, and silence is my only response. He lives for baseball. If that's taken away, what's left?

Me.

In his mind, it's only me left in his life.

"They'll have you back. They'll make it go away. You're their weapon, their strongest team member, the highest-paid first baseman in baseball. For a reason. They won't risk losing the season by losing you."

"They already have."

"Talk to them."

A fist slams against the closet door, causing me to jump. "I have. I have a failed drug test and that scene your boyfuck caused on the red carpet and they don't want the bad publicity. Do you know what this means to my contract?"

"Your contract should be safe. I heard—"

"There's a code of conduct clause, Lara. I've broken it under these allegations."

Allegations... *truth*. He's completely unhinged.

"What are you doing with me? You show up at the bar, threaten me and others, and you want me to what? Sympathize? Help you? I can't. Not with that threat still out there."

"Be with me. The coaches like you. The owner's wife likes you. America loves you, Lara. They love us together. Why can't you just pretend to like me?"

My glare should be enough. It's not as he looks at me so expectantly. I stand up, willing to take whatever he rages my way. I swallow down the quiver in my voice and speak firmly. "You're leaving, but before you go, you are going to delete that email. And then when you get home, you are going to delete the photos you stole from my phone. You're going to delete every video you have of us, and every image we ever took with or without consent. You are you going to walk to the front door and leave as if you were never here. Do you understand me?"

"Why would I do that when you're my only hope to come back from this?"

"Because you aren't going to mess your life up any further. You have damaged me in ways I will never recover from, but if you don't leave right now, you will have to kill me. I will never help you. I will never let you get away with hurting Kaz. I will never let you have another night of peace on this earth if you hurt either of us again. Do you understand, Mark? This is it. We are over and we will never be again."

"What am I supposed to do?"

"Fix your life. Stop using steroids. You didn't enter the major leagues a drug user. You didn't get MVP for three seasons doing drugs. You didn't become Mark Renner, the great baseball player, because of the drugs. You had talent. You still do. Be the person you know you can be. Make your parents proud again. Prove the naysayers wrong and win their hearts all over again."

Standing before me, in all his height, his hands twitch at his sides and inside I flinch. My phone rings and I look back at the floor.

Kaz.

For a very brief second, I feel hope. And then I hear Mark's angry roar.

NO UPDATES.

No calls.

No Lara.

I push the curtain to my bunk to the side and get up. The bus is quiet, the lights out as the guys sleep, and we rumble our way to the next city. I can't remember where we're going as I make my way to the small galley kitchen. Pulling a beer from the fridge I need something to help me sleep. This won't help, but since I have no idea what's happening with Lara, I don't mind if my thoughts are numbed until I do.

Sitting down in the co-captains seat, I ask, "Where are we?"

Doug, our driver, has a smile in place, appearing happy to have some company in the middle of the night. "Somewhere in South Carolina. We've got about two hundred miles or so to go." His eyes return to the road and he asks, "Can't sleep?"

"No."

"Great show earlier."

"Thanks." I take another long pull from the can, set it in the cup holder, and rest back. The monotony of the dark road, the soft road noise as we drive, does a good job of relaxing me. I don't know how long my eyes dip closed, but I'm startled awake by a hand on my shoulder. "What?" I ask, looking up.

Dex is there, lit by the little light coming in from the dashboard. "Rochelle just called me."

I stand, wiping the sleep from one of my eyes. My phone is in my other hand and I flip it up to see the screen. No call. "What'd she say?"

"Come on. The guys are up."

I glance to Doug whose grin is gone. Patting him on the shoulder, I walk back. Derrick is leaning his head out the top bunk bed. Johnny's leaning against the wall near the sink. Tommy has moved to the table, and Dex takes a seat on the couch. Bent forward resting his arms on his knees, Dex looks up at me. His usual bravado and charisma not seen, so I ask again, "What did she say?"

"Lara was in an accident."

What the fuck? "What do you mean?"

"She's alive, but she's in the hospital."

I didn't need a beer to numb myself. Those words do a damn good job all on their own. Not a heartbeat to be felt. No breath leaves my mouth. No words escape my lips.

But my thoughts are thrown into chaos.

I look to Derrick. We've been through a lot together over the years and I need to know what he thinks. This is a big decision. If I leave the band and go to her, I'm potentially cancelling two shows. He hops down and says, "You need to go to her."

"Can you go on without me?"

"No. We don't go on without you. She's important to you, she's important to us. We're a band. That means we band together." Johnny stands with his feet planted firmly in place, and says, "We're going back to LA. Tommy will have a plane waiting for us at the nearest airport."

Tommy stands and moves toward the front of the bus. "On it."

WARMTH KISSES MY shoulder, fingers strumming down my spine. I shiver from the delicious chill that follows as a hand cups my ass, and whispers fill my ear, "You're safe, baby."

I want to burst with flowers and hearts, love songs, and romance. The emotion is strong inside, cradling me in its depth. Rolling over onto my back, his fingertips dance across my chest, his lips kiss mine, and an audible hum awakens me.

"Lara?"

I try to open my eyes, but they're heavy.

"Lara?" A familiar voice calls my name. "She's awake."

Bright lights and shadows come into view. I close my eyes tight searching for the man that keeps me safe—protects me from the bad—in the back of the orange-red of my lids.

"Wake up, baby." The warmth of a hand holds mine and that voice draws me to lean to the right. "Lara, can you hear me?"

My lids flutter open and I see a man. My body, faster than my sluggish thoughts, moves instinctually against the far side of the bed, a cold railing digging into my back. My throat is rough, and gasps and coughs replace the words I want to scream.

"She's awake." I'm startled by Rochelle. "I'll get a nurse."

As my vision clears, I jump again, sitting up in the process. "Stay away," I work out, my voice scratchy while tears flood my eyes. I scream, "Help!"

"Lara?" He reaches forward to touch me and I scream again.

I run from the bed, the IV ripping from my arm and causing more pain. Holding my wrist, I run for the door just as it opens. A nurse and Rochelle are there and I drop to my knees and plead, "Help me."

As I sob at their feet, the nurse calls for help and Rochelle kneels down next to me. "Honey, you're safe. Kaz and I will take care of you."

I look into her eyes. "No. No. No. No. No. Please. Please. Help me."

"We will." She looks over her shoulder. "Kaz and I are here for you."

My gaze slides up the white linoleum, higher up his jeans, and into that bastard's eyes. A pain reflects into mine, but I know what happened. *I know how he hurt me.*

I'm on my feet as fast as I can scramble up and run out the door. I only glance back once to see him fast on my heels. I'm grabbed before I reach the turn. His hand covers my mouth just as I scream. Two orderlies grab me and the nurse starts saying, "Calm down. You're safe, Ms. Kessler."

The man holding me contradicts that. *I'm not safe. Why doesn't anyone realize that?*

My thoughts run wild.

Dreams.

Reality.

Which is which?

Rochelle is sitting bedside when I float into daylight. My body is numb, my desire to fight escaping me. I give up and roll my head to the side. "Where am I?"

"You're in the hospital."

"Why?"

"You were hurt in a car accident."

"What? I don't remember."

227

There's no smile on her face, not even a comforting one. "The doctor said that would probably be the case. Your parents are getting coffee. They'll be right back."

"Are my injuries that bad?"

"No," she replies sadly.

I don't understand her reaction to me. "Then what's wrong?"

"We should wait for the nurse. I'll go get her."

She reaches the door quickly. "Rochelle?" With her hand on the doorknob, she wordlessly looks back. I ask, "Is everything all right?"

One nod. That's all she gives me before she disappears and I'm left alone in this hospital room.

Where the IV is attached stings, and I have bruising up and down my arm. My wrist looks swollen. I see the marks on my chest and a flash of light hits behind my eyes and I close them. Headlights.

The door is opening and I look up. My parents rush to my side and smile. "Hi," I whisper, tears forming just from the sight of them.

"Sweetie," my mom coos. "You're awake. How do you feel?"

"Groggy."

My dad says, "That's to be expected. The nurse said she can give you something if you're in pain."

"My legs are stiff," I tell my dad.

"They say that's normal. You've been in the same position for hours and your body has been through a lot."

"What happened?"

"You were in a car accident," my mom says. "We're lucky you're alive." *A car accident? Why can't I remember that?*

"So it was bad?"

Dad shoves his hands in pockets, clearly uncomfortable. It must be hard to see your only child in a hospital surviving a car crash. "It was. Do you remember anything?"

"Headlights."

"Do you remember who you were with?"

228

"Michael? The nurses said not to interrogate her right when she wakes up."

I laugh at the admonishment. "It's fine. I don't remember anything. Who was I with?"

"Mark. Mark Renner."

Sitting up, alarmed, I ask, "Is he okay?"

They glance to each other before looking back at me. "He's in a coma."

"Oh my God. I need to see him."

"What?" my dad asks. "No. You can't."

"Dad, I need to. He needs me."

My mom says, "Get a nurse, Michael." She sits on the side of the bed. "Honey, why do you want to see him?"

"Because he was trying to protect me."

"From what?"

"From Kaz."

25

Kaz

THE REFLECTION IN the window stares back at me. Night had come crawling back before I had a chance to appreciate the day. I don't know the time, but my body's tired. My mind is worse. I lower my head and rub my temples as if this nightmare is just that and I can wake up from it.

As if Lara running to escape me, screaming in terror because of *me*, wasn't enough, her words shattered my heart. The nurses say this is a normal side effect from a traumatic event, but I'm calling bullshit. *How could she think I would hurt her? Does she not know I did everything I could to protect her?*

How does she not see me? The one who loved her through the worst thing to happen to her? How does she not see the man who made love, real love, with her, to her?

"Kaz?"

I look back at Rochelle. "Is she asleep?"

"She is. It's not peaceful, even under sedation. I don't know what happened to her, but she's struggling."

"I want to help her."

"But you can't."

"She remembers me as a monster. Why?"

Rochelle sits in a chair. The waiting area is busy, but it's large, so we have privacy in the corner. "I don't know. Whatever happened before the accident is what has messed with her mind, but she doesn't have amnesia, so this will pass. The doctor even thinks it will be soon."

Glancing at the guys, I stand and go over. "You guys can go home. She's safe and the media presence will rise with the sun."

Dex steps forward and shakes my hand. When I take it, I'm pulled in for a hug. "She's going to be okay."

Nodding, I step back. Johnny shakes my hand next and brings me in again. These guys are softer on the inside than they let on. With a pat on the back, he says, "We're family. Remember that."

"I will." I return a few pats before we part. Holli slips between us and hugs me tight. I wrap my arms around her waist, but Johnny stands there watching us, so I loosen my hold. "Thank you for checking on her last night."

"I'm sorry. The lights were out. We knocked and didn't hear—"

"You're not to blame. You did what you could."

"I'm sorry," she replies, sniffling. "I'd like to stay."

"Go home. Get some rest. You've had a long night."

When we separate, she says, "So have you. I'll stay if you want to go home."

"I can't leave her." She nods. "Go home with Johnny. Rochelle will keep you updated."

"Okay. I'll be back in a few hours too. I want to shower and change clothes. Maybe a few hours sleep."

When she moves under Johnny's arm, I slap hands together with Derrick and we bring it in for a chest bump. I say, "Brother."

"I'm sorry, man."

"So am I."

"You want me to stay? Keep you company? Get some real food or coffee?"

"Nah, go home. We'll keep in touch."

"Call if you need anything."

"Why?" I ask with a grin. "Your lazy ass won't leave that bed once you hit it."

He laughs. "True. Call Holli or Tommy."

"Ha!"

They start walking toward the garage where they can avoid the paps that have been waiting outside basically since we arrived. Tommy offers, "I'll stay. For real. You go home and get some Z's."

"I can't leave her."

"I'm gonna head to the coffee shop next door and grab a cup. I'll bring you one."

I could try to convince him to go home, but I know Tommy. He's a giver. He sees us as the family he needs to protect. I know he's not going anywhere. Maybe he will in a few hours. I'll try then. For now, I reply, "Thanks."

Rochelle walks Dex down the hall. They stop at the far end and hug. He touches her cheek, lifting her chin. Her long hair hangs down her back, and then he says something that brings a small smile to her face before they kiss.

I want that.

Back.

I want that *back*.

With Lara.

I want that back with Lara.

Sitting down in the hard chair, Lara's dad sits across from me. "She's asleep."

"Rochelle told me."

"Tell me something, son."

Looking up, I stare into his face. I see Lara in some of his features, but she resembles her mom more. Worry creases across his forehead. "What do you want to know?"

"You love my daughter."

"Are you asking?"

233

"No. I can see you do." I watch him as he stands and walks to the window. "Why was she with Mark if he had done what Rochelle told us?"

"That's a good question. I'm not sure I have the right answer."

He tucks his hands in his pockets. "What answers do you have, Mr. Fabian?"

"I don't think she was with him willingly. And I know she loves me... loved. Maybe I don't have the answer to that anymore."

"Rochelle said she loves you. Lara's mother says she does. Lara told her. She's been more secretive with me. I think she knows I wouldn't have reacted well to the news of what Mark did to her."

"I didn't."

The right side of his mouth rises and he looks back at me. "I know. Thank you."

"It was actually my pleasure."

"So the bastard is in a coma."

"Seems that way."

"The police think he was trying to kill them, that he purposely crashed the car. What do you think?"

I rub my temples, tired and angry and tired of being angry. My stomach twists thinking that he tried to kill her. The thought has crossed my mind more than a dozen times. "I think they might be right."

"He tried to kill my daughter."

"Twice."

"He's right down that hall."

"In room thirteen sixty-four and unguarded."

Our eyes meet and we nod. There's no sympathy when Mark Renner is the topic of conversation.

"For the time being." He exhales and walks to the waiting area. "I should get back to Lara's mother."

"Good talking to you."

"Good talking you." With a nod, he walks back to Lara's room.

I'm tempted to follow, but since the last incident, I stay. Leaning back, I try to get more comfortable in the chair. Eyes are on me, so I can't relax. I get up. Rochelle comes toward me and gestures. "Come on." I enter Lara's room quietly, following Rochelle inside. "Wait in here with us."

Lara's mom says, "We're going back to her townhouse for a few hours. She's stable so we'll come back in the morning. Will you be staying or would you like a ride home?"

"I'll stay."

Coming straight up to me, she hugs me. "Thank you for taking care of our daughter."

I hug her back, dropping my head to her shoulder. "I love her," I whisper.

"I can see how much." We part, but her kind yet tired eyes, so much like Lara's, stay on me. "Maybe in the morning we can sit down and you can tell me about it. Lara confided in me. She said you were the one."

She said I was the one? If my heart didn't ache so much, I think I'd be overjoyed by that. I just hope she feels the same when she wakes, because I'm not sure I'll cope if she doesn't. "She's afraid of me now."

She reaches up and touches my cheek. With a soft smile, she says, "Her heart knows you. It will work out." Walking to the door, her husband joins her. "Good night."

Rochelle and I both answer, "Good night."

When we're alone, I go to Lara's side and take her hand. Raising it to my lips, I kiss it, letting my lips linger against her skin.

Rochelle says, "Maybe I should get some sleep."

"I'll stay up."

"All right. Wake me up if she wakes up."

"I will."

Rochelle lies down on the small sofa against the far wall and closes her eyes. I pull up a chair and sit, resting my head so her hand is under my cheek. The quiet room insists on sleep and I reluctantly close my eyes. After being up for a day and flying across the country, I give in.

Comfort caresses me, fingers weaving into my hair. All the love I've ever felt for her is there and I see it in her eyes. She rests her head on my shoulder and I hold on to her, not wanting to lose her again. My arms come up empty and I cry out for Lara. But the darkness falls away, replaced by light when I open my eyes. I look up. Lara is looking at me. Her eyes aren't wide with fear like before, the corners easy with concern. *For me?* She whispers, "You don't scare me."

I sit all the way up, hating that her hand falls to the bed when I prefer her touching me. I don't push her, although all I want to do is hold it. "I hope not."

"I know what we had. I just don't know what happened last." Her voice is too steady, and distant, her emotions held firmly at bay.

"You will. You have to give yourself time to heal."

"I'm sorry."

"For what? You have nothing to be sorry for."

She exhales and looks up at the ceiling. "For earlier. I don't know why I reacted like that." When her eyes meet mine, she adds, "Well, I do, but I don't at the same time. It makes no sense. I know I loved you."

Loved.

Her gaze leaves mine and she pulls at a loose thread on the hospital blanket. "What happened at the end?"

"There are only two people who can answer that: you and him."

"He's in a coma. Is he going to live?"

I'm afraid so. "Yes."

"Maybe I should visit him."

We turn to the far side of the room when Rochelle speaks, "I don't think that's a good idea, Lara." She stands and comes to the other side of her bed, opposite of me. Briefly glancing to me, she tells her, "He's responsible for the car crash."

"The accident hurt us—"

Rochelle's voice raises just a notch. "It wasn't an accident."

Lara turns back to me, then closes her eyes. "How do you know?"

When she looks back to Rochelle, Rochelle replies, "Because the evidence suggests otherwise."

"Ro."

She looks at me. "I know the doctor said to wait, but I won't sit here and let her believe that psycho wasn't trying to kill her."

A gasp draws our eyes to Lara. Her hand is over her mouth and her eyes wide. "He tried to kill me?" she stutters as the heart rate monitor blips faster.

Shit.

"He didn't," I say.

"He didn't try to kill me?" she asks with the innocence of a child.

"No, he tried, but he didn't succeed. You lived with no permanent damage."

Rochelle says, "You've got to remember something, Lara. The police need to know any detail you can remember."

"I only remember being at my place. Kaz was there. I took him to the airport to meet the band."

"That was four days ago," I say. "Do you remember anything after that?"

"Lane. We were at your house. Two chairs arrived and a buffet, your dining table, but only three of the eight chairs. Don't worry though. I called the manufacturer. They're going to rush the chairs."

I smile. "It's okay."

"No, it's not. I wanted those two rooms finished before you got home."

Rochelle's mood has lightened like Lara's and mine. She asks, "Do you remember going to dinner with Holli and me?"

Lara shakes her head and looks down.

When Rochelle covers her hands, she says, "You will. Just give it time."

"Why have I forgotten?"

Sitting down next to her, I take her other hand gently, but she pulls it away. I try not to let her reaction hurt me, and stay strong in the belief that she'll come back to me. I try. "Because it was that bad."

"My mind's blocked it out." Her bottom lip wobbles. "I don't want to remember then."

"You must," I insist, my heartbeat lurches into panic mode. *I can't lose her.* "Just give it time."

"Take it easy," Rochelle tells her.

Lara turns her back to me, pulls her hand from Rochelle, and closes her eyes. "I'm tired."

"We'll let you rest," Rochelle says and walks to the end of the bed. Taking me by the arm, she gestures toward the door, knowing my heart's just been ripped out. "Come on. We'll get coffee."

When we walk out, I look back once. Lara's eyes—the beautiful blues I fell in love with—stare back into mine just over her shoulder. But there's no love seen in hers, only curiosity.

And then the door closes.

26

Lara

My MIND IS playing tricks on me, but I see the truth.

Sort of.

Kind of.

I sigh, frustrated that I've lost days somewhere in the back of my mind. The memories are there, they're just locked away, so I just have to find the key.

When I woke up, I was quiet, wanting the time to think, but Rochelle walks in with a nurse, both wanting to check on me. I've slept for hours. The nurse smiles and greets me, but goes about her business checking the monitor and my IV. "Are you in any pain?"

"A little on my left side."

"You're bruised, but your ribs aren't broken. It's a miracle you walked away." Her eyes land on mine. "Well, not walked, but you're in one piece and you'll be good as new. That's what counts. You have a concussion but we're monitoring things. If you need anything, just call for me. I'll be here all day. Shift change and you're stuck with me." A kind smile appears.

"Thank you. How long do you think I'll stay in the hospital?"

She takes the chart and starts writing. "The doctor will check you out later. If all goes well today, I bet they discharge you tomorrow." Looking to Rochelle, she asks, "You'll arrange transportation?"

"Yes."

"Good." The nurse walks to the door and says, "Buzz me if you need me."

"Thanks again."

When the door closes, Rochelle asks, "How are you feeling?"

"Tired. Some pain."

Sitting on the edge of the bed, she rests her hand on my leg. "He's in a lot of pain too. It may not be obvious, but he's hurting out there."

I look away, not able to bear the accusations in her eyes. "I'm sorry. I don't mean to hurt him."

"You remember him. You remember how much you love him, but you're scared of him. What happened?"

"I don't know." The pressure to find that key in my thoughts weighs on me and tears fill my eyes. "Why don't I know?"

"Your brain is protecting you from something horrific. You've got to realize that you're not alone. I'm here. Kaz is here."

"My parents are here."

She smiles. "Yes, they're here." When the smile fades, she rubs my leg to comfort me. "Your parents know what Mark did to you."

"I figured. Has my dad killed him yet?" I cover my mouth and shake my head. "I shouldn't have said that when he's in a coma."

She snaps, "Stop worrying about him. He's going to live."

"I just meant—"

"I know what you meant, but you need to hear me. Whatever Mark did to turn you against Kaz is wrong. You shouldn't feel anything but hate for Mark. He tried to kill you, Lara. I know it. The police know it. You know it. You just can't remember. You will though. And then you're going to need that man out there in the waiting room who has stayed despite the pain he's feeling from your rejection."

"Don't yell at me, Rochelle. I'm trying—"

"Try harder." She stands. "I won't sit by and let you defend that psycho while pushing away the guy who took care of you when you were abused by Mark Renner. Kaz was the one drying your tears. He was the one who had us check on you. He was the one that called the police. It was him that had everyone searching for you." Walking to the door, she says, "I need fresh air and you need rest."

"I'm sorry."

"Don't apologize to me. It's Kaz who's been hurt."

The door closes and I turn to the window. The sun is rising, the sky getting brighter. The start of a new day should bring hope. Not today. The door opens and I sit up when I see two female officers walk in. A dark-haired officer takes the lead. "Hi, I'm Officer Rodriguez and this is Officer Caprusso. Is it all right if we ask you a few questions? We need to fill in some blanks on our report."

"Sure. I already told the other officers what I remember, but I'm happy to help if I can."

After pulling out a small notepad from her shirt pocket, she reads, "We don't have much information on Mr. Fabian. We do know he's been living under the alias of Fabian, but his last name is Petrowski."

Petrowski, I repeat in my head. *Petrowski.*

Officer Rodriguez says, "He called nine-one-one. Would you recognize his voice if we played you the call? Can you identify it?"

"Yes."

"Do you mind verifying it for us?"

"No. As I said, if I can help, I will."

Officer Caprusso holds out her phone. "Just press play."

The other officer presses play and the operator begins talking. When Kaz speaks, panic is heard in his voice, *"I need the police. I think my girlfriend has been kidnapped."*

The monitor speeds up along with my heart while I listen. I

recall snippets of a conversation I had with him.

"When did you last speak to the missing person?"

"Maybe ten or fifteen minutes ago."

"Sir, do you know it's illegal to file a false report?"

"It's her ex. He's hurt her. I'm afraid he's got her right now, taken her against her will."

"And why do think that if you just spoke to her?"

"She left her friends at the club. She left her purse there. How'd she get home? And she said 'Later gator' to me. She never says that."

Later gator? Do I really say that? When it's over, I close my eyes.

Later gator.

Later gator...

Later gator!

"He knew!" I say, popping up in the bed.

"Who knew what?"

"Kaz," I tell the officer. "He knew I was in trouble."

"How?"

"The code words. Later gator. We don't say that. We always say goodbye. Just in case."

"Just in case of what?"

"Just in case someone dies."

Both of their gazes hit me. I wave my arm. "Morbid, I know, but we say it."

"One other question. You said you don't remember that night. Have you remembered anything? Any detail, even small, can really help fill in the blanks."

Later gator.

"I remember talking to Kaz." I close my eyes, the key to unlocking the events of that night within reach. I stretch my mind and take hold of it. "I remember. I talked to Kaz. I was in my closet and Mark was blocking the door."

"Of your closet or his?"

"Mine. Kaz had a show in Atlanta and kept calling to check on me, so Mark told me to call him to get him to stop."

"Did it work?"

"He knew." My heart starts inflating again, filling with the love I held on to when my head couldn't. "He knew I was in trouble and that's why he called nine-one-one."

Officer Rodriguez leans against the end of the bed, watching me intently. "Anything else?"

Looking off to the side, I try to focus internally. A shiver runs the length of my spine and I squeeze my eyes shut. The bruises. The pain in my side. My throbbing eye. Kaz. My hands start to tremble, but I fight the urge to close my mind off. I fist the sheet and persevere...

The phone rings and I look back. Kaz. I knew he wouldn't give up on me.

"That's him?"

I turn back to Mark, and reply, "Yes. He won't stop until he believes I'm safe."

"Safe from me?"

"Safe, in general."

When his phone rings, he looks down at it. He turns his back to me and answers it, "Tell me good news, Coach."

I back away and grab my phone from the floor. I've missed his call, but I can text.

A thunderous, "No," scares me. It's more like a roar. Mark punches the wood frame of the door. His death glare is latched on to me. There's no escaping. I know it. He knows it. "No pay and they're dropping my contract effective immediately."

I'm trapped in here, so I try a different route. "I'm sorry." All the moxie I had mustered a minute earlier is gone, like the fight from my body.

"I'll lose my sponsors, my titles. They want my World Series ring back."

Panic was understandable earlier. It was a reactionary emotion that could be dispelled by asking the right questions. What

I see in Mark's eyes is wild and untamed. There's no going back for him. This is the moment where logic needs to win out.

"It's just a ring. You'll have the memories and the record."

An anarchist fire burns in his eyes. He rubs his temple, then says, "Let's go."

Fear has returned, and knows no bounds. "Where?"

I thought the "No" *earlier was stormy. He's a hurricane brewing out in the wide-open ocean, looking to destroy our peace on earth.* "Get in the fucking car."

The voicemail on my phone chimes. I look back once wishing I could grab it but I'm yanked by the nape of the neck. We walk while I cry out, "Please. Stop, Mark. You're hurting me."

"Not for long."

Not for long? He's going to let me go.

I was a fool thinking he was going to let me go. He has no plans to do that. That much is crystal clear. We've been driving for twenty minutes. He's mumbling in the driver's seat, buried so deep in his head. "It will be okay. You'll play somewhere else."

"No, I won't. No one will touch me now. My ball career is over."

He tosses the phone to me and I look at the screen. The email he threatened to send earlier is up. "I'll never take your side, but if you blame him—"

"Don't tell me what I can and can't do. I can end you."

Looking at the phone in front of me, I say, "You can, but you'll never end my love for him."

"I will."

I'm confused. One minute I'm holding the phone, the next it's flying into the windshield. I reach up to stabilize myself, but my seatbelt cuts into me.

Opening my eyes, the nurse rushes in the door and past the officers to the machine. "Help me up," I plead. "Please." I struggle to sit up, but once the nurse assists me, I move my feet over the side of the bed. "Agh." My ribs. I cradle my taped middle and use the steel stand of the IV to level me to my feet.

The nurse protests, "You need to get back in bed, Ms. Kessler."

"I need to see him." I head for the door to her dismay.

"You won't catch him. He's just left after I updated him on your condition. I told him to go home to get some rest. Anyway, you're going to hurt yourself if you're not careful."

"Please help me. Please," I cry. "I love him. I don't want to lose him."

She shakes her head, and then says, "I can't help you. I'll get in trouble." My hope deflates until she adds, "But I'll look away. You've got five minutes and then I'm coming for you."

"That's all I need." I manage the door and she holds it with her foot, keeping her back to me. "Thank you."

"Go."

I tell the security guards, "I'll be right back." They don't listen and step forward to follow. Looking down the corridor, I don't have time to waste with them and pick a direction, going with the one that leads to the parking garage. I move slowly but steadily hoping he stopped to talk to anyone, maybe Rochelle, someone that could slow him down. I round the corner and that's when I see him. Kaz is standing at the elevator doors waiting for them to open. I keep moving, but the doors open and he steps inside. "Kaz? Wait." Right when I reach the silver steel doors they are closing. It's too late. Our eyes meet and the doors close.

The stairwell is to my left, but I can't take the stairs in this condition, so I remain in the last spot where he left me. Dropping my head down just as tears start to fall, I cry. "Please don't leave me. Please don't."

Ding.

When I look up, he's standing there. His arms go wide, holding the offending doors open, and he says, "I would never leave you."

My tears are still falling but now in happiness, each filled with hope. "I know. I remember everything."

27

Kaz

THE ELEVATOR BUZZES in protest as I hold the doors wide open. The most beautiful woman I've ever seen, the one who holds my heart, controls my emotions, stands before me in an ugly hospital gown somehow even making that look incredible.

Lara's eyes are wide with anticipation, tears filling them, hope written into her soft smile. Pride swarms the blue of her eyes as if she's solved the world's problems, not knowing she's solved mine with three simple words: *I remember everything.*

"You do?" I ask.

"I do." She takes a step closer and quietly says, "I love you. I think I loved you before I even knew I loved you, Kaz."

I drop my arms to my sides and step out of the elevator. She takes one more step and the distance between us closes. Taking her by the back of her head and her waist, I kiss her like I've wanted to kiss her for the hours, days, and years that existed but were never complete without her in it.

When we part, I close my eyes and our foreheads come together. I whisper, "I love you, Lara. I love you. I love you. I love you." The words are a chant so her heart never forgets our love again, even if her mind can't remember.

Her breath warms my chest as I hold her close, so close, never wanting to let her go. "You saved me."

I'd confess that I feel at fault I couldn't be there, that I left when she needed me, that I couldn't stop him from taking her. The confession lumps in my throat. I'm so grateful I can hold her now and that she's here, she's alive, she remembers. I take her hand carefully from my arm and bring it to my lips, kissing near where the IV pricks her skin. "Let's get you back to bed. You need rest. You need to heal."

"Stay with me," she says, looking up into my eyes. A halo of light is reflected in them, brightening her plea.

I smile. "I'm not going anywhere, baby."

We walk back to her room together. My arm stays wrapped around her waist but I'm cautious. I don't want her in any more pain than she already is.

The nurse is standing outside the door, tapping her foot. Her smile gives her away though. "Ms. Kessler, you need to get right back in bed. They won't discharge you if you're not better."

"I had important business—"

"Mr. Fabian *may* be important business, no doubt, but healing is more important." Stepping inside, she holds the door wide open for us. "I'm sure he understands. Right, Mr. Fabian?"

Spying her nametag, I smile to get us on her good side. "Yes, Nurse Martin."

She cracks a wider smile as she takes Lara's side and helps her back into bed. "Food will be brought around soon. I suggest you eat. You must be starved. Can I get you anything else in the meantime?"

Lara glances to me. "I'm good. Thank you."

Nurse Martin scolds playfully, "Mr. Fabian, let her rest please."

"I'll make sure she does." As soon as the nurse shuts the door, I tell her, "Scoot over. I'm coming in." Lara wriggles to her right and I slip off my jacket and then my shoes. When I climb in, I wrap my arm under her and she turns on her side, snuggling against me. "I love you."

"I love you, too. I'm sorry for last night."

"Do you know why?" I don't finish the question. It hurts me to even say it, but I need to know why she was so scared of me.

"There's an email. He wrote an email that included the photos you took of me."

Anger sweeps through my veins, but I try to remain calm so I don't worry her. "What did it say?"

She's still, so still that I tighten my arm around her.

"He was going to send it to the press saying you did that to me. I remember reading it, seeing the photos, trying to convince him not to when we crashed."

"It was the last thing you saw." *The bastard. Sick, fucking bastard.*

"I'm sorry."

"Don't apologize. Your mind played tricks on you. It was the last image you had, the words that said I hurt you. You knew, deep down, you know I wouldn't."

"I know you won't."

I kiss the top of her head. "Get some rest. I'll wake you when the food is delivered."

She nods wordlessly, closing her eyes. It doesn't take but a few minutes in my arms for her to fall asleep, her slumber even and her breathing steady. If she gets real rest so she can heal, I'd stay like this forever.

It wasn't food that woke Lara from her sleep. It was a doctor. He knocked lightly disturbing my sleeping beauty. We turned and although I know I should trust doctors, I still kept my hold around her firm enough to protect her and light enough not to hurt her.

"I'm Dr. Herman. I'm sorry to interrupt but I needed to speak with you."

Lara readjusts and sits up, my body remaining her support. "Hello."

"I'm Mr. Renner's doctor."

She shudders. Our peaceful space invaded by the name alone. "We want nothing to do with him."

"I understand that, Mr. Fabian, but like we ask our patients to follow doctor's orders, we try to follow our patients requests if we can."

Lara clears her throat. "He has a request? I thought he was in a coma?"

"He's woken up."

Our sanctity—that Mark Renner was unconscious—is broken. Violated by the news, I can feel it in my girl, the way she's shaking. Her heart monitor beeping.

I'm firm. There is no room for any misunderstanding. "We don't want anything to do with him. You do realize that he not only kidnapped her, but tried to kill her, right?"

"I'm not here to judge. I'm here to heal. I won't be put in a position to be judge nor jury on this issue."

"I will. I will be judge, jury, and executioner if he even utters her name."

The doctor shifts and puts his hands in his pockets. "I will pretend I didn't hear that—"

"You don't have to pretend. I'll say it to his fucking face."

He looks at the chart in his hands, then back to up. "I'm only here to let you know he's woken up and he would like to see Ms. Kessler."

"No way!" I state, unflinching in my stance.

The doctor turns to Lara. "Ms. Kessler, the decision is ultimately yours. I understand the situation is heated, but I do need to tell you that he's not in great condition."

She replies, "Because he tried to kill us. I don't owe him anything despite his health. I won't be seeing him ever again if I have my way."

The doctor goes to the door. "Very well." He leaves, but Rochelle shows up before the door closes.

"Hey, you two. I heard there was good news in here and seeing you together like this—this is very good news." She walks around to Lara's side of the bed and they hug. "How are you feeling?"

"Better. Much better. Memories intact."

"Your parents will be so happy. I'll let them get a few more hours sleep before contacting them."

"Thank you. Do you know when the doctor will be around to check me out? I don't want to stay here any longer."

She replies, "I'll check for you. What's going on?"

I say, "Renner's awake."

Rochelle's eyes widen. "How do you know?"

Lara says, "That was his doctor. Mark has requested to see me."

"No," Rochelle responds adamantly.

I always liked Rochelle.

Looking down at her hands, Lara speaks low, but we hear when she says, "I can't rest knowing he's down the hall from me. I just can't."

"You don't have to," I say. "We're getting you released today." I ease up to my feet.

Rochelle looks at me. "We need to talk about the two shows that were cancelled and the interview."

"Shoot."

"Tommy and I thought it was best to flip things around since the shows were pushed to next week. The interview will be postponed, but I don't know how long. Do you think you're up for it?"

"I can't think about that. We need to push it until Lara's better."

Lara sits up. "You should do it. If you don't, the speculation will get worse and they'll start digging deeper. This is your chance to put the rumors to rest." Turning to Rochelle, she adds, "I still want to be there."

"You're not going to be there. You're going to rest. The interview can wait."

"I don't want you to have to wait on me. The paparazzi are hounding you as it is."

"I can handle them. You focus on healing. We'll get you home and settled, so you can recover in comfort."

"I don't want to go to my townhouse."

I'm not even sure if it's showing, but I feel that damn cocky smirk on the inside. "Who said anything about your place, beautiful?"

A squeal erupts but not from Lara. We both look at Rochelle who is smiling ear to ear with excitement oozing as she bounces. "Oh my God. You want Lara at your house?" Turning to Lara, she says, "Say yes, Lara. Yes to love."

Lara looks to me. I nod. "Say yes to love, Lara."

There's a pause as she looks between us. Her eyes settle on mine, and with the first unburdened smile I've seen on her in a while, she says, "Yes. Yes to love. Yes to you, Kaz." *Best four words I've heard in a long time.*

THERE ARE TIMES you should go with your gut. Correction: always go with your gut. It will never lie to you. It may trick you. It may even be wrong sometimes. But it won't lie.

I trusted the wrong thing. The bodyguards said they were "On it." They weren't. One small slip in their judgment and Lara was put at risk again. I was only gone an hour, details of the upcoming shows organized, the interview questions approved, a call to Lara's parents placed.

Nodding to the bodyguards, I open the door. Lara gasps, then relaxes when she realizes it's me. I rush to her bedside. "What's wrong?"

"He was here."

"What? Who was?"

"Mark. He was here." *What the fuck?*

"What do you mean he was here? How?"

"I don't know. He was wheeled in by some man, and we were left alone despite me telling him no." Her strength caves and she starts to cry.

I hold her. "Did he hurt you? What happened? What did he say?"

"I'm fine. I am. It was just so unexpected. He took me by surprise."

My teeth grind together. "Lara, what did he say?"

"That he's sorry. He said sorry."

"What else?" I hold her tighter, trying not to lose my shit. *That fucker was in here.* "I know there's more. Just tell me."

"He wants something I'll never do for him. He asked me to lie to protect him."

"Lie about what?"

"You."

"What did he say?"

"That we had broken up after a bad fight. You were irrational and hit me. I ran to Mark for help. He was driving me home and a deer ran in front of the vehicle causing us to crash."

"What? That's not plausible on any level. What did you say?"

She takes my hand, removing the pressure from my knuckles as I grip the railing of her bed. "I will never lie for him and I will never betray you."

Hugging her, I try to comfort her as best I can. "I know. You sure you're okay?"

"I am," she replies while I rub her back.

"Rochelle will be in to pack up your stuff. I'm going to get you discharged. You're not staying here any longer."

I start for the door, but she calls me, "Kaz?" When I look back, her gorgeous eyes are on me. "You can't protect me from everything. I know you're trying to, but I'm okay. We're okay. Please stop worrying."

"I'll never stop worrying. Not while he breathes."

"All of this, this isn't how we're going to live. I can't live like this.

You can't put your life on hold to helicopter around me."

"I'll feel better when we're home."

"I like when you call it home." *It's only home because of her.*

"It was never home without you."

With a shy smile, she asks, "Just so I'm clear, are you wanting me to stay or live there?"

"What would you like to do?"

"I want to be with you, and I want what you want."

"I love you, Lara. Live with me then. Let's just do this. Let's be together."

If only I could capture the smile on her face and keep it forever. She's so incredibly lovely. She's also giggling in giddiness. "You love me enough to make that offer so freely?"

"I do. What about you?"

"I do. I do, too."

I'm hoping it's only a matter of time before she's saying I do to me forever.

28

Lara

SPENDING TIME IN bed with Kaz is the best medicine. We talk, we cuddle, we watch movies, and we sleep entangled in each other—our bodies and emotions. He's healed my soul as much as my wounds.

It's only been a few days since being discharged from the hospital, but so much has happened that I've decided to stay disconnected from the world a little bit longer. Kaz had my townhouse packed up and my stuff brought here. Two of the spare bedrooms are filled with boxes and my furniture. My clothes have taken over his closet, and both bedroom closets. And he has not complained once. Though I have. I feel bad, but then he makes me feel so much better with his kisses, and hugs, and afternoon delights. That's when he talked me into staying and two days later, my townhome was on the market.

It's just after midnight. Kaz met with the band for a few hours earlier in the evening, but he's been home since. And score one for me—he made me a Russian dish called Pelmeni. I'd like to say it was good, but it wasn't just good, it was amazing. He's quite the chef. "Where did you learn to cook?"

"My mother. She said it would drive the girls wild."

Smiling, I lean my head on his shoulder. "She's right."

"That was a big motivator, but I also found it relaxing. It's a process to follow. You can get creative or get lost in the process. It's nice to be lost in your thoughts sometimes. I get that when I play guitar too."

"What about the piano? You never talk about playing, you never play, but yet, a beautiful piano is the centerpiece of your home. The whole house revolves around it."

"It's a ghost that haunts me."

"Will you play for me?" I ask nervously. I don't want him to feel uncomfortable, but I want to help him like he's helped me.

He leans his head to the side, far enough over to look me in the eyes. "I'll play for you, but not right now." His lids are heavy with sleep, worry and the world weighing them down. "Let's go to sleep."

"Okay." I lift up just enough for my lips to reach his and kiss him goodnight, hoping to kiss away his troubles. But I have a feeling his troubles run deeper than he lets on. "I love you."

"I love you, Lara."

ANOTHER DAY PASSES and no piano. Another night arrives and we're cuddled on the couch in the bedroom, an old movie is on the TV, but I don't think either of us is really watching.

I say, "I got a call that his computers were taken as evidence and the videos found. They asked me what to do with them once they were done."

"What did you say?"

"I told them to destroy them. I just hope they didn't watch them. I can't worry if they did though. It is what it is. As long as they don't go public..."

"And the photos?"

"They'll be gone with the videos, the computers destroyed."

"Are you okay?"

I lean my head on his shoulder. "I'm fine." I entwine my fingers with his and ask, "Why did you walk away that day in Luxembourg?"

"I knew I wasn't living the life I wanted to. I was convinced at one time it was, but I knew. I woke up. I showered. Got dressed and went to the concert hall. I was watching the symphony warming up. Just stared at them, thinking."

"About?"

"About my life and how I saw it going. My hand was injured and I was struggling with the slow healing and the intense touring schedule. I thought *what if I didn't play*? What if I walked away? What would happen?"

"You injured your hand protecting your mom and sister."

"I've never thought for one second it was a mistake."

"But you lost everything—your piano career and your family because of it."

"I didn't lose it. I left it behind to discover what was ahead. I'd do it again. It was never about them choosing me over him. It was about stopping someone from hurting others. Unfortunately, it didn't work."

"Kaz?" He keeps his eyes on me when I say, "Thank you."

"You don't have to thank me."

"I want to, for me and for them. Your heart is so big, right and wrong, so clear to you when it's a fuzzy line to everyone else."

"It's not to you, but your soft heart might cause you problems sometimes. Here's the thing though—stay soft, vulnerable, open. Don't let anyone harden you against what matters."

"What matters?" I ask, whispering.

"Love."

THE LIGHTS HAVE been out for an hour or more. I've been tracing the design on his T-shirt with my finger and thinking a lot about his life before he walked away. I have so many questions, but I start with some obvious ones. "If you didn't want to perform, why are you in one of the biggest bands in the world?"

"I never said I didn't want to perform. I just didn't want to do what I was doing anymore. I wasn't happy under that spotlight and public interest was growing in the press back home."

"But you're in the spotlight now."

"It's different now. Johnny Outlaw is the frontman. Dex gets his own fair share of attention. I'm a guitarist in the shadows of their spotlights and I'm good with that. I don't need the attention. I just want to play music that people enjoy." He smiles, then winks. "And being in *The Resistance* pays damn well." He slides farther down under the covers and ends my questions for the night.

The notes are heavy, the melody trickling into my dreams and gently coaxing me awake. My eyes are tired, but I turn to check the time anyway. 2:47 a.m.

Lying there in the dark, I hear him. For the first time. And I know he wants me to, so I get up and pad across the floor, dragging the sheet with me as I go. I tighten the corner into a knot above my chest and continue down the hall until I see him. I had full intentions of going closer, but seeing him stops me still. Moonlight lights the room, but Kaz is a shadow in its night. His head is lowered as his fingers play from a memory that captures the vividness of a life once lived.

The familiar music gets darker hitting a crescendo of emotion, and I call to him. "Kaz."

His fingers stop moving, his head rises, and his eyes land on me, and a smile that weakens my knees appears. "The piano was a spontaneous purchase. I haven't played it before."

Leaning against the wall, I watch him as his fingers run along the top of the keys. "Tell me about it."

"I'd just bought the house, but we had flown to New York for a show. It was late, maybe around midnight and I was with some friends, Derrick was there. We passed a piano store and a guy was playing it. Only one light on, but the music could be heard from the street. I stopped and watched, missing that feeling of getting lost in it."

"Do you not get lost when you play guitar?"

He looks up with a smile that's so sincere it's hard to believe so much weighs him down. "I do. I love the guitar. I couldn't choose if I had to, but I missed playing piano. I knocked on the door knowing the store was closed. When he answered, I told him I'd buy it, but I wanted that one. The richness of the timbre was what I'd been missing." He taps a black key. "But I've not touched it since it's arrival."

"Why?"

"I was worried I'd forgotten the music."

"You didn't. I heard you play by heart."

His smile grows, pride seen in his expression. "Since it was moved cross country, I didn't even know if it was in tune."

Standing next to him, I run my fingers through his hair. "I had it tuned while you were on the road."

"Thanks," he replies shyly. "I woke you. I'm sorry."

"Wake me anytime you need me." His arms come around my waist and he rests his cheek to my stomach. I cradle his head to me.

"I wanted to play something more romantic for you the first time, maybe Tchaikovsky? But Beethoven has a way of capturing the music that plays inside me tonight."

"You played the music inside you that needs to be heard."

His arms tighten around me. "You've saved me in ways I didn't know I needed saving, filling the holes where pieces escaped, and the light exposed me for the fraud I am."

"You're not a fraud. You've lived two lives. Those lives don't have to be separate. You can be whole again."

"I don't want this attention, for people to see the gravity of my old life."

"We all have skeletons we want left buried. You have nothing to be ashamed of. You have nothing you need to hide."

"What if..." He doesn't say anymore. He just closes his eyes and holds me.

"It's going to be okay," I whisper, the hour growing longer, my body wearing down, not recovered yet. "You're going to be okay."

"You'll be there tomorrow? You'll come with me to the interview?"

Despite how I feel physically, I will be there for him like he's been there for me. "I will be there however you need me to be."

THIS. IS. *INSANITY*.

Word got out, though no one accepts responsibility for the press leak.

The doors can't open because of the crush of people surrounding our vehicle. When I look around I expect to see *The Resistance* fans. What I don't expect to see are the Kazimir Petrowsky fans out in force. Russia's great prodigy has returned and they are here in droves of support. Tommy tells the driver to go around to the parking garage.

Once we're safely inside, three bodyguards wait just outside our door. Rochelle stands by the door waiting, another woman with a harsh black haircut and deep red lips is beside her on the phone. Tommy hops out and I unlatch my seatbelt. Kaz remains still, the same debate I saw in his eyes earlier playing in the intense expression. I squeeze his hand and the door opens.

The driver says, "*S'vasrasheniyem*, Petrowski."

Looking back over my shoulder, I watch his mouth form the words, his lips speak the language. Before my very eyes, I watch Kaz Fabian become Kazimir Petrowski.

TWO HOURS EARLIER...

So tense.

"You're tense." I rub his shoulders, but they don't ease under my touch.

"I'm nervous and I don't get nervous." Kaz sets his coffee mug in the sink and fills it with water to soak. *He's so damn neat.* He puts me to shame.

I follow him into the bedroom and farther into the en-suite bathroom. He turns on the shower and I sit on the edge of the tub. "Opening up about my life... I've hid it for so long that it feels foreign to me now."

"You don't have a Russian accent, not even traces of one. I thought I heard something a few times, but nothing to make me think twice."

"I let it go and watched a lot of American movies. I binged on Christopher Walken for a while, but I was told that was not typical. It was just easy to mimic. I watched Ryan Gosling movies, listened to *The Resistance* ironically, and went to a voice coach a few times. It was really just being here, blending into the culture that helped. I met Derrick and focused on his. That might have been a mistake. He's got a laid-back Southern California dialect going on." He laughs and it's good to hear the sound. "Come in with me."

"And make you feel better?"

An eyebrow is cocked and he smiles. "You always make me feel better."

We undress and go into the shower together. The hot water washes away the worry that plagues me and I move in hopes that it does the same for him. His head falls back as the water covers him and his broad shoulders. He moans and I get dirty ideas just from the sight of him.

His heart is all giving. His kindness to me can never be repaid to the extent he deserves. I'll do my best to show him how I care through love and devotion, through actions and words. I kiss his chest and he lifts to look at me and kisses my temple. I place another just a bit lower and his breathing picks up and I start to go down.

Strong hands stop my descent. "Wait." When I look up at him, he says, "You don't have to do this."

"I want to do this for you. Do you want me?"

"I want you, so much." He squeezes his eyes tight when he says the last part. Looking back into my eyes, he says, "But I don't want you to think that I can't wait for you to feel better. I can. I will. For you, I'll wait until you're ready."

"I'm ready. I want this."

His mouth opens but no words follow, just the sound of his breath as it deepens. I take him into my mouth slowly, enough to tease, enough to keep him on edge, to maintain control so he loses himself for a few seconds at the end. The same hands that held my arms rest on the back of my head as I take him deeper. Soon our movements are synchronized, his pleasure at the tip of my tongue and then engulfed until I'm swallowing around him. It doesn't take long for him to let go, to release himself and his burdens, letting me carry them for a while.

Taking me by my elbows, Kaz helps me to my feet. The water rains down over us and I close my eyes letting it drench me completely. I don't know how long we stand there, two bodies melded together as one.

Hearts beating together.

Breaths short and quick until long and even.

Tender strokes of fingertips and palms soothe our souls.

It could have been seconds, but I wish it could be hours. I wish we could stay cocooned in this sanctuary, protected within these walls for just a few more days. The world outside is deceivingly pretty with its blue skies and fluffy clouds. Birds can be heard chirping. Despite the beauty of the moment, tears still come.

"Why are you crying, baby?" he asks so softly it almost breaks my heart.

"I cry for you."

"You don't need to cry for me. Hiding who you are can never be hidden forever. The truth always comes out."

"But it came because of me."

"My hitting him brought the attention on me, not you." My chin is lifted. I never hide from him. He's seen me at my worst and loved me through it, healing me from the inside out. "But you need to know what you mean to me. Everything I do is because of you now and I have no regrets. This life is worth living because of you. The air crackles in excitement because you dared to enter the room inside my heart. The blood that flows through my veins flows because of you. Can't you see, Lara? I'll take any bad because I've tasted and savored the good. I feel alive again." He kisses me wholeheartedly. "Because of you."

29

Lara

"*S'VASRASHENIYEM*, PETROWSKI."

Kaz replies in Russian, *"Spasibo tebe, moy drug."* He follows me out of the large SUV and wraps his arm around me, holding me against his side. I'm not sure if the closeness is for him or me, but I feel the same, so I slip my arm under his jacket and around his taut middle. Rochelle leads, Tommy by Kaz's side, the woman with the harsh hair behind us. She's still on the phone, her smoky voice matching her hair.

"I don't give a fuck. Make sure it's done or you're fired."

As we're whisked through an employee's corridor of a hotel in downtown LA, I ask, "What did the driver say?"

"Welcome back."

"And you?"

This time he looks down at me, and smiles. "I told him thank you."

"That sounded like a lot of words for thank you."

"We called each other friend. *Drug* means friend in Russian."

"Really? That's interesting. I guess that's where our culture got the word from."

He laughs. "Yes, probably."

Tommy halts us and the entire group stops, waiting to move forward. The bodyguards are on full alert and block us from view. We're given the all clear and collectively start moving again.

Thinking back on the crowds and the driver, I ask, "You were more than a prodigy, weren't you?"

"A prodigy isn't enough?"

"It is, but the crowd outside. They weren't Resistance fans. They were Petrowski fans."

"The name carries the weight of a blue bloodline. Russians are very loyal. As a people, we've ruled the world and been at the mercy of it. We are strong through and through and when one does well, it's a reflection of the people themselves. Even if that person was born into royal society. Petrowski an extension of a great time in history, but in today's society it just means we were born into wealth."

Ms. Harsh Hair starts to talk to Kaz and Rochelle steps to my side. "We'll be in the room, but across it. I'm told it's a large suite where many interviews are held. You cannot say anything when they're filming."

"I won't."

She looks at me. "Nothing. Not even if you know it makes him uncomfortable to answer." When I don't reply, she adds, "We've gone over the questions several times, had some marked off, and others replaced, but we are bystanders only from this point on."

Kaz's hand finds mine and though we're looking in opposite directions, our fingers mingle together. Together. We're together in this. And we'll get through it together.

A service elevator is waiting with doors wide open. Kaz has to get up to the suite and get mic'd. Unfortunately only half of us fit, so Ms. Harsh Hair asks me to wait for the second one along with Rochelle, a hotel manager, hotel security, and one of Kaz's bodyguards. When the elevator door opens for us, I wait knowing the security guard is probably anxious to get to Kaz and do his job, but he holds out his hand and says, "After you."

"Thanks."

Rochelle and I step on and he walks on before the manager. The button is pushed and we're off. Once we're off, I whisper, "I need the restroom," to Rochelle.

The manager answers, "Right this way. There's one down the hall you can use."

We start walking and the bodyguard follows behind us. I glance over my shoulder surprised to see him with us. The manager opens a suite and we all go inside. I offer, "You can go first since you need to get back to Kaz."

"I'm assigned to you, Ms. Kessler."

"Me? What do you mean?"

"My job is to cover you, to protect you. I'm part of your security detail."

"You are? Who hired you?"

"Mr. Fabian."

"Oh. Well, thank you. I feel much safer with you here." What am I saying? I inwardly roll my eyes at myself. Do bodyguards like to hear that or was that creepy? I bet it was creepy. Ugh. I just go to the bathroom and try to block out my embarrassment.

The three of us head back to the other suite and enter quietly. It's just about to start when I find Rochelle off in the wings watching. Kaz looks handsome in his button-up shirt and jeans. His hair is a damn sexy mess of dark that looks like he just rolled out bed.

The female reporter seems to think so too. She has the nerve to stand from her chair and touch his hair that's hanging down over his eyes at one point.

And I want to break her fingers for it.

Taking a deep breath, I try to relax. I'm definitely more nervous about this than he is. With his legs spread wide, he owns the space around him, sitting calm on the outside. I wonder how he's doing on the inside.

The signal is given and the interview begins. Misti Roberts introduces herself and the segment before introducing him as Kaz Fabian, member of the rock band, *The Resistance*, and missing pianist child prodigy, Kazimir Petrowski. He doesn't react to the names, but smiles and greets her. Always the gentleman.

She starts in rapid fire. "Do you prefer to be called Kaz Fabian or Kazimir Petrowski?"

"Kaz is fine."

"Let's go back to your days in Russia."

He interrupts, "I was born in Russia, but I spent most of my life traveling to different countries."

"So Russia is not home for Kaz Fabian?"

"Russia is my birth country. I love Russia, but it's not been my home in a very long time."

"Where do you call home?"

He glances my way. *Home.* Then he answers, "Los Angeles. I've lived here almost nine years." I know he can't see me in the dark back here, but he knows I'm here. He knows I'm his home as he's mine.

"Are you here on a visa?"

"No. I got my citizenship three years ago."

"Before you were a member of *The Resistance*?"

"Yes."

"So Johnny Outlaw, the band, and management never knew that you weren't an American?"

"I am in all ways except by birth. As I said, I'm an American citizen."

She leans in as if the conversation is between friends, intimate, just the two of them. "So tell us, a star by fourteen, talent that was unmatched by others who had studied and performed for years, and you walked away."

He stays the course and remains how he's sitting, not

responding to the leading statement, but waiting for the questions as instructed prior to coming here.

Misti continues as if repeating his life back to him will be news to him. "You attended Julliard at age twelve, living in New York City that year with your parents and sister. The Petrowskis have managed to maintain wealth and status for hundreds of years, through wars, and transitional times in your birth country. How does your family make their money?"

"That would be a question to ask them."

"You're not close with them?"

"When I left, I knew what I was walking away from—"

"A life of luxury from what our research has determined. You walked away with nothing. Why would you do that? Why would a boy of sixteen walk away from a burgeoning musical career, his family, status, and wealth, Kazimir?"

He stares at her. Unblinking.

I don't realize I'm holding my breath until Rochelle releases the one she was holding. He replies, "I am part of one of the greatest bands to ever play music. I would have played guitar for them even if I had to do it free. That's success. I didn't have success when I was fourteen, fifteen, or sixteen. I had fame. I don't need fame, Misti. I need purpose. I started a journey that brought me around the world and set me in the middle of the land of opportunity. So I don't think of myself as leaving wealth, status, or a career behind. I didn't leave those things. I found them right here."

"You didn't mention family."

"The band is my family. My girlfriend is my family. I have everything, so it's not what I left behind. It's what I have now and that's all I'll ever need."

Misti shoots a look my way. "About your girlfriend—"

Rochelle nudges me, and whispers, "You were off limits."

"Seems I'm back on."

Kaz is firm when he states, "I don't talk about my private life now. I'll answer the questions we agreed to about me and the speculation surrounding my disappearance, but my girlfriend is not something I'll discuss publicly."

"Since you brought her up, I thought we could clarify a few things. Mark Renner, for example. When his rep was called, they released a statement to us. Would you like to know what it says?"

"No," Kaz replies coolly.

She reads it anyway, "Mr. Renner is deeply saddened by the turn of events that has caused Ms. Kessler any pain. He apologized to her in person recently and wants to take this opportunity to apologize publicly."

"I don't want to hear anymore."

"It's not that lon—"

"I don't. Want. To. Hear. It."

"Maybe Lara Kessler does," she insists, turning to me.

Kaz's fingers start moving along his hip. What appears to be a meaningless motion to some is noticeably a nervous habit to me. Rochelle grabs my arm and pulls me farther back. Ms. Harsh Hair intervenes and flips off the reporter. Offense is heard in Misti's gasp and seen in a forehead that I would have bet money couldn't wrinkle. It is though, causing me to smile.

Clearing the silence, Kaz asserts, "This interview is about me, not the ones I love."

"Love, Mr. Petrowski? Lara Kessler is embroiled in a bizarre event with Mark Renner. How does love factor into this situation?"

She's poking. *Poking. Poking.* He'll only remain cool for so long before he loses his patience with her questions. Whispering to Rochelle, I ask, "Is she allowed to ask him these kind of questions?"

"There's no law. It's a guide. We've seen a lot of reporters pull this bullshit. We can stop the interview."

Tommy's hand rises. "One moment, let's see how he does."

Kaz shifts in his seat. "I thought we established that Fabian is my last name?"

She falters under his glare. "My apologies."

"As for Ms. Kessler, you can contact her PR rep after our

interview and ask the question I don't have a right to answer."

The reporter stands. "I have a surprise for you."

Rochelle and Tommy are on alert. The three bodyguards are focused.

Tommy rushes forward. "He was set up."

The double doors to the suite open wide and just as I look from Kaz to the people walking in, it clicks.

He's been ambushed.

The bodyguards are in motion. Rochelle jumps over cables to get to Kaz, and I do the only thing I know to help. I hurry to the producer, and say, "She can interview me. Anything. She can ask me anything."

Kaz stands. "No."

Misti is beaming. "Join us."

"No, Kaz goes if I do this."

She seems to debate so I spell it out for her, "Kaz Fabian, Kazimir Petrowski. Mystery solved. Me and Mark Renner, the famous baseball player-turned killer. What will sell more commercial spots?"

"Your story."

"There's your answer."

Kaz shakes his head. "No. You're not doing this."

"*Zdravstvuyte*, Kazimir."

We turn toward the thick accent of an older woman. I know who it is. Her hair is lighter, her eyes darker, but the love for her child is evident. Spinning to face him, I place my hands on Kaz's chest. "I'm here for you, Kaz. Whatever you need. Remember, I'm here for you."

His gaze is fixed over my shoulder, a deep line forming between his eyes. Confusion is the heaviest dose of reality and I know anger or pain is next. "What are you doing here?"

With her hands holding a large leather purse, his mother speaks to him in English, "We are invited guests."

Misti smiles proudly. "We organized a reunion. The camera is still on by the way, so we've captured it all."

"Stop recording. We've revoked all rights to do anything with this footage." Ms. Harsh Hair is my hero. I need to find out his publicist's real name, this one not fitting anymore.

Misti's shoulders square and she glares at her. "You can't. We already own the interview. He's already been paid."

His publicist wins the battle when she retorts, "Read the fine print, princess. A stunt like this terminates the contract and we retain the fee, so bye, Misti."

Rochelle jumps in between Misti and Kaz and tells him to go. Her voice rises as she talks to the bodyguards. "Get them out of here."

Kaz takes my hand. "We're leaving."

Walking wide around the camera equipment, I'm well aware that we're avoiding his mother. Debating if it's best to leave or to face his mother, a woman who looks sad watching her son leave without the reunion she hoped for, I ask, "Your mom, Kaz?"

"My parents want their prize back. They don't care about me or they wouldn't have shown back up like this. It's all for show. Playing it up for the cameras."

His mother cries, her words slipping between Russian and English. One phrase is clear: "I love you."

"Kaz?" I hesitate.

He doesn't. "No, I won't give them this. If they want to speak with me, they can do it privately."

I don't argue because he's right. I don't know what they want or why they're here, but it's not a good place for him to be— emotionally or physically. We make it down the elevator to the bottom floor and down the corridor that leads out the employee entrance when Kaz jerks us to a stop.

Before us stands a woman a few years older, not by much, maybe five, with a lifetime of sorrow written on her face. Taking what life has given her out of the equation, the resemblance is remarkable. Her eyes match the unique color I've fallen in love with.

Her hair is the same dark shade as his that recalls midnight over the Mediterranean. "Hi," she says.

Looking to Kaz, I wait to see what he wants to do.

"Hi," he replies. His hand tightens on mine as they stare at each other.

"Please don't leave," she pleads. "We need to talk."

"I have nothing to say to you." His tone slips into an accent that hits the letters more intensely.

We start walking again, sidestepping around her. The door is pushed open, the SUV waiting for us just beyond it. But before we can leave, his sister says, "*Otets* is dead."

30

Lara

KAZ STOPS.

Standing beside him, I wait, letting him make the final decision. The door in front of us is wide open. We can leave, forget all this, and try to live the life we had this morning. Or we can turn back and fill the holes that make up the emptiness in his heart.

Will we keep walking, leaving his sister behind, or do we stop and face the ghosts of his past life?

"Father is dead. You don't have to run any longer."

Kaz turns his head toward me, but speaks to her, "I haven't run in years."

"We couldn't find you."

"Because you weren't looking." Our eyes stay locked on each other's.

Even with my back to her, I can hear her say, "I'm looking now."

"Maybe it's too late," he replies, looking down, away from me. I miss his eyes already. The pain filling them makes me want to hug him until it's gone again, but I don't dare move. Not an inch.

Her voice sounds closer when she says, "Maybe it's not. I miss you."

His head lowers forward and he closes his eyes, his emotions seeming to overwhelm him. Our hands separate and he turns around, staring straight at the woman he once tried to protect. "What do you want from me, Katerina?"

"I want my brother back?"

"Why? Because father's dead?"

"No, because I love you. I miss my younger brother."

I take a step back, feeling intrusive standing so close to the two of them as they try to find peace between them.

Rochelle, Kaz's mother, and a few other people come off the elevator. Tommy taps Kaz's arm. "Time to go."

Kaz turns to leave, but I stop him this time. "You'll regret leaving them behind. Maybe not now, but one day."

The back of his hand runs over my cheek. "You're too forgiving."

"You might benefit from that one day."

A smile appears. "True." He takes a step, but stops again. Looking back at Tommy, he says, "Make sure they arrive at my house safely."

"Will do."

I take hold of his arm and we head for the SUV. The door is open and we settle in quickly before Misti comes after us with a cameraman in tow. The door is slammed closed and the vehicle takes off. Kaz looks out the window as we pass the fans on the sidewalk. "Well that went to shit fast."

"Did it?"

He looks at me surprised. "You think that went well?"

"I think there's an opportunity for it to turn out well."

"Jesus, Lara, have we not been through enough?"

"More than our fair share. That doesn't change that your mother and sister are here to see you."

"For the publicity. If they wanted to see me before, they could have. My dad is dead and they need someone else to take care of them. Don't let that soft heart of yours blind you to the facts."

"You walked away. You said that. Now you want to punish them again for it. What if they made a mistake? What if they are here to make up for it?"

"Don't turn this on me." His hand fists at his side. The other fist goes up tapping against his closed eyes. "I felt the loss for years. I finally don't and look who shows up." He lowers his hand and his fingers flex. Looking at me with eyes that plead for mercy, he says, "I know you want to see the good in everyone, much to your detriment, but there are not two sides to this story. There's one and the facts remain. They chose the man who hit them over the kid who would have fought to the end for them."

Reaching forward, I hold his right hand in mine. "Fight for them now, Kaz. This is your chance to do what you didn't get to do before. You may call my heart soft, but you fought for me. Before you loved me, you fought for me. That's who you are. That's the man you are. Your family is back and this is your chance to find your way back."

"What if I don't want them back in my life?"

Covering his hand that rests on my thigh, I feel safe talking to him about this. Someone has to and he's open to hearing my thoughts. "I think you do more than you let on."

Turning to look out the window again, he says, "Maybe."

My phone rings. My lawyer. I hired a business lawyer while in the hospital. I knew there would be "stuff" to deal with that I needed to have handled for me. "Hello."

"Lara, I've got news."

Grabbing hold of the door handle, I brace myself and turn my back to Kaz. He has enough problems of his own to continue to take on mine. "And?"

"He confessed to the police."

"Mark did?"

"Yes. He's now being held in county until a judge can make a ruling in his case."

Stunned. I blink several times. "What did he confess?"

"To taking you against your wil—"

"Kidnapping?"

"Sort of."

"Sort of?" I close my eyes and focus on my breathing.

"You walked out of the club willingly, Lar—"

"Because he threatened to hurt Kaz."

The sound of disappointment fills the line. "He's going to fight. You know that."

"What else?" I snap.

"He admitted that he tried to commit suicide."

Correcting him, I ask, "You mean homicide?"

"He's arguing temporary insanity and that he gets treatment instead of prison time. There are still a few outstanding issues with his case."

"He's going to win. I know it."

"We can hold out hope, present the evidence and your testimony from the hospital." There's a pause. "He has very good lawyers."

"If he's found guilty on the charges, how long will he serve?"

"That's for the judge to decide based on the state laws, his confession, and the charges filed against him. Your statement will be used, but with his confession on the record, you shouldn't have to testify. I have good news though."

"I need good news right now."

"The restraining orders against Kaz and Derrick have been dropped. Yours remains in place against Mark."

"Okay. I'll tell him."

"Look, Lara, we've presented a file backing our recommendation for a longer sentence. I would recommend putting this behind you and moving forward the best you can at this stage. It's out of your hands. I'll keep in touch with details as things move forward, and I suspect they will fairly quickly now. Lie low. The media will hear of the confession within hours and they'll be looking for a statement from you. Don't say anything. Direct them to me."

"Okay."

"Take care of yourself and we'll be in touch soon."

"Thank you." When I hang up, I peek back at Kaz.

His gaze is burdened, his shoulders stiff. "What's going on?"

That is the million-dollar question. I have no idea what is going on. How do I put this behind me when it still stands squarely in front of me? I can't talk to Kaz about it now. He doesn't need extra worry. Just give him the basics. "Mark confessed."

"Really?"

I release a deep breath and relax for the first time in months. "I can finally move on." Reaching over, I wrap my hand with his. "We can finally move on."

Kaz moves across the leather seat and puts his arm around me. I rest my head on his shoulder and he kisses me. "Finally."

I hope.

KAZ PACES.

Anxiety courses through him, his fingers tapping at his side, his jaw tensing, his eyes focused on the floor but his mind so obviously on something else.

I sit in the middle of the couch in the living room and watch, giving him peace before the storm arrives. The gate buzzer rings his phone. He stops and looks at me before punching in the code. I see his lips purse and he blows out. Then he comes and sits next to me. "So this is it," he remarks and looks down at his shoes.

"What do you want, Kaz?"

"I want to believe that we can be a family again."

I kiss his shoulder. "It's not about believing. It's about knowing. You know deep down they love you. They were put in an impossible situation. I don't think they chose him over you. They chose to survive the best they knew how."

"I feel betrayed."

Putting my arm around him, I whisper, "I know. You have every right to feel that too. Just don't let that feeling make decisions for you. This is a new opportunity. You can take or leave it, but at least listen—openly—with your heart and head."

A knock on the door pulls us back to the moment. He pats my legs and we kiss quickly. I stand when he goes to answer the door.

It's not a boisterous reunion in the entryway, but quiet and cautious on both sides. Kaz hugs his mother and then his sister bringing tears to everyone in the room. He leads them into the living room and introduces me, "This is Lara Kessler, my girlfriend. My mother, Vera Petrowski, and my sister, Katerina Petrowski."

I reach forward to shake their hands. Despite their smiles, they don't accept right away, but then I realize the mistake I've made. Oh my God. They're royalty. Maybe I insulted them by not curtsying. So I try my best to recall every Disney movie I ever saw with a princess in it, and curtsy.

Kaz chuckles and reaches down to take my arm. "No, you don't have to do that."

His mother and sister are giggling. Rochelle is laughing.

Shit.

"I wasn't sure."

Kaz rubs my lower back. "It's okay." He signals to the sofas and chairs. "Let's sit."

His mother eyes the piano and asks him something in Russian.

Kaz says, "English."

Tension sucks the air out of the room with that one word. I feel I should go, that I've become an obstacle for them to climb their way back into each other's lives. His mother glances to me, and smiles when she looks at him. "Do you still play?"

"Occasionally," he responds not missing a beat. I've gotten to know Kaz well enough to read the emotions he tries to bury. His expressive eyes always reveal his true feelings.

He's trying so hard to keep them out, to keep them at a distance, to protect himself. His mother's interest is natural though he's fighting receiving it. His reluctance to pretend he's not hurt is also natural. Was it only his talent that held them together? If that's all that bound them together, it's also what tore them apart. If they only understood how fighting for them effectively sabotaged his ability to play. And he lost them anyway. With a shattered hand, he left, but the true shattering was in his heart.

When he looks at me, I see more pain. Conflict.

Perhaps sensing his unease, Kaz's mother asks me where the restroom is, and I direct her to the guest bathroom. She says nothing until she comes out, and then I see steel in her expression, one so similar to her son.

"You love my son."

"With all my heart," I answer. She closes her eyes and then a wistful smile overtakes her beautiful face.

"I've never forgiven myself for letting him leave. I've never stopped loving him, praying he was safe and happy. Seeing him... happy..."

I want nothing more than to reassure her, but I can't make it about her when I need to protect him. "I think he wants you back in his life, but he needs answers. He feels abandoned. But he also needs honesty. Don't lie to him to get back in his good graces. You need to apologize."

"I failed him for so many reasons he has never known." She whispers, "I'm so incredibly proud of him for what he did. So proud of him for the man he has become."

"Tell him."

My gaze lifts over her shoulder and I can tell from Kaz's expression that he heard her. As we slowly walk toward him, I see him take a deep breath, possibly for courage to attempt reconciliation.

"I haven't played much over the years, *Mamasha*." He takes one of his guitars from the corner and wraps the strap around his neck. "I taught myself to play guitar. It was more portable." Shrugging while he strums, he says, "I think I'm a better guitarist these days and my work keeps me on the road. I've seen the world with the band."

His sister perks up. "You are friends with Johnny Outlaw?"

All eyes in the room turn toward her, then a small backing of laughter replaces the heavy. Kaz nods while smiling. He rubs the back of his neck and says, "Yes, but I'm not sure how I feel about my sister asking about him."

She's about to say something, a smile appearing and then disappearing just as quick and she hesitates as if she isn't sure she can joke with him. But a determination I've seen set in his eyes flashes in hers and she slips into a typical girl. "He's dreamy."

"He's married," Kaz counters.

She shrugs. "Still nice to look at."

"Let's make sure he never finds out you said that."

I tease, "Kaz has many admirers himself."

Katerina laughs but makes a sour face. "I can never see my baby brother as a what do you call them—heartbeat?"

I jump in again. "Heartthrob. And that he is indeed."

Kaz frowns. "Hey! I'm right here." He may be griping from the teasing but I can tell he enjoys the back and forth with his sister. It's apparent he missed the camaraderie that comes so naturally between siblings.

His mother smiles. "They always fought. It's good to hear it again." She hiccups a small sob, and I can see how much this has broken her. Losing her child. Losing her family.

Katerina pats her arm lovingly. "We went through a lot with *Otets*. His death and funeral seemed easy in comparison." She looks at Kaz. "I hope you understand why we stayed."

"I don't," Kaz replies, his pain finally cracking in his voice. "I've never understood why you would stay under those conditions."

His mother says, "We would have been penniless. We would have had to leave Russia. Where would we go?"

"Anywhere. We would have survived together." He stands and walks to the piano. Tapping one key twice, he looks back at them, and adds, "I've done well?"

I don't know why he's asking the question. It's obvious he's done well on his own. Maybe... my heart starts to ache for him. Maybe he still needs acceptance from them, reassurance for the little boy inside him that he has made them proud.

His mother stands and walks to him. Leaning against the other side, she says, "You've done well, my son. You were meant for greatness. It's who you are. You have a good life?"

"I've had a good life."

"I was living the fate life gave me. I was too old to survive without any comfort. Your sister..." She looks down, shame breaching her soft features. "I told her to stay. I promised to find her a good husband and that she'd live a good life." When she looks to her daughter, they both have tears in their eyes. "I should have sent her away. She should have gone with you. She's had a life, but not an easy one. With the Petrowski last name, there's always interest in our family. Katerina is single and beautiful. The media hounds her. They call her cold as ice. She's not. Her father..."

"I'm fine," Katerina demands, standing this time. "It doesn't matter what has happened. It's time we heal what we can." She walks to Kaz and cups his face. "You were right to leave. You got out. Look at you and the beautiful life you've created for yourself. I'm so proud of you, Kazimir."

Holding her upper arms, Kaz softens before us. "You have money, right?"

"We have more money than we can spend."

The insecurity in his voice is heartbreaking. "You're here for me?"

She nods. "We don't expect miracles. Healing takes time. But we don't want to live without you any longer. We had no idea where you were until we were contacted by the press. And then suddenly, there you were. Right there in plain sight. My brother, the amazing musician." She hugs him and when he embraces her, she says, "It's okay if you're not ready to be part of this family again, but please don't close the door."

His mother comes to them and wraps her arms wide around them. "This is what I've yearned for."

Healing does take time, and together, I think they'll be fine. Seeing them makes me miss my parents. I take my phone out and send them a text to come over.

The gate buzzer sounds again and Tommy says, "I'll handle it." He gets up and goes to the security camera and phone near the door. I hear him say, "Come on up."

Tommy joins Rochelle in the kitchen. They're talking in low voices and settle at the table. I turn my attention to Kaz and his family. His sister is looking me over. When she smiles, it's kind, so I return one.

Somewhere in the conversation, his sister and mother apologize. He doesn't need to hear the words, but I know he likes that they took responsibility. I like hearing them laugh and seeing the tears shed between them. Joy and love. No tension lives here.

Tommy goes to the door and when it's opened, we all turn toward the voice I know instantly. "I refuse to stay away any longer. She's my girl too." Lane and his exaggerated arm flailing come my way. "Now where is she, you big handsome lug?"

Signaling toward us, Tommy rolls his eyes.

"I've missed you too," I say to Lane, walking around the couch to greet him properly with a big hug.

With his arms around me, Lane says, "Damn, he's so good-looking, but he makes me so mad."

"Why?" I ask, leaning back.

"He stole my friend."

I hug him again. "He didn't steal me. He's healed me. I'm right here, better than ever."

Lane smiles, flashing his pearly whites. "That's wonderful to hear because Calliope is driving me mad."

"Wait, what? We finished her project already."

"Nope. We're starting on her boudoir and let me tell you, the woman is divine. We've never decorated a playroom before and I'm going to need guidance from someone who understands the kinks of the heterosexuals."

Surprisingly, Kaz speaks up, "I've got a friend who would be happy to help her out."

Lane's finely shaped eyebrows go up. "You do?"

"My best friend in the band."

I laugh. "Derrick?"

He smiles. "Yup. I think he just might be what that princess needs."

Katerina whacks him in the chest. "Forget about Hollywood princesses. You have a sister with a royal title who wants to meet your friends. Especially friends in the band."

I nudge his sister. "Trust me on this. Let Derrick go for the actress. They are complete opposites and perfect for each other."

Tommy comes back into the room. "Why can't I date a kinky actress?"

Rochelle pats his arm. "Because you have too much heart for someone so shallow. Your girl is out there. Don't worry. You'll find her right when you need her most."

He huffs. "I'm getting a drink. Anyone else?"

In unison the whole room says, "Me," then erupts in laughter again.

Within the hour, my parents have joined the party. BBQ is delivered and the kitchen table is covered. Friends and family are spread around the living room, the kitchen, and outside. Everyone is eating and drinking, talking and laughing.

I like Kaz's sister. She's good people. A tad star struck by the mention of the band, but I've been there so I let her giggle and burst with excitement. It's not every day you find out that your brother is part of such an amazing band.

When I come inside the house from the backyard, Kaz is standing in the kitchen showing my mother how to make Pelmeni. My father is watching a game on the TV and I take the seat next to him at the bar. He smiles when he sees me. "He confessed."

"Yes, he did."

"I didn't protect you. I think... You know what? I didn't think. I would have never guessed that someone so well known would hurt my daughter. I'm sorry."

I lean my head on my dad's shoulder. "No one did. I didn't either. I'm here though and I want to focus on the good things in my life."

"I suspect this is your life now."

Sitting up, I watch Kaz. "He's the man my soul belongs with."

"Love is funny like that. We think we know better, but it has a plan of its own. You were in one place and he in another—worlds apart. Love changed everything, brought you to where you were meant to be, brought you together."

"You and mom weren't worlds apart and you're still happily married twenty-eight years later."

He chuckles as if remembering a secret that amuses him. "Her father said I was a rotten, no-good kid who wouldn't amount to anything."

My mouth drops open. "What? I've never heard this before."

"Yep. I was the man her mother warned her about."

"A bad boy? Mom fell for the bad boy?"

"She sure did." He winks.

I look over at my mom—my cute little homemaker mom—and suddenly I see her in a whole new light. My dad runs a successful business. They have a beautiful home in the suburbs where they raised me. I was never spoiled but I never went without. I always felt safe in their love growing up, so to say I'm shocked is an understatement. "So how do you feel about me being with a bad boy?"

Nodding his head toward the back of Kaz, he replies, "He's not as bad as his rock-star reputation would lead you to believe."

"So you approve?"

"He was there for you when you felt you had no one else you

could turn to. He is helping you heal, not just your bruises, but also your heart. I see how you look at him, but I also see how he looks at you. Love. It's a funny thing."

Smiling just from looking at Kaz, my heart is filled with happiness. "It sure is."

Epilogue
Kaz

THREE MONTHS LATER...

Fucker.

Six months.

Mark Renner only got sentenced for six months in county jail and six in a treatment facility. No actual prison time. It was deemed an unsafe environment for him after taking his fame into consideration. He didn't take Lara's life into consideration. *Asshole.*

"Attempted" means he wanted her dead. The judge saw things differently. I assume he's a baseball fan. I suspect we'll see him with some primo box seats next season. Fucker.

Renner's just fucking lucky he didn't succeed.

So am I.

I look over at my sleeping beauty, not knowing where I'd be if she hadn't survived. She thinks I saved her, that I healed... that I'm healing her. She doesn't see the truth.

She saved *me.*

When I walked away from what everyone called a life of

privilege, I knew where I was heading. Not physically but I knew I had to leave, that something better was calling me. I thought it was *The Resistance*. I can't lie. It's a sweet gig, but finding your soul mate, even in the middle of chaos, is sweeter.

I'd sacrifice my soul for this woman. She knows she has me wrapped around her little finger, but I think I have her all wrapped up too, so all's fair.

Leaning over, I kiss her, and then slip out of bed. I leave the bedroom and walk down the hall. The house is finished. Lara decorated every last room. It's exactly her taste and it's perfect. She captured the two of us in the details. I see her pride when she looks around at what she's accomplished. She doesn't see my pride when I look at her.

When I reach the living room, I struggle to shake off the breaking news of her ex getting off so easy. She did though. She went straight to sleep and has slept soundly. She tells me I give her peace. Maybe I do. I hope I do.

I lift up the piano bench, grab the small box inside, then sit down. When I reach for my guitar in the corner, I stop and turn, deciding to play piano instead. I've been working on a song. It's lighter than I used to compose. I happily blame her for my changing mood. I take the box out and open it, then set it on top of the shiny black surface.

It only takes a few notes before she appears from the hall. Naked in the moonlight as it shines in her eyes. Hair hanging down, messy from sleep. A smile graces her face.

My gorgeous girl.

"C'mere," I say and pat the bench next to me.

She does. A moonbeam follows, as she comes toward me, a guardian angel to save my soul. "Can't sleep..." Her gaze falls on the ring. Her eyes flash to mine.

"What do you think about that?" I ask, trying to sound casual. My stomach is twisted in knots, waiting, hoping she loves it.

Swallowing hard enough for me to see her struggle, her eyes fill with tears. I always hate seeing her cry, but I'll take her happy tears any day. "It's beautiful."

I take the box in hand and get down on one knee, kneeling before her. With her delicate hand in mine, so small and soft against my large and calloused hand, I see our differences. Yet, we fit together so well, perfection found in the details of our past and present. "I want a future with you. I want late-night talks, early morning sex, a soft place to land in a hard world, a wife to come home to, and if we're fortunate enough, a family with you. Lara," I say, and then kiss her hand, "I love you, baby. So much. I want you in my life. I need you. Will you marry me?"

Nodding, she says, "Yes. Yes, I love you so much, Kaz."

Her arms come around me. I stand, lifting her into the air with me. Our lips come together and we kiss, our destinies sealed as one. I set her down on the top of the piano. Taking a blanket from the couch, I cover the flat surface. "I'm going to make love to you on this piano. I've dreamed about it since I walked into this house and saw you bent over it."

The tips of her nails drag lightly down the back of my neck. "I've dreamed about it too. So many times."

"Lie back."

When she does, I lift her legs by the ankles and rest her feet on the top. They part for me and I lean forward, running my hands up her stomach and over her breasts to her shoulders. Taking hold of her, I move down and kiss her pretty pussy, using my tongue to taste her inside and out. She squirms but I hold her in place.

It doesn't take long before she's calling my name on the peak of an orgasm. When she's wholly mine, limber under my touch, I angle her body toward the keys, then yank her closer. She slides easily across the slick surface while on the blanket.

Her pretty blues are trapped in desire. "I want you inside me."

Lifting her just enough to bring her down lower, the keys ring in retaliation as she lands softly down.

"Kaz?"

I place my forehead against hers and whisper, "Shhh." Maneuvering between her legs, I kiss along her temple down to her ear. "I love you. I love you." Her body clings to mine as her warmth takes me into its soft embrace.

Deeper.

Deeper.

Pressing deeper until we're connected in ways that feel too good to ever leave. Lara leans back, her head on the top of the piano. I grab her hips and thrust faster and harder. Our breaths combat the music we're making, fighting to be heard, to be felt, to be freed.

"*Ty vladeyesh menya. Serdtse. Telo. Dusha.*"

This is freedom.

With her I can be who I am completely. She loves me as I love her—deeper than physical, stronger than emotional, longer than this life will allow.

"Tell me what that means," she says. Her eyes are closed, our bodies slick with sex and sweat.

I kiss her neck and drag myself out of my head. "You own me. Heart. Body. Soul."

A smile appears and I kiss the corner. She holds on to my shoulders and moves, fucking me. "I love that. Say it again."

"*Ty vladeyesh menya. Serdtse. Telo. Dusha.*"

"God, that's so sexy, Kaz."

Moving faster, I warn her, "Hold on."

Her hands go to her side, the tips of her fingers on the keys. I lose myself in her love, her body, her scent, her moans, until I can't hold on any longer. Grabbing her hips, I fuck her until nails dig into my shoulders and her pussy tremors from another orgasm. I fuck her until I find my own release, blinded by the brightness of ecstasy.

With a chest full of heavy breaths, I exhale, and sit down on the bench. I bring her down with me holding her body across mine as we both try to catch our breath. Reaching forward, I tap a few of the ivories.

"Look at that. We made music together."

She giggles and it's the best sound in the world. Then she looks up at me with love in her eyes and says, "Play for me."

"Anytime." I reach my other arm around her and start playing the song I know so well as if I've known it my whole life, even though I wrote it for her recently.

Kissing my cheek, she says, "It's beautiful."

"Like you."

"I already said yes, charmer."

"Better get used to the compliments because you're gonna get a lot of them."

"I can get used to it." She wraps her arm around my neck while I continue play. "Kaz?"

"Hmm?"

"Do you think we got together because of what we went through? I kind of dragged you into my mess."

I stop playing and rest my hands on her lower back, holding her to me. Looking into her eyes, it's easy to see why I fell in love with her, but it was more than her beauty that drew her to me. I saw her soul that night—vulnerable and exposed. In her weakest moment she showed me her strength. She fought back. She survived. She came to me at her worst and gave me her best. "No. I think we came together because we connected on a level we knew was unique. But I think we'll stay together because of what we went through. We fought for this. We fought for love."

"Love is funny like that." She rests her head on my shoulder and I finish playing the song for her.

I've not felt this content, this peaceful, this happy in years. The notes flow from fingers to keys with ease. Having Lara here has made all the difference. She's helped ease the transition with my family as we try to fit the pieces of our puzzle back together. I was never responsible for their choices, but I feel better from this outcome. Having them back has meant more to me than I expected. Lara even helped them find a house in Beverly Hills. Temporary, but it's nice to have them here. Maybe one day, they'll leave Russia and stay. I think they like being out of the public's eye here and by how much my mother has doted on me, I think they like having me around.

I finally introduced Katerina to Johnny. Shaking my head at the memory, I have to realize she's not just my sister, but a woman now.

Derrick asked me about her the other day... I breathe out. That fucker is not going anywhere near my sister.

When I play the last note, I wrap my arms around her and hold her. Lara whispers, "I have a surprise for you in the grotto. A little housewarming gift now that it's decorated."

Getting up, we walk into the bathroom and clean up. After slipping on some boxer briefs, we hold hands and go outside. "You didn't have to do anything. It's your home too."

"I wanted to."

When we reach the grotto, I see a box and peek over at her confused. "Why is it out here?"

"Just open the box," she replies slyly.

I lift the lid and there inside is the best gift I've ever received... next to her, of course. "You bought me a smoking jacket?"

She shrugs. "Figured you can't have a grotto unless the image is complete. A young Hugh Hefner in the making."

Chuckling, I remark, "I'm thinking I'm not going to get away with his lifestyle."

"You get the jacket and the grotto. That's the most similar to Hugh I want for you."

I take her by the waist and pull her to me. "I don't need anything or anyone else. You're all I need, baby." I plant a firm one on her lips until she's weak in the knees. When she holds on to me, I know I've done a good job of kiss-vincing her.

Twenty minutes later, I'm lying next to her under a sky full of stars. I turn in the lounge chair just to admire her. I can't believe she's my girl. She's more stunning than the stars could ever be. "Thank you for saying yes."

She touches the lapel of the jacket. "Thank you for asking," she says, amusement in her eyes and playing out in her smile. "You know people will say it's too soon."

"I don't care what people say."

Her body stretches next to mine and she moves against me. "I don't care either. We've lived a lifetime in a few months, more life than most live in years. I was so lost until I found you."

"I was found until I thought I lost you. I knew then and there that I would do whatever it took to give you the life you deserve." Cuddling with my girl, I say, "How about we take the next sixty years easy?"

"Make it seventy and you've got yourself a deal."

I kiss her nose. "How about I give you life?"

"Plus eternity and you've got yourself a deal."

"Done. Now let's fuck on it."

Giggling, she says, "I love you, Kaz."

"I love you, Lara."

The End.

Keep reading for excerpts from
The Resistance* and *The Redemption
by S.L. Scott

The Resistance

S. L. SCOTT

Prologue

I'M A FUCKING fool.

I'm not even sure how I got into this mess, but I know I need to get myself out of it. I look down at the hand on my thigh inching up higher and my stomach rolls. Squeezing out from between the tight confines of the third row in this van, a girl on each side wanting a piece of me, I fall over the seat into the cargo area and move away from their astonished stares. They're speaking German and I don't know what the fuck they're saying, but I've been in this type of situation enough to know how it will end, if I let it.

Everything has changed... or sometime around my last birthday I changed.

I didn't invite these chicks. Dex did. He'll fuck'em all before the night's through and the bad part is, they'll let him. Thinking they're special, that they'll be the one to tame him. They'll let him do what he wants just to be close to him.

Beyond this set up being predictable at this point, it's really fucking old or I am, probably both. I ignore their taps on my shoulder and them calling my name. I ignore everything to do with them and focus on my phone.

On the inside, I'm freaking the fuck out that I'm sitting in the cargo hold of a huge van in Germany with attractive girls willing to do anything I want them to, but I prefer to look at a photo of a little blonde with hazel eyes. Freaking the fuck out might be an understatement.

I'm a player or was, supposed to be, maybe still am. I don't keep score or anything like that, but I've slept with plenty of women, sometimes more than one at a time. I used to blame my lifestyle, but more recently, I realized I'm the common denominator in the bad relationships I've had.

The car comes to a stop and the driver rushes around to the back to let me out. I stumble while climbing out, and hurry inside away from the sound of my name being called. The girls will be upset when they realize I'm not staying to play, but Dex will be thrilled— more pussy for him.

Cory hops out from the front, and follows me. "Wait up," he says, jogging to catch up.

When we reach the elevators, we look back. Dex is helping the girls out of the vehicle one-by-one. With a cigarette hanging from the corner of his mouth, he's sloppy, already drunk. He never lacks for female companionship. By the way he acts, I don't see the appeal, but I don't think that's why they're hooking up with him anyway.

Cory looks at me and nods once. "What's up? What happened back there?"

The elevator doors open and we step in, pushing the button for our floor. "Over it. Over it all."

"The girl from Vegas?"

"She's not from Vegas, but yeah, I've kind of been thinking about her."

When the brass doors reopen, we walk down the hall to our rooms. Cory and I don't do small talk. We've been friends for years, best friends if I think about it.

"Maybe you should call her," he suggests as we open our doors.

"Maybe I will."

"Night."

"Night," I mumble and shut the door behind me.

1

Holliday Hughes

"Comfort zones are like women. You have to try a few before you find the one that feels right."
~Johnny Outlaw

THAT DAMN LIME and coconut song has been playing on a loop in my head, driving me nuts for hours. I make a mental note: Fire Tracy in the morning for subjecting me to that song twenty-thousand times yesterday. She called it inspirational. I call it torture after the first two times.

Rolling over, I look at the time. 4:36 a.m. I have four hours before I need to be on the road. This may be a business trip, but it will still be good to get away for a few days. I need a break. I've been in a bad mood lately. The spa and I have a date I'm really looking forward to. The thought alone relaxes me. I close my eyes and try to get a few more hours of sleep before I need to leave for Las Vegas.

I get two tops.

I tighten my robe at the neck. Just as I open my front door to get the paper, I hear a male voice say, "Hello?"

Peeking through the crack, I hold the door protectively in front of me just in case I need to close and lock it quickly. "Hi."

"I'm your new neighbor. I just moved in last week. I'm Danny."

Curious, I slowly stick my head out to get a better look at this Danny. Strands of my sandy blonde hair fall in front of my eyes, so I tuck it behind my ear and get an eyeful. To my surprise, he's quite handsome and has a big smile. "Oh, um," I say, dragging my hand down the back of my hair, hoping to tame the wild strands. "Hi. I'm Holli. Welcome to the neighborhood."

He nods toward the paper on the bottom of the shared Spanish tiled steps that lead to our townhomes. "I'll get your paper since you're not dressed."

"Thanks." I watch him. He looks like he just got back from a run or workout—a little sweaty, but not gross, in that sexy kind of way. Or maybe Danny's just sexy. He's well built with short, brown hair and when he bends over, I notice his strong legs and arms. Well-defined muscles lead to—*Oh my God!* Not just my face, but my entire body heats from embarrassment. Hoping he doesn't say anything about me checking him out, I turn away and start picking at a piece of peeling stucco near my house number. "Um, so are you settled in, liking your place?"

His chuckling confirms I was busted. But he's a gentleman, so he acts as if it didn't happen. "I like the neighborhood. The place is great," he says. "I like all the space, especially the patio. I'm thinking of having a party to break it in, maybe in a few weeks after I finish unpacking." He hands me the paper and takes two steps back. "You should stop by."

Nodding, I look into his eyes. I think they're brown, lighter than mine, more honey-colored. His offer is friendly, not a come on, which is good since we're neighbors now. "Thanks for the invitation."

Walking back to his door, he steals one more glimpse over his shoulder. "Have a great day. See you around, Holli."

"Yeah, see you around."

I shut the door, paper in hand, and fall against the wood with a smile on my face. One of my golden rules is not to date where I sleep, but I still appreciate that my new hottie neighbor is easy on the eyes. He might know it, but he doesn't seem arrogant.

I lock the door and get ready to leave.

Los Angeles is hot, smoggy, and grey at this hour and I have a feeling it won't be much different a few hours from now. I close the patio door and lock it, double checking for safety. After pulling the drapes closed, I take one last look around to make sure I'm not forgetting anything. I text Tracy and let her know I'm leaving. She doesn't reply, but I'm not surprised. Her boyfriend proposed last night after six years of dating. Being the kind boss and friend I am, I let her out of this trip, so she could spend the weekend with their families to celebrate the engagement.

There are selfish reasons as well for letting her off the hook. I really don't think I can handle hours of sitting in the car with her as she reads bridal magazines and plans every detail of her big day. After too many dud dates in the last couple of months, I'm not in the right frame of mind to plan her happily ever after.

With my garment bag in one hand and my suitcase in the other, I click the button, disarming my car's alarm as I walk to my parking space. I've lived here a couple of years. I wanted a place near the beach that also had space for my office, and I was fortunate enough to find both in this townhome.

A meme I created went viral three years ago this month. Who knew a snarky-mouthed fruit would be the way I make my fortune. I took it though and ran with the brand, building it into a small empire I named Limelight. The company is lean and I keep my costs under control. My fortune has grown by a few million in the last year alone.

I back out onto the street and take the scenic route, one block up to the beach. Driving slowly along with my windows down, I let the sound of the waves and the smell of the ocean center me. At the first stoplight, I take one deep salty air breath, roll the window back up, and leave for Vegas.

An hour into the trip, Tracy calls. I answer, but before I have a chance to speak, she asks, "Can I please tell you all about it again?" Happy laughter punctuates her question.

"Of course. Tell me everything." I'll indulge her wedding fantasies because that's what friends do... and because I have four hours to kill in the car. Listening to her takes my mind off the time and the miles stretching ahead of me as she relives every last detail of the proposal. Fortunately for me, she skims over the engagement sex.

Her excitement is contagious and because I've known her and her fiancé, Adam, for so many years, my happiness exudes. "Congratulations again."

"Thank you for letting me stay home this weekend. You'll be great and don't be nervous. It's just a rah-rah go get'em presentation and cocktail party. The rest of the time is all yours."

"You know how much I hate these kinds of events."

"You don't have to prove anything to anyone. Your company's success speaks for itself."

"Thanks. I'll try to remember that."

"Drive safely and squeeze in some fun."

I laugh. "You know I'll try. Bye." When we hang up, I turn on some music and let the miles drift behind me.

After a stop for gas half-way and a coffee later, I enter the glistening city in the desert. Pulling up to my hotel, I valet my car and take my own luggage to my room after checking in. I like this hotel because of the amenities, but the men aren't bad to look at either—a little edgy, a lot sexy—lucky for this single girl.

I spend a couple of hours checking emails and work on a proposal before I realize the time and need to get ready for the night. It's Vegas, so I mix business with some sexy. I pull on a black fitted skirt that hits mid-thigh, an emerald green silk camisole with spaghetti straps, and a short black jacket. I slip on my favorite new pair of stilettos and after one last check of my makeup and hair, I head out.

The meet and greet isn't long, but I slip out at one point to use the restroom. As I'm walking back toward the ballroom, I'm drawn to a man standing with a group of people nearby. His magnetism captures me. He might just be the best looking man I've ever seen—tall, dark hair, strong jaw leading me up to seductive eyes aimed at me. His head tilts and for a split second in time, everyone else disappears. I break the connection by looking away, everything feeling too intense in the moment. When he laughs, I add that to his ongoing list of great attributes.

When I pass, the feel of his gaze landing heavy on my backside warms my body. With my hand on the door, I pause, wanting to look back so badly. I resist the urge, open the door, and return to the party. The presentation portion of the evening is interesting. Despite that, my thoughts repeatedly drift back to the hot guy in the corridor—fitted jeans, black shirt, leather wristband. *Damn I'm weak to a leather wristband.*

I'm mentally brought back to the presentation when my company is recognized as one to watch. The acknowledgement is nice, and it feels good to be among my peers.

The dinner becomes more of a party as everyone wanders around instead of taking their seats. I'm not hungry and need to psych myself up to mingle. Tracy is awesome in these types of situations. Me, not so much.

The ballroom is dimly lit, I'm guessing to set the ambiance, but since this is business, I can do without the romance. I head straight for the bar just like everyone else—one big cattle call to the liquor to make the rest of the night a little more bearable.

"I usually hate these things," I hear from the guy behind me. When I look over my shoulder, he gives me a half-smile—half-friendly, half-creepy. "But they don't usually have attractive women either."

I roll my eyes while turning my back on him and his cheesy pick-up line.

"I'm sorry. That was bad. I know," he says with a weird nasally laugh.

His breath hits my neck and I jerk back. "Do you mind? Ever hear of personal space?"

"Sorry. You're just really pretty." He shrugs as if that makes everything better. "Your beauty is making me stupid."

"You think?" *Big mistake.*

He actually takes my sarcastic comment as a conversation opener. "Yes, I do. But I can't be the first to be dumbfounded by your beauty."

Standing on my tiptoes to see how many more people are in front of me, I exhale, disappointed by the long line. One person in line would have been too many at this point. "Excuse me," I say and slip out of line. I find the table with my name tag on it, set my purse down, and take off my jacket. This hotel ballroom is crowded and too warm.

Saved by a friendly face, I see Cara, a marketing strategist I know from L.A. Weaving between the tables, I sit down in a chair next to her. With her eyes focused on the paperwork in front of her, I ask, "Working during the party?"

She looks up, smiling when she sees me. Opening her arms, she leans in and hugs me. "Holli, it's so good to see you."

I went with a different company than hers for a campaign a while back and glad she's not holding it against me. "Good to see you again."

"Congratulations on your success. Well deserved."

"I'm not sure if a smartass lime deserves the success it's gotten, but I'll take it."

She taps my leg. "You deserve it. It's funny and quite catchy. Just take the accolades."

"Thanks."

Looking over my shoulder, she leans in and whispers, "I'm

skipping out of here early, but I'm meeting a few people for dinner tomorrow. If you're still in Vegas, you should join us."

"I'd love that. Thanks."

She stands up and grabs the papers in front of her. "Fantastic. I'll text you the details tomorrow. I'm so glad we ran into each other."

"Me too. See you tomorrow."

I'm left sitting alone. When I look around the room, like Cara, I'm thinking that skipping out early might be the way to go. If I do, I know Tracy will kick my ass, so I decide to suffer and give this party one last chance. But I definitely need a drink and the line for the bar in here is still way too long.

I head for the doors to buy a drink in one of the many hotel bars—any bar without a line. Guy from the bar line jumps in front of me as I try to exit, startling me. "Hey, hey, hey. You're not leaving already, are you?"

Since my glare and earlier hints didn't work, I reply, "I'll be back, no need to worry yourself."

His head starts bobbing up and down, confidently, and a big Cheshire cat grin covers his face. I start walking again as he keeps talking... again. "Cool. I'll see you later then."

I feel no need to respond to the come on, and will try to avoid him when I return. Following the wide-tiled path through the casino, which reminds me of the Yellow Brick Road, guiding me to what feels like Oz, a bar in all its gloriousness with no lines in site. Inside the darkened room, the sounds of the casino fade away as current hits play overhead. Still on a mission for a cocktail, I step up to the bar and wait.

The Resistance is available now!

The Redemption

S. L. SCOTT

Prologue

SADNESS SURROUNDS ME and I feel bad for not feeling worse.

I stand at the back, near a tree, separate from the families and friends that have gathered. I stay back here, away from the crowd, and watch her. She tries to hide her devastation and tears behind big sunglasses that she slipped down over her eyes minutes before.

Her hair is down, hanging over her shoulders and longer than I remember from the last time I saw her. It's been too long since then. But even in the middle of a sea of black, she still stands out, strikingly beautiful and I'm drawn to her, wanting to be with her in ways I can't.

With all of these people around, I'm finding it hard to swallow despite being outdoors. A lump formed in my throat earlier this week, making me wonder what caused it. *Maybe guilt.* Squeezing my hand tightly around the coin, I realize a tragedy has given me hope where none existed before. And despite one of my closest friends dying, an uncertain future, and the realization that with his death, my life has been forever changed, I can't stop thinking about the woman he left behind.

1

Rochelle Floros

THE FUNERAL WAS... it was what it was. Johnny and Holli drove me and the kids home. There were too many people staring at me, waiting for my breakdown. I needed the silence of the ride to be able to face the waiting mourners at my house, and they gave that to me. Just after we park, Johnny turns to me and says, "The Resistance is a family. We take care of one another. I'll always be here for you, Rochelle."

I nod, not sure I can speak under the weight of my emotions. I want today to become a distant memory sooner than I should. I don't want to remember Cory's death. I want to remember his life, his life with me, his life with our four-year-old. It's a life that our newborn will never get to experience and the significance of that drags me under. I rush out of the car right before the first tear slips down, but I wipe it away before anybody can see.

But he sees.

Antonio Dexter Caggiano sees right through the facade I put on for everyone else, but doesn't move from Neil's side. He knows where he's needed without me saying. They sit on the tire swing together, spinning slowly, talking, bonding in a way that seems almost abnormal for the man I've always known Dex to be. A magic trick reveals a pair of drumsticks and Dex hands them to Neil. My oldest son starts banging on the tire and up the chains, happily distracted from the sadness of the day.

Staring across the lawn—faded black jeans, long, shaggy hair, bandana back in place after we left the cemetery—I find the most unlikely ally on such a depressing day. He's just here, silently supportive without asking anything of me.

Dex is kind to spend time with the boys. He has a playful smile on his face, and assuming from Neil's laughter, which I hear echoing across the yard, Dex is also funny. He left his ego at home, an anomaly from every other day. He's fascinating to watch. Kids are genuine in their emotions and Neil seems to like Dex.

Neil deserves laughter and fun, but he also deserves his father. I get up and move to the side of the yard where I plant my small garden each year. My tears water the lettuce that is just starting to grow. Cory planted that. I wanted strawberries.

I stomp on it. With both feet, I jump up and land down on the plant because he didn't live to see it grow. "Damn you!" Picking it up, I rip it from the ground and throw it against the fence. "Damn you, Cory!"

A burning regret coats my insides as I panic and rush to pick it up. Through watery-vision, I drop to my knees and take it in hand, holding it to my chest. Suddenly strong arms wrap around me from behind, pulling me into his lap. Dex's body against mine feels so foreign and yet, like the only place safe for me to grieve.

The sobs break free, the ones that I've been holding back all day, and my body is wracked with every emotion that I don't want anyone else to see. My breakdown feels like a failure. I should be the one to comfort others today. Pressing my head against his shoulder, the light hum in his chest is soothing. "He left me, Dex. He left me here all by myself to raise the boys on my own. I can't do it."

"You can. You will. I'll be here for you."

He's the least expected person to find comfort in, but he's the only one that feels right. I nod. My head is tucked under his chin while his fingers gently but firmly open my fisted hand. He takes the lettuce that is destroyed and sad, just like me, and says, "It's gonna be okay. Maybe not for the lettuce, but you're gonna be okay."

We sit there a few minutes, the slight breeze feeling good against my hot face. Maybe he's right. Maybe I will be okay. It's hard to tell right now. With a deep breath and even heavier exhale, I look up into his eyes and all that he said is repeated in his expression. I get up and start walking to the backyard again. He follows, but he stops and plants the lettuce back into the garden, and says, "It's worth a shot."

"Yeah, it's worth a shot."

We come from around the corner and Dex goes inside without another word and I join Neil on the swing. No one's the wiser that I almost fell apart, or that Dex held me together. My strength is back on display for everyone else. His bad boy reputation as the drummer for one of the biggest bands in the world is back intact.

SIX MONTHS LATER...

It's hot in here. I need fresh air; the crowded party is steamy from all the bodies crammed into the living room. Looking out at the pool area, it's not any better. "I'm gonna walk around," I say, leaving the safety of Johnny's side.

"I'll be here," he replies before taking a drink of his beer. Johnny Outlaw may be one of the most famous musicians in the world and the lead singer of The Resistance, but he's also been a shoulder for me to cry on. He's like the brother I never had. Along with that role, he's become very protective of me in public settings and these types of situations. Holli, his wife, is usually here to keep me company, but she had a business trip and is out of town. So I'm here with the guys from the band. That's a lot of testosterone to be around while drinking your sorrows away.

Remembering there's a small balcony off the master bedroom, I head for the stairs. The balcony has a great vantage point overlooking the pool. Dex is the master of throwing awesome parties and he's gone all out for his birthday. Everyone from Academy Award winning Directors to young starlets jumping at any casting couch opportunity that comes along is here. Current rock musicians are mingling with Pop Princesses, and I just spotted Tommy, the tour manager with some of our roadies at the bar. I used to be more of a free spirit, comfortable in social settings... when Cory was alive. But my happiness died when he did. I never imagined I would be expected to live in a world without my heart. I'd gotten good at hiding my sadness, but lately I've been struggling to put on a happy face for others.

Dex's party is a sea of beautiful people and definitely intimidating. The heat and drinks making my mind blur into a mixture of emotions. I start walking faster, hoping to stave off the panic attack I feel coming on.

I pass some familiar faces, saying hi as I walk by. Seeing other people, the ones I don't know, makes me want to lower my gaze to the floor and block out the stares. Sometimes the stares bother me. I was relatively unrecognizable before Cory's death, but I made headlines as the 'Poor Widow' and my photo was everywhere. So I see the looks, the sideways glances, and feel the sympathy lying heavy from their curiosity. Nights like this usually help me escape the sadness of losing the only man I ever loved. Alcohol also helps, so I down a shot and slowly make my way upstairs, trying not to let the liquor knock me off-balance.

The double doors of the master bedroom are closed along with the other bedroom doors down the hall. Taking the knob in hand, I turn slowly. It opens and I'm greeted with darkness. I'm hoping no one is in here doing something I don't want to see or hear, so I enter with caution. Although there is no light except for the moonlight coming in from the balcony doors, I walk in when I hear silence. Closing the door behind me, I don't bother looking around. I just go to the French doors and open them wide. The night is clearer up here, the miles of LA lights laid out before me with a stunning view of the city. The area around the pool below is more crowded than I realized when I was in the mix of it.

A heavy exhale of smoke draws my gaze to the left. Dex sits forward resting his elbows on his knees and eyes me.

He doesn't look bothered that I'm here, but I feel the need to explain anyway. "I wanted... I needed to get away."

"From what?" he asks while stubbing his cigarette into an ashtray on the Spanish tile.

I lean against the doorframe, my head resting back, my eyes lulled closed by the voices carrying up from below. Over the last six months, we haven't spent a lot of time together, but he's stopped by a few times to talk, reminisce, or just sit with someone who knows what he's going through, empathizing through moments of silent understanding. He makes it easy to just be, to be whatever I need to be. "Everything... from me."

"It's hard to escape yourself."

"I know. I've tried."

"Me too." The ice in his glass shifts, clanging against the walls of the double old-fashioned. I look just as he sets it down, and asks, "Drink?"

"Sure," I reply. "Why are you trying to escape?"

"Sometimes being the bad guy sucks."

"You're not a bad guy."

"Everyone else thinks I am."

"I like to think you just play one on TV... or in your case, on stage. The infamous bad boy drummer of The Resistance isn't all that bad, you know."

He hands me his glass and I hold it up to toast him. "Happy birthday, Dex." The straight bourbon feels thick as it slides down my throat.

His expression changes and he stands, moving behind me, his chest against my back. "Do I get a birthday wish?"

I feel his every breath coming in and out, each one hot against my neck. My heart starts beating faster, the air that felt freer moments before now ripe with innuendoes. This tension between us is new, but I like it. The hesitation I thought I would feel drowned with the last gulp of his drink. I take one last breath before turning, my gaze now meeting his. "Make a wish."

The warmth of his hand covers my cheek and his lips are pressed to mine and mine to his, connecting us like never before. I would have thought I'd get careful, gentle, tentative. I get pressure swarmed with confidence, a wanting that feels more lustful, caressed in need. My body reacts, moving closer, edging into the kiss, wanting it, needing it. I'm pulled inside, the doors shut behind and he whispers, "Too many people can see up here."

I nod, though I'm not sure he can see as I stand in the shadows of the curtain. He's seen clearly, the window panes reflecting an abstract design across his body. Taking a sip, his eyes find mine. There's nothing hurried about his movements as he takes me in. While setting his glass down on the table nearby, he says, "I've wanted to kiss you longer than you'll understand, longer than I had a right to."

Licking my lips, the action involuntary, I'm starting to think that maybe I've wanted to kiss him longer than I had the right to as well. But I see him. I've always seen the real him and not the showman or the manwhore he wants everyone else to see. I see the way the light reflects in his brown eyes, giving them more life than one would expect when labeled just "brown." The liquid tone of where sand meets the ocean at night might do them more justice. His eyes are lighter than mine, and hold a history completely different. But they draw me in, his body wagering me closer.

When I go, I lift up this time to kiss him. With a tilt of our heads, our mouths open and our tongues meet. I shouldn't want him like I do. It's wrong to feel this way, but every physical urge I have overrides my thoughts and deepens as our breaths become each others.

Immersed in a passion that alleviates other burdens I've carried for too long, I enjoy the loss of control, my tension slipping away as he maneuvers me back toward the bed. I go willingly in all ways, wanting to grab hold of this feeling of freedom and release it sexually. I sit as he stands in front of me. The expression on his face highlights his handsome structure—a cut jaw, strong when juxtaposed against his soft gaze. I realize he hides behind his sunglasses so much that I'd forgotten how truly striking he is. His hair is shorter than a year ago, but still hits just below his chin in a jagged-style, carefree and uncalculated.

He slips his shirt off, dropping it to his feet before leaning down and popping open the front of my jeans. I let him as I lean back on my elbows. My shoes come off and then my jeans, slowly, but with no doubt. Neither of us are naïve to what's happening or what's to come. I sit up and take my shirt off before lying back down and asking for the drink. When he hands it to me, I finish the amber liquid and take an ice cube into my mouth, finishing the remaining traces.

Standing up, I demand, "Take your jeans off and lay down." I set the glass back on the dresser across the room and when I return, his lean, muscular body, all six-foot-three of him is on the bed. Crawling up the large mattress, I sit down on his middle, his hardness feeling so good between my legs. I take the ice from my mouth and it drips on his abs, making them twitch. Another drip and another.

"You like to tease," he says, not a question, just an observation.

I lean down and run my tongue over each drop, my chest pressed to his erection.

Lifting my eyes up to watch him, I drag my tongue lower and slower before hearing him mutter, "Fuck."

His head falls back and his eyes close. I drag my fingers over the ups and downs of his defined muscles, appreciating every sit up he does for this exact reason. When I blow across his stomach, his reaction is felt everywhere. Sitting up, he pulls me by my arms and flips me under him in one smooth move. Desperate lips are pressed against mine as his hips flex down, his knees maneuvering my legs apart. Ten inches taller than me, but our bodies seem to fit in so many ways. He kisses my neck and I moan unexpectedly, well aware I just made the only sound in the room. Lifting up, he looks at my face as his hand gently squeezes my left breast. "You're beautiful. The most beautiful woman I've ever seen."

If I thought the moan was unexpected... that tops it.

Never knowing he thought this about me, I'm not sure what to say, so I lift up and kiss him instead. I let the bourbon take over for a bit and enjoy the other ten inches he has on me. His hips come down again, and my body tingles from the contact, my hips reacting by moving against him.

My chest presses against his as his body weighs down on top of mine. Another moan escapes me as our tongues caress. The slightly rough skin of his hand slides under my bra and he takes me firmly, massaging and peaking my nipples. Rolling onto our sides, our mouths part and our eyes meet again. With a soft whisper between us, he asks, "You sure?"

I reply with a kiss to his cheek before I roll onto my back and unfasten my bra. After dropping it to the floor, I lift my hips up, removing my thong. The moonlight streaks in, accentuating the want found in his eyes as he stares at my body. Boxer briefs are removed and he lies next to me. When I look over at him, the reality of the situation is clear even through the wavy goggles of alcohol. His penis is long, thickly attractive, smooth, but hard. He reaches for a packet from a drawer next to the bed and rolls a condom on before turning to me and staring at me without reservation. His gaze is heavy enough to feel as it envelops me in desire. The way his tongue slides over his bottom lip while looking at me makes me anxious for more. But I remain still, letting his lust linger between us, building, just like my yearning for him.

Patience has no concept of time, but cravings do, so I touch his arms, encouraging him closer... closer... until he's centered on top of me. He leans down resting on his elbows and kisses me. Pushing in, my body welcomes the stretch and burn, desiring the long lost sensation. Deep inside our bodies, our feelings emulate the intensity of the act. Our pace picks up in a frenzy of kisses and caresses. Heated bodies move together in sync, out of sync, and everything else that feels good and natural. A bite to my neck, a nibble to his earlobe. We cover each other in panting breaths over skin that becomes slick with passion.

Every thrust elicits sounds from our mouths we can't contain. Guttural. Sensual. Every thrust purposeful and rough, sexy, and caring. Our connection is not casual but filled with an unbridled passion I wasn't aware lay deep beneath the surface.

Pushing his hair back with my hands, I look up at him as a sheen of sweat starts dotting his forehead. His body moves fluidly, his experience showing. I push him over and readjust on top, slipping down slowly. His three gun tattoos wrap around the muscles of his arm and flex when he steadies me on top of him. Our pace slows. I don't want this to end too soon, but my insides urge for more. I close my eyes, willing the darkness behind my lids toward the imploding light I know is buried, longing to be seen.

Fingers rub assuredly, a confidence in the action. I feel. Feel. Feel. My head drops back as his touch drives me closer. I want. Want. Want. I move, rocking on top of him, increasingly selfish in pursuit of my own ecstasy. With a gasp, I catch that elusive sensation that makes me feel Heaven and Hell equally. "Oh God! Cory!"

Everything stops.

Just when I peak, I fall back into reality, well aware of the damage I just caused. I open my eyes, seeking his out. It's not a soft gaze I find but a glare cloaked in hurt and shock. I'm still, afraid to move at all, but the words come tripping out. "I'm sorry.

I'm sorry. So sorry."

Then shame fills my racing heart. "Oh my God! What have I done?" I'm swift to my feet as disgust fills my soul. "What have I done?" I mumble again. Cory's face flashes in my head, memories of his laughter ringing in my ears as a torturous reminder. "Shit. Shit. Shit." Not sure what to do, I stand there mortified.

"You wanted this," Dex says, sitting up. His voice sounds as confused as I feel. "You fucking wanted this. You wanted me."

His words are messing with my head as guilt slithers in, drenching me on the inside. How could I betray Cory like this and with Dex, his friend? "Fuck. I've gotta go." I run for my jeans, pulling them on, then drop to my knees to feel for my shirt. I slip it over my head and stand, my thoughts are like broken nerves, the pain of what I've done covering the raw ends like pinpricks of shame. I feel Dex's gaze heavy on my backside as I put my shoes on and run out of the bedroom, slamming the door behind me.

Down the staircase and through the party-goers, I run for the front door, not bothering to shut it or look back this time.

Outside, I stand on the stairs that led me away from his bedroom and the disgrace, hoping I can escape the cramping in my chest. I hate Hollywood and their fucking valets and mansions. Humiliation like this needs a quick escape, but I have to wait for my car to be pulled around. When it is, I jump inside, relieved that I didn't run into anyone I know while waiting. I leave through the gates of the neighborhood and speed home. My hands are shaking, so I hold the wheel tighter.

What would Cory say? I've disrespected his memory. *What will Johnny say? He barely tolerates him since his drug use almost destroyed the band. He would never support me and Dex being together.* Shame coats me. *And Holli? Will she be disgusted that I gave into a physical desire instead of using my head and mourning quietly like I've done for the last six months? Will I be able to face them if they find out? What if Dex tells them?* I'll become one of his many, but this time with a face, a name for them to judge. *Will I be able to face myself? Look in the mirror without feeling disgusted for a lapse in judgment?*

I flip the visor down and open the mirror. The lights are bright, making me squint. When my eyes adjust, mascara is smeared on the left corner. My cheeks are flushed, not from the night or the rash exit, but from sex and lust, desire, and dishonor—everything I had managed to avoid until tonight.

Flipping the mirror back up, my eyes fill with heavy tears. I hope to find physical safety in the distance from him before they fall. But no distance will protect me from betraying the memory of the man I loved so much.

The Redemption is available now!

A Personal Note

Dear Readers, Bloggers, and Authors, your continued support touches my heart and stokes my fire of creativity. Thank you for always being there and for the love you share when you read, review, and share my books with others.

To my sweet family –
You are everything to me. I love you!

To my friends, this journey wouldn't be the same without having you a part of it. Thank you to Adriana, Amy, Andrea J., Annette, Ashley, Flavia, Heather, Irene, Jessica H., Kerri, Kirsten, Kristen, Kiersten, Lara, Liv, Lynsey, Marion, Marla, Mary, Ruth, and Serena, The Playwhores, and to my awesome group of Scotties on FB—SL Scott Books.

Special thanks to N. Michaels Author for the translations. Spasibo.

I love you and adore each and every one of you.

Thank you for taking this journey with me.
Suzie

From the Author

The domestic abuse portrayed in this story is a work of fiction, but not taken lightly. Please, if you or someone you know is being abused, please contact The National Domestic Violence Hotline www.thehotline.org /1-800-799-7233, or reach out to someone you trust for help.

S.L. Scott

New York Times and USA Bestselling Author, S. L. Scott, was always interested in the arts. She grew up painting, writing poetry and short stories, and wiling her days away lost in a good book and the movies.

With a degree in Journalism, she continued her love of the written word by reading American authors like Salinger and Fitzgerald. She was intrigued by their flawed characters living in picture perfect worlds, but could still debate that the worlds those characters lived in were actually the flawed ones. This dynamic of leaving the reader invested in the words, inspired Scott to start writing journeys with emotion while injecting an underlying passion into her own stories.

Living in the capital of Texas with her family, Scott loves traveling and avocados, beaches, and cooking with her kids. She's obsessed with epic romances and loves a good plot twist. She dreams of seeing one of her own books made into a movie one day as well as returning to Europe. Her favorite color is blue, but she likens it more toward the sky than the emotion. Her home is filled with the welcoming symbol of the pineapple and finds surfing a challenge though she likes to think she's a pro.

To keep up to date with her writing and more, her website is www.slscottauthor.com or to receive her newsletter with all of her publishing adventures and giveaways, sign up for her newsletter: http://bit.ly/1pF049r

Find S. L. Scott on social media:

Facebook: https://www.facebook.com/slscottpage

Instagram: https://instagram.com/s.l.scott/

Twitter: @slscottauthor

Goodreads: goodreads.com/author/show/6467114.S_L_Scott